Paid i

Susan Handley

To Valerie,
Happy Reading!
Love Susan Handley xxx

Published by Sunningdale Books

All rights reserved
© Susan Handley, 2021

Susan Handley has asserted her right under the Copyright, Designs and Patents Act 1988 to be identified as the author of this work.

This book is a work of fiction and any resemblance to actual persons, living or dead, is purely coincidental.

Cover includes adaptation of photograph created by jannoon028 courtesy of www.freepik.com

1.

Lucy Stirling peered out of the window of the black limo as it pulled up to the kerb, causing a murmur to ripple through the crowd.

'I suppose it's too late to change my mind and get someone else to do tonight?' she said, on the back of a nervous laugh.

The rest of the car's occupants returned benign smiles, apart from Tom Morrelli, lead singer of Nevermind. He peered at her from beneath a dirty blond fringe and gave her hand a squeeze.

'You'll be fine.'

Lucy let out a long breath and nodded. The door swung open. She looked past the chauffeur to the crowd beyond.

'Here goes,' she said, setting a slender foot clad in a red-soled shoe on to the pavement and emerging from the car's dark interior.

Long hair the colour of sunlight cascaded down her back. She smoothed out her dress with manicured fingers; the Ralph Lauren gold creation showed off her toned figure and tastefully left as much to the imagination as it laid bare. The clicks of a multitude of cameras filled the air; photographers yelled her name, vying for attention. She paused, kicked out a hip, while radiating a smile guaranteed to make it onto the cover of every lifestyle magazine to grace the supermarket shelves.

Tom clambered out after her, sporting an easy looking grin. The cameras' stutters were lost beneath a tidal wave of screams as a throng of teenage girls fought amongst themselves for a glimpse. Felix Lee was next out. After sashaying over to Lucy and Tom, he thrust a hand into the pocket of his Versace silk suit and tipped his chin at a jaunty angle, surveying the crowd from behind a curtain of sleek black hair.

As the trio posed for the paparazzi, back at the limo, Carla Porter, a young woman remarkable only by her ordinariness, peered out, radiating uncertainty. Not that she needed to worry. Her lack of celebrity was as good as a cloak of invisibility. She slipped out of the car, shyly skirting around the group of three, and started up the steps to the iconic white box of concrete and glass better known as the Stirling Gallery. Inside, a woman with a tray of champagne-filled flutes approached. Carla took a glass and turned to watch her companions slowly make their way up to the entrance. They struck a final pose for the cameras, waved to the crowd, then swept inside.

'Whose idea was it to leave my throw in the car?' Lucy said, rubbing at lean arms stippled with goosebumps.

'You'll be thanking me when you see the shots in *Hello*,' Felix replied.

'Champagne?' the waitress asked.

Felix's elegant fingers took two glasses. He handed one to Lucy then lifted the other to his lips, his green eyes half-closing as he took a sip.

The waitress proffered the tray to Tom. He shook his head.

'Not for me, thanks.'

'Miss Stirling...' the waitress gave Lucy a warm smile. 'I hope you don't mind but I wondered, if it's not too cheeky, could I have your autograph? I'm such a big fan.'

'Of course,' Lucy said.

'I've got a pen and paper in my pocket. If someone could hold this?' the waitress gestured to the tray in her hands.

Felix looked at Carla, who glared back at him.

'Here...' Tom said, taking the tray and earning himself a coy smile in return.

'What's your name?' Lucy asked, pen poised.

'Molly O'Leary,' she said, in a fitting Irish brogue. 'If you could just make it to Molly.' As Lucy dashed off her signature, Molly continued, 'I thought you were fantastic in Rio. You must be so fit. I tried diving from a really low board when I was on holiday once. I thought I was going to break my neck. If I had a gold medal, I think I'd wear it all the time. Like you did in that shampoo advert. I wish I had hair like yours... I'm sorry. I'm babbling, aren't I?'

Lucy gave Molly an inquiring look as she slipped the signed sheet in between two glasses.

'You seem familiar. Have we met before?'

'I work the reception here. I started a few weeks ago.'

'Of course.'

Tom handed the tray back.

'Actually, if it's not too much trouble, I was really hoping...' She glanced down at the sheet, then back up at Tom, a warm smile on her lips.

He picked up the pen and paper and added his own hastily scribbled signature before returning them to the tray.

'Don't bother to ask for mine then,' Felix muttered behind Molly's back as she returned to the reception desk.

Just then the door to the main hall swung open and Jackson Cope, the gallery's manager rushed over. A tall, slim man; he flashed a smile revealing teeth as white as his wing-collared shirt.

'Lucy, darling. At last. I was beginning to worry.' He leaned in for a customary air kiss, both sides — very European, despite his Australian heritage. 'Come, take a look...'

He propelled Lucy towards the door he'd come through, pausing at the threshold.

'Well...' He flung out an arm. 'What do you think?'

The vast space, usually devoted to whatever themed exhibition the gallery was running, had been transformed into a decadent dining area. Silverware adorned large round tables cloaked with crisp white linen. Gold napkins and crystal glasses completed the look. At the front of the hall someone fussed with a swag of gold satin adorning the makeshift stage on which sat a lectern, tall marble plinth and several artist easels. On the wall behind, two huge canvases — photographs of Helen and Gordon Stirling in tasteful monochrome — smiled benevolently over the room.

Lucy clutched her chest with both hands.

'Oh my God, Jackson. I love it!'

'The VT's all set to run,' Cope said, pointing towards the stage. 'Do you want the screen down from the start or shall I lower it after your welcome speech?'

'From the start. That way the film can run as soon as I finish.'

'That's what I thought. Also, I know you said you wanted your pieces to be up last, I hope you don't mind, but I've taken the liberty of putting them first in the listing. I thought if they came straight after the video, you'd be able to take advantage of the sentimental mood created by the film. Perhaps one of your party could start the bidding, get people in the mood?'

Lucy turned to Tom.

He gave a shrug. 'Sure.'

Cope looked at his watch. 'Good. Well, I think that's everything. I'll nip upstairs and get your pieces, then if you'd like to join me on stage in, say, ten minutes, I can take you through the programme.'

Before Lucy had time to reply, a harried-looking man, short and round-bellied and sporting a greasy comb-over, rushed towards them.

'Mr Cope, sorry to interrupt but there's a problem. The vegetarian and vegan options—'

Cope promptly lifted a finger, stopping the man mid-flow.

'Excuse me one moment.' He dragged the man away to a safe distance where they consulted in a close huddle. A minute later, he was back. 'I'm sorry, there's a small problem with the catering. I don't know how long it will take to sort out and... well, I had hoped to have your pieces on the stage before the first guests arrive...'

'I can go and get them if you want?' Tom said, turning to Lucy.

'You won't be able to carry all three.' She looked at Felix. 'Would you mind helping?'

'Of course not. Anything for you darling Lucy, you know that.'

After filling them in on where to find the items, Lucy produced a small key card from her Dior clutch bag.

'You'll need this...'

Felix took the card and while he and Tom started for the lift, Lucy slipped a hand through the crook of Carla's arm.

'Come on, let's go and find our table.'

Cope was about to follow them into the main hall, when he spotted Molly at the reception desk, next to the tray of welcome drinks.

'What are you doing girl? Don't just stand there looking gormless. Get rid of those glasses. The first guests will be arriving any minute.'

As Cope hustled off, Molly set the tray on the reception desk, lifted the autographed sheet from between the glasses and, wearing a wide smile, slipped it into her pocket.

2.

'Here you go mate,' the taxi driver said. DI Matt Fisher held onto the door, swaying in his seat as the car came to a stop. 'That'll be nine-fifty.'

Fisher held out a tenner. He felt the note slip from his fingers. 'Keep the change.'

'Cheers. Need a hand?'

'No. I'm good thanks.' Fisher pushed open the door and followed his yellow lab, Luna, onto the pavement. They walked around the house and entered at the back into the kitchen where he unclipped Luna's harness, hanging it on a hook by the door. The dog set off down the hall, the tip-tap of her claws on the hardwood floor mapping out her path.

'Alexa! Turn on the lights.'

On the opposite side of the room a high wattage, unshaded lamp marked out the location of the fridge. Fisher set off towards it, aiming to the right of the dim glow, his hands held out in front of him. Luna pattered back into the kitchen and came to sit beside him, tail swishing energetically across the floor. He reached down and gave her a quick stroke of her head as he pulled three letters from her mouth.

'What have you got for me today?' His voice seemed to echo around the quiet kitchen. 'Alexa! Play my Friday playlist.'

An energetic Foo Fighters track drove the silence out of the room. Fisher placed the letters on the worktop and reached into the cupboard where the dog food was. Ten minutes later, with Luna tucking into her dinner, he grabbed a bottle of lager from the fridge, cracked it open and headed for the lounge. He had just set the beer down on the table next to his favourite chair when the doorbell rang.

Luna ran to the door, barking enthusiastically. Fisher started across the room. Seconds later, a dull thud marked the moment his toe struck the doorframe.

'Ahh, you...' Pain radiated up his leg. How long before he'd learn where the fucking door was? It wasn't as if it kept moving.

The bell rang again, more insistently this time.

'You alright in there?' came a shout through the letterbox. 'It's Geoff from next door.'

'Keep your knickers on! I'll be there in a minute,' Fisher yelled back, hobbling across the hallway and opening the door.

'What happened to you?' Geoff asked at the sight of Fisher: shoulder against the wall, balancing on one leg and rubbing his toe.

'Just smacked my foot on the way through.'

'Won't hurt when the pain's gone,' Geoff said, ever cheerful. 'Parcel came for you earlier. Where do you want it?'

Fisher heard the hollow tap of cardboard.

'Just stick it in the lounge, on the coffee table.' He pressed into the wall to let Geoff pass.

'Keeping well, are you?' Geoff said as he returned to his spot on the doorstep. 'Apart from the toe, obviously.'

'Can't complain. Well, I could but, you know...'

Not in the mood to socialise — rarely was, these days — Fisher let the conversation wither. Soon, he was on his own again, settled in his chair. He was about to crank up the music when his phone started to trill. It was the reminder he'd set for Josh's birthday. Shit! He'd nearly forgotten. How was that possible?

He picked the phone up and scrolled through his contacts. A stilted voice read out the names until he got to the number he was after. He hit dial and waited.

Shortly, a boy's voice rang out, 'Hello?'

'Josh. It's Dad. Happy birthday son.'

'Hi Dad. Thanks for the card.'

'It came, did it? I was worried I'd posted it too late.'

'Yeah, it came this morning. I thought you might have brought it over.'

'I was planning on stopping by on my way home, only the boss called me in as I was leaving. I've literally just this second got in.'

'Oh. Right,' Josh said, his voice thick with disappointment.

Fisher's guilt took his heart in its tight grip. Why lie? There'd been no meeting with the boss — no point; there was no case to update her on. Since *it* had happened, he hadn't been let anywhere near anything that actually needed a detective's prowess, despite his pleading.

He forced his negativity aside and said, 'So, have you had a good day so far?'

'It's been alright. I've had school all day.'

'Of course. Well, what about tonight? Your mum got anything special lined up for you?'

'Nah. She's going out with... err, a friend.'

The pause was long enough for Fisher to get a fair idea what sort of friend.

'You're staying in on your own, on your birthday?'

How long would it take to get a taxi over there? But then there was the present... the present that had only just been delivered and would probably take all night to wrap. He should have ordered it sooner. Yet another thing he should have done but hadn't. Story of his life these days.

'No. It's alright,' Josh said. 'I'm going out. Nando's and then the cinema — some comedy.'

The only difference was, the dealer here wore black leather shoes rather than the latest Nike trainers.

On returning to the main hall, Carla headed back to the table. On seeing everyone gone, she slowed and cast a look around, quickly spotting Lucy and the rest of the crowd at the bar.

'Look what I got!' she said, joining them. She reached into her handbag and retrieved what appeared to be a dirty napkin, pulling it taut to reveal an inky scribble.

'Soiled napkin by Tracey Emin?' Felix said. He let out a laugh, a staccato stuttering sound like a child's attempt at machine gun fire. Oliver Heath laughed along.

Carla frowned. She looked down at the object in her hands, as though doubting what she had. 'It's Shane Harman's autograph. I didn't have any paper on me.'

Felix leaned towards her and theatrically put a finger to his lips.

'Shh! Don't let Tom hear you say that. He and Shane are arch enemies. Think Damon Albarn and Liam Gallagher, only worse.'

Tom rolled his eyes and reached for his pint, turning his back on Felix.

Carla continued, 'He's over there with some woman I kinda recognise. I wasn't sure who she was, so I didn't dare ask for hers. Didn't want to embarrass myself.'

'Too late for that, darling,' Felix said starchily. 'You really shouldn't stalk the guests like some commoner.'

Lucy went to say something but the arrival of a large woman sheathed in a colourful kaftan that clashed with her mauve hair caused the conversation to stall. With promises to boost the appeal's coffers even more, she led Lucy away to a waiting table of middle-aged women whose combined wealth was more than the national debt of some third world countries.

After she had gone, Carla turned back to Felix.

'That woman asked Lucy and Tom for their autographs when we got here,' she said, sounding petulant. 'No one said anything about that.'

Felix treated Carla to a condescending smile.

'She's staff. Whereas we are here at the invitation of the patron.'

Carla hurriedly stuffed the napkin back into her bag.

'You can be a mean sonofabitch sometimes Felix,' Tom said. 'I've been asked for my autograph loads of times tonight; didn't hear you say anything then.'

'They wanted your autograph? Oh, I thought they mistook you for a waiter and were trying to place a drinks order.' He gave another stuttering laugh before turning back to Carla. 'If you're really interested in collecting autographs... you know the woman you thought you recognised? That's Georgia Bellucci, star of film and theatre. She only works classy productions, which is probably why you didn't recognise her. I'm sure Tom could get you her autograph. Perhaps on a pillowcase rather than a dirty napkin.' Felix treated the others to a sly wink.

Tom snatched up his pint from the counter.

'Why don't you just fuck off, Felix?' He pushed away from the bar, grabbed his cigarettes and disappeared into the crowd.

4.

Carla watched Tom's retreating back.

'What's up with him?'

'They used to be an item,' Fran said. 'She ditched him to marry Shane Harman.'

'Tom and that actress...?'

'Ahh, you really do inhabit a different world, don't you?' Felix said. 'Have you even heard of *Hello*?'

Ollie laughed and Carla glowered at them both but said nothing. Fran's attention had already drifted. She scanned the room lazily. Seconds later, a smile tugged at her lips.

'Chelsea and Karina are here,' she said, waving furiously into the crowd. 'I won't be long.' She grabbed her glass and an open but full bottle of champagne off the bar and was about to rush off when Ollie grabbed her arm.

'I don't think that's such a good idea.' He looked pointedly at the bottle. 'You're supposed to be starting training tomorrow, remember?'

She looked down at his hand, a scowl taking shape.

He exhaled noisily.

'Fine.' He released his grip. 'Have it your own way, but don't blame me when Lucy leaves you dead in the water in next month's trials. She's not even back in the squad yet and she's already hitting the pool more than you.'

15

Fran threw her head back and started across the floor with long, hip-swinging strides. On reaching her supermodel friends, she brandished the bottle of bubbly with a giggly scream.

'She'll be lucky to get selected, let alone a medal, next time,' Ollie said, watching as his wife filled her glass until froth spilled over its sides.

'What was that about Lucy diving again?' Felix said.

'A little white lie. I'm hoping a bit of healthy competition might spur Fran on.'

'What if she asks Lucy if it's true?'

'She won't. That would mean admitting she's worried.'

'Maybe it's time Fran ditched the diving? Focus on the modelling instead.' Felix looked back over to the leggy blonde and raised his eyebrows. 'Though if she keeps knocking the drink back like that, she'll have to rethink that too. Nobody wants a nelly elephant thundering down the catwalk.'

Ollie gestured to Felix's almost empty glass and hooked an eyebrow.

'I've got a fast metabolism and fantastic genes.' Felix zig-zagged a finger down the front of his body. 'Ain't an ounce of fat on me, baby, don't you just know it,' Ollie broke into a laugh. Felix laid a hand on his arm. 'Seeing as little Frannie is busy with her friends, why don't we go take a look around the rest of the exhibition? Maybe I'll see something that takes my fancy.'

From her position at the bar, Carla watched Ollie and Felix saunter away. She picked up her glass of Coke and sank onto a stool, inconspicuous in the gloom.

***

Tom shunned the designated smoking area, choosing instead a walled courtyard that on warm days was full of the casual chatter of diners eating alfresco at the gallery's popular café. After propping the door open with a bottle, he took a seat at a small

16

bistro table hidden in the shadow of a wall. He leaned back, stretching out his legs, lit a cigarette and blew out a long, thin stream of smoke. The sky was bright with stars and the air fresh. He shivered. Sitting up, he hunched forward and thought about fetching his jacket. The jacket Lucy had picked out for him. He thought back to when they'd first met, some nine months ago. Lucy Stirling: billionairess, gold medal Olympic diver and successful artist; beautiful, kind, intelligent. Her confidence had excited, even intimidated him. It was all part of the thrill. He took another deep drag. The cigarette's end glowed red in the blackness. He exhaled, watching the smoke disappear.

A sound over by the door caused him to look over cautiously, half-expecting to see Lucy standing there, wearing her disappointment openly. But he knew she'd be too busy schmoozing the guests to even notice his absence. A shaft of light spilled across the floor, growing slowly, before shrinking back to a thin a sliver. Tom's heart thrummed in his chest.

'Thought you might have changed your mind,' he said, lifting the cigarette to lips that curved into a smile.

***

Jackson Cope stepped into the service lift and hit the ground-floor button. Finally, he could relax. It had been a long day; he'd been on his feet since five a.m. All those people, all that money raised, and all down to his organising. Sure, it had been Lucy's idea, but he'd been the one to actually breathe life into the plan. While she was up in her studio playing at being an artist, he was the one making it all happen.

Making his way to the main hall, he found himself drawn to the bar. He'd told himself no drinking, knowing he'd need a clear head in the morning, but one little glass of something couldn't hurt, could it? He weaved through the thinning crowd, passing celebrities dotted around like a constellation of stars. At the bar, he ordered a red wine. A large one. He casually took in the room as the barman cracked open a fresh bottle. A huddle of willowy, super-skinny women with waif-like faces caught his eye. They were leaning in close, as though sharing some secret. One of them, a friend of Lucy's, threw her head back and brayed with laughter, before lifting a glass to her lips. Nearby, a florid-faced American ranch owner, something to do with almonds or avocadoes who had bid in a spirited fashion, waved. Cope let his gaze slide by, making out he hadn't seen him. Further along, a voluminous head of titian waves stood out like a beacon in a sea of grey. Cope tried to see through the gaps between bodies, until he saw hers — a very good body it was too. She was talking to an elderly couple: French vineyard owners with a penchant for modern art, if memory served. A quick check told him there was no obvious partner hanging in the shadows and no obvious drink in her hands. A smile slipped across his lips.

Clutching his own red wine and a glass of champagne — always a safe bet — he turned, about to head in the direction of the redhead, only to discover Carla standing right behind him. He stopped abruptly, sending the drinks sloshing over his fingers.

She took a step back and threw him a look of disgust.

'Watch it! I've already had one idiot chuck his drink all over me tonight as it is.'

He looked down at her white blouse with its pink-tinted damp patch.

'Maybe you should watch it? Sneaking right up behind me like that.' Impatient to make his acquaintance with the redhead before someone else could, he started to walk away.

'Wait...' Carla called.

He turned back.

'Have you seen Lucy?'

'No. Sorry.'

He went to leave a second time. Carla took a step towards him and said, 'It's just that I want to leave. I'm supposed to be going back in the limo but I want to go now.'

He gave a shrug. 'So go. I'll tell Lucy you've gone when I see her.'

'I can't. I didn't bring any money with me.'

'What do you expect me to do?' He wasn't going to offer to pay for a damn taxi, if that was what she was angling for.

'I thought you might know where she is. She's not in here, or in the exhibition room, or the ladies. I don't know where else to look.'

Cope darted a look back over to the titian goddess; saw her splendid cheekbones subtly lift as she smiled. The elderly French couple were gone; in their place stood a silver-haired man sporting a blue tartan kilt and matching bow tie. Cope watched him usher the redhead into the corner, out of the way of passers-by. He returned to the bar and slammed the glasses down onto the counter and growled, 'Just wait here.'

Half an hour later, Carla was still waiting. Twice she had circumnavigated the hall, craning her neck, looking from face to face. She returned to the walk-through exhibition set up in a neighbouring room, being enjoyed less by avid art fans than ardent lovers squeezed into dark corners. She strolled slowly through, looking from couple to couple, but to no avail. Back in the main hall, Ollie and Fran were at the bar. Fran looked at Carla, surprise only just visible on her Botoxed brow.

'What happened to your top?'

'Some idiot tipped wine all over me. I tried to get it out but...' Carla peered down at the obvious stain, pawing at it with nail-bitten fingers. She looked back up at them. 'It looks better than it did.'

Fran attempted a sympathetic smile that stopped short of her eyes. Just then her gaze flitted over Carla's shoulder.

'Where've you been?' she said to Tom as he joined them.

'I went for a smoke then got locked out. I only managed to get in when—'

Someone Tom recognised as a daytime TV presenter rushed past, knocking into him, appearing too preoccupied to notice. Tom was still watching their retreating back as Felix arrived.

'What's going on?' Tom asked him, gesturing towards the entrance, where a small crowd was beginning to gather.

Felix shrugged. 'No idea.'

Tom wandered over and tapped one of the gathering on the shoulder.

'What's happening?'

'It's Lucy Stirling. She's been murdered.'

5.

'Hang on. Tight corner coming up,' DC Beth Nightingale said.

Fisher reached up and grabbed the handle above his head just as the car banked into the bend, tyres squealing. It was nearly three a.m. and they were on their way to an exclusive art gallery, racing along country lanes that twisted and reeled as unpredictably as a rollercoaster.

'Easy,' he said, as they straightened up. 'I'd like to get there in one piece, if you don't mind.'

'Sorry sir.'

He'd been enjoying a dream-filled sleep in glorious technicolour when the call had come in. Yet he'd happily traded his quilt for a suit and tie at the prospect of working a live investigation. At last, a chance to escape the office, the odour of which was as stale as the cases he'd been working on. He didn't care the only reason he got to go was because the other two DIs in the major crime unit were out of action. Jen Marshall was sunning herself somewhere in the Caribbean. The other, a guy called Dave Beswick, was similarly prostrate. Only, rather than lying on a sandy beach, he was laid up in a hospital bed, recovering from a heart attack.

Another corner. Fisher rolled in his seat. Gentler this time. A whisper of perfume, something fresh and clean, conjured up an image of Nightingale leaning into the curve, drawing close, before the car steadied.

'Are you nervous?' she asked.

'What?'

'I just wondered if it was normal to feel nervous.'

Fisher thought about it. His heart danced a jig in his chest in reply. That was excitement, right? It was his first case since the incident; a chance to prove he still had it in him. It's what he'd been waiting for.

'You'll be alright,' he said. 'Just remember to keep your eyes and ears open and your mouth shut. Don't go putting words into people's mouths.'

'Will the DCI be there?'

'The Falcon? Unlikely. Not at this time of night.' In his experience, Detective Chief Inspector Anita Fallon had no desire to dirty her hands on an actual crime scene. 'Why's that?'

'I just wondered. I'll be honest, I'm a little bit terrified of her.'

Fisher wanted to tell her the Falcon was all bark and no bite, but he'd be lying. Instead, he said, 'I wouldn't worry. She won't want to miss out on her beauty sleep.'

'Even if there's a chance of meeting some celebrities?' Before Fisher could answer, she went on, 'Do you think there'll actually be anyone properly famous there? Like someone I actually recognise.'

Celebrities and the media were a dangerous mix, meaning the case was likely to attract an undue amount of attention. As lead detective, how soon before he found himself under the microscope? Not exactly the ideal circumstance for him to prove he could still hack it. His stomach rolled, and not because of the road. Maybe it was too soon?

He felt the car slide beneath him as it took another tight corner.

'Will you slow down,' he snapped. 'If the dog doesn't throw up I will.'

'Sorry.'

on her front; on her chest. A small round pad. Like a medical thing.'

'That'll probably be from the ECG, from when the paramedics pronounced her dead. They often leave them attached.'

'There's something else...' Another rustle of scene suit. 'It looks like she's got some brown paint or dirty water on her. There's a puddle of it underneath her.'

Fisher sniffed the air, delicately, trying to detect a certain aroma.

'Is this your first dead body, Beth?'

'No sir. I worked No Hope when I was in uniform. Why's that?'

Knole Hope, otherwise known as No Hope, was a notorious estate where more drugs changed hands on a daily basis than in Boots.

'I just wondered if she'd soiled herself — the puddle — dead bodies have a tendency to purge.'

'It's in the wrong place. This is more around the head area.'

'Okay. Carry on then. What's she wearing?'

'A long evening dress, gold and glittery, with a low back that drapes all the way down to the waist.'

'What's her back like?'

'Her back?'

'Yes. Her back. What's it like?'

'I can't see any marks on it. It looks very toned, from what I can tell. But it's kinda hard to tell from the way she's lying.'

'But you'd say this could be the body of an Olympic diver?'

'Yes.' A confident reply.

'Okay. What else can you see?'

'An open handbag. Looks like Chanel. And there's a phone on the floor about three feet away. It's been stamped on or hit with something heavy.'

'Murder weapon?'

'I was just coming to that. There's a bronze figure of a swimmer, or rather a diver. Could be whatever the equivalent of a self-portrait in sculptures is. It's...' She rustled as she moved and Fisher heard her breath catch in her throat. 'There are chunks of flesh on it, as well as blood and hair.'

Fisher committed to memory the layout as far as he could. 'What else?'

'There's a big stainless-steel sink in the middle of the workbench, and jars with brushes and knives — like craft knives — in them and tubes of paint and a roll of paper towel at this end. At the other end, there's a couple of metre's gap before the far wall. A bit further along there's a huge full height window with an easel in front of it. Next to that is an industrial-looking machine. There are some shelves with sculptures on them that look like they're being worked on. Then over at the back of the room, to your left, there's another door that looks like it goes into a small room. That's pretty much everything.'

'Any signs someone came up here from the party?'

'What sort of thing?'

'An empty glass or an ashtray with a cigarette stub. Maybe someone asked to see more of her work, then when they got her in private, something happened and things got nasty. Or maybe she had a falling out with someone and wanted to avoid arguing in public so brought them here.'

'There's an empty mug by the sink,' Nightingale said. 'No glasses though.'

'Okay. Carry on.'

'The sink in the middle of the workbench has got a cupboard underneath. The door's open. I can see a bottle of turps and some cloths. Just looks like it's full of cleaning materials.'

Fisher nodded then shifted uncomfortably, trussed up like a turkey in the scene suit, with his suit jacket and shirt beneath. A trickle of sweat ran down between his shoulder blades.

'Is it just me or is it warm in here?'

28

'The kiln is on,' called a woman whose voice Fisher didn't recognise.

'Who said that?'

'I don't know,' Nightingale said quietly. 'One of the CSIs, I guess.'

'One second,' the woman shouted. A moment later, 'Sorry, I was in the middle of dusting the kitchen for prints.'

Fisher could hear the woman make her way over.

'Carrie Finch. I'm the senior CSI here.'

'DI Matt Fisher. You mentioned a kitchen.'

'Kitchenette, really: sink, kettle, small fridge.'

Fisher imagined her taking in the dark glasses, noticing his hand clutching Nightingale's arm, but whatever she thought, unlike her colleague, she kept it to herself.

'So, what can you tell us at this stage?' he asked.

'Initial observations are the victim was struck over the head with a heavy object, most probably the bronze sculpture on the floor next to the body. It looks like she was kneeling or bending down when she was hit and died where she fell. Obviously, we'll need to do a full blood spatter analysis to be sure.'

'Prints?'

'The place is full of them, including on the bronze figure, though most of those are smudged, suggesting your killer wore gloves.'

'Do you think gloves mean whoever did it came here knowing they were going to kill her?' Nightingale asked, after the CSI left to return to her work.

'Not necessarily,' Fisher said. 'Though I doubt they brought them to help with the washing up.'

6.

Fisher stepped out of the studio and forced a deep breath out of his nose, flushing the tang of violence from his nostrils. He held onto the wall and started to tug the scene suit down his body, peeling it off a limb at a time, taking special care not to get his feet caught. Finally free, he scrunched it into a ball and passed it to Nightingale, then called Luna to him. He reached down, the tension leaving his shoulders as he felt the familiar grip of her harness in his hand.

'Right, let's see what we've got downstairs then.'

'The main hall is over on your right,' Nightingale said, as they stepped out of the lift on the ground floor.

Fisher followed the sound of voices; letting himself be guided by Luna. Nightingale went ahead and opened the door for them. After crossing the threshold, he took a few steps to one side, then said, 'Right, Beth, quick visual.'

'It's a big room, full of tables and chairs and a stage at the front. There are still tons of people here, waiting to be interviewed. I can see some of our team taking statements and quite a few uniforms.'

'Any sign of Andy?' The very next second, he heard the sergeant's resonant voice cut through the chatter. 'Talk of the devil. Is he free?'

'He's talking to someone on the other side of the room. Oh, it's the DCI.'

'The Falcon's here?' Fisher said, failing to hide his surprise.

He should have known. She'd spent the last few months telling him how everyone had the utmost confidence in him. And most of the time, she even managed to avoid adding 'despite your disability'. But when it came to putting her money where her mouth was and trusting him with a case, her actions spoke louder than words. Not surprising, seeing as DCI Anita Fallon had one foot poised on the next rung of her ambitious career ladder and the other ready to boot out of the way anyone who might cause her to slip from it.

'She's seen us,' Nightingale said. 'They're coming over.'

Soon Fisher could hear the tip-tap of heels, accompanied by Wickham's firm tread. He clenched and unclenched his jaw.

'DI Fisher,' DCI Fallon said, in a cool, bordering on cold, tone.

'Ma'am.' He nodded. 'I wasn't expecting to see you here.'

If the Falcon picked up on his choice of words, she chose not to comment.

'Really? At a murder scene where I'm SIO?'

Like that meant anything. Fisher had worked countless murder cases where she'd been the senior investigating officer and hadn't deemed it necessary to actually visit the crime scene. Why should she, when she had a comfortably appointed, heated office and minions she could call on to give detailed briefings?

'So, what's your assessment?' she asked.

'Bit early to be hypothesising.'

'No ideas at all?'

'Like I said, it's early days.'

'Hmm. DS Wickham…?'

Fisher felt a jolt of anger grip his gut at her decision to consult the more junior officer.

'I think…' Wickham paused. Fisher stiffened; either the sergeant was going to make himself look an arse as he tried to make something out of nothing or there was some detail of the scene that Fisher hadn't been made aware of. Wickham went on, 'DI Fisher's right. It's too soon to say.'

31

Fisher relaxed. Maybe he was being paranoid?

'Okay,' DCI Fallon said. 'Well, I'm going to be around a while longer — try to give the guests some reassurance — shout if you need to run anything by me.'

Only after the sound of her heels had diminished to a quiet click did Fisher trust himself to speak.

'What the hell is she doing here? Andy, did she say anything to you?'

'Something to do with resourcing issues.'

Fisher nodded but the grim set of his jaw made it clear he was anything but happy.

'Well, it is what it is. I suppose we'd better do what we're told and crack on. Beth, go see if they've sorted that room out for us yet.' As soon as she left, he challenged Wickham. 'Resourcing issues?'

'I didn't want to say in front of Beth, but why do you think the Falcon's here?' He set a heavy hand on Fisher's shoulder. 'Sorry mate. I told you before, people are going to have a hard time believing you can do this job blind. You'd better get used to it — she's going to be all over this case like the mother of all rashes.'

***

Nightingale arranged for them to work from one of the managers' offices. A warm, quiet room that smelled of lily of the valley and was furnished with a good-sized table and four chairs with padded seats. In the past, Fisher would have bestowed himself no favours, conducting witness interviews in the main hall, along with everyone else, but these days, with his senses down by one, he found noisy environments difficult to work in.

Fisher's chair squeaked as he sat down. With a strong black coffee by his elbow and Luna at his feet, he waited for Nightingale to fetch the first interviewee.

The door clicked open. Nightingale's voice filtered in, 'If you'd like to go through, Mr Cope...'

A muffled movement of feet on carpet was followed by the sound of a chair being pulled back on the other side of the table.

'DI Fisher, this is Mr Jackson Cope, general manager of the gallery.'

Fisher picked up a hint of apples as Nightingale took her seat next to him.

'I was also a close family friend,' Cope said and Fisher caught a trace of an accent hidden under the lofty tones of an expensive education. Australian? New Zealand? He wasn't sure.

'Mr Cope, I understand you found Miss Stirling.'

'Yes. Something I won't forget any time soon. If there's anything I can do to help you catch whoever did it....'

'I appreciate that, sir,' Fisher said. 'Let's start with tonight, shall we? It was a fundraising event?'

'The Indonesian Tsunami Appeal set up by Gordon and—'

Fisher clicked his fingers.

'Gordon Stirling... Gordon Stirling was Lucy Stirling's father?'

Gordon Stirling was a household name. The founder of a particularly successful dot com business, which had gone from strength to strength, affiliated companies growing almost as fast as Gordon Stirling's bank balance.

'Yes,' Cope said. 'Both Gordon and Helen, Lucy's mother, died in a helicopter crash earlier this year. They were in Indonesia helping direct the efforts of the appeal when it happened. Lucy was holding tonight's auction in their memory.'

Reminded of it now, Fisher recalled hearing the breaking news of the disaster as he'd lain in his hospital bed, bandaged eyes preventing him from seeing the tragic footage. That was in the days where he'd still retained some slim hope of recovering his sight. It seemed like a lifetime ago.

'The room where the murder took place: it's some sort of art studio. Is that right?'

'Yes. It was Lucy's studio.'

'She'd given up the diving then?'

'Yes. She retired after Rio.'

'How old was she?'

'Only twenty-four. But she didn't quit because of her age. A bad landing in the preliminaries in Rio left her with a fractured disc in her neck. She shouldn't really have competed — she could have ended up paralysed — but she wanted that gold. Afterwards, Helen encouraged her to return to her art; she'd been studying it at Cambridge when she got into Team GB. Helen had already established the gallery and made Lucy artist-in-residence.'

'That was lucky. Mummy owning an art gallery like that,' Fisher said. He thought he heard the breath catch in Nightingale's throat.

'Lucy didn't need luck.' Cope said drily. 'She had natural talent. You've been up there, seen her work for yourself.'

Fisher let the silence stretch for a moment, before lifting his hand to his head and raising his dark glasses. In his mind's eye he could see the other man take in the empty stare, perhaps noticing for the first time the dog with its harness on the other side of the table.

'How was I supposed to know you're blind? You could have said.'

Fisher let the glasses drop back into place.

Unruffled, Cope continued, 'Look, Lucy was a damn good painter and, in my opinion, an even better sculptor. Some of her work went for considerable sums.'

'How considerable?' Fisher asked.

'Anywhere between two and eight.'

'Hundred?'

'Thousand.'

Fisher was grateful he hadn't just had a mouthful of coffee. It might have ended up sprayed all over the table. For someone who had once moved in a world of millionaires, he was surprised to find himself so easily shocked. But the amount mentioned did open up one line of enquiry — at eight grand a pop, could they be the reason she was killed?

'I don't suppose you noticed whether any of her work was missing from the studio?'

'You can't seriously think she was killed for something so petty?' Cope said in a voice that suggested he was wrinkling his nose in disgust at the suggestion.

'It's not often I hear eight grand being referred to as petty,' Fisher said.

'Sums of that size are inconsequential to the sorts of people here tonight.'

'People have killed for a lot less. And presumably her work will be worth considerably more now that she's dead.'

'I find your attitude really quite offensive.'

'I'm only stating the facts.' Fisher waited a beat, then continued, 'Putting motive aside for a minute, when you entered Lucy's studio did anything catch your eye or seem out of place?'

'You mean other than the fact Lucy was lying there dead?' Cope sounded surly now.

'Sometimes, even in the face of horror like the scene you witnessed upstairs, the human brain can still notice the smallest anomalies. What I want to know is, did yours?'

'No.' After a minute, it was clear Cope was not inclined to offer more.

Fisher kicked himself. He'd antagonised the man. Great start. Time to change tack.

'You clearly thought a lot of Lucy,' he said, adopting a softer tone of voice.

Cope cleared his throat and Fisher wondered if he was tearing up.

'I had worked for Helen for many years, since coming over to England from Australia in the nineties. So I'd known Lucy most of her life. She was an incredible woman. I can't imagine anyone intentionally hurting her.'

'Well someone did. And they did more than hurt her.'

Fisher could hear sniffing now.

'Excuse me,' Cope said, before blowing his nose.

'Okay,' Fisher said. They were getting nowhere. 'What about other relationships? Was Lucy seeing anyone?'

'She'd been dating Tom Morrelli for a while.'

Fisher hitched his eyebrows and felt the skin around his eyes pinch.

'The singer from Nevermind?'

'Yes.'

'Any problems between them?'

'Not as far as I know. Though I was surprised it had lasted as long as it had.'

'Why's that?'

'Lucy took her parents' deaths very badly. She went through a bit of a rough patch and resorted to going out a lot. And not necessarily to the sorts of places she would ordinarily have frequented. I think she hated being on her own, so said yes to any invitation that came her way. As a result, she started to rub shoulders with a lot of people that... well, let's just say, weren't her usual type.'

'Like Tom Morrelli,' Fisher said.

'Don't get me wrong, Tom's nice enough, but there's no denying he's a bit rough around the edges. Likes a drink and a smoke. Not at all cultured. Spends most of his time playing that guitar of his. Lucy was refined, hardworking. And she kept herself fit, despite the fact she was no longer training.'

'Was Mr Morrelli here tonight?'

'Yes. He came with Lucy.'

'Anyone else with them?'

'A few of her friends. Oh, and her sister.'

'What's the sister's name?'

'Carla. Carla Porter.'

'Married, is she?'

'Married? No, I don't think so.' Cope sounded confused by the assumption, then, after a beat, 'Oh, you mean because of the different surname? No. Helen and Gordon adopted Lucy. Her birth mother's name was Porter.'

Fisher made a mental note to find out what that meant in terms of inheritance, then asked, 'I don't suppose you know who Lucy's next of kin is?'

'I believe that would be Lucy's aunt, Mrs Eleanor Morgan. Helen's sister. She was also here tonight.'

Fisher sat up.

'Do you know if she's still around?'

'I doubt it. You'd know it if she was.'

'Why's that?'

'She would have insisted on speaking to you before anyone else.'

Fisher knew the type. He nodded, then said, 'Nightingale, could you go find out, please?'

Fisher heard a chair scrape across the floor. After the door had clicked closed, he asked, 'Did Lucy have any problems with any of the guests that you know of?'

'No, but then she was the sort of person to get along with everyone.'

While Fisher considered where to take the questions next, Cope took advantage of the gap. 'Look, I'm supposed to be overseeing the shipping of the auctioned items first thing tomorrow. Will that be a problem?'

A case of the show must go on? Fisher banked the observation.

'It shouldn't be, as long as you steer clear of the studio and any other areas that are sealed off.'

'What other areas?'

'I can't say at the moment. It's possible we might need to expand the crime scene depending on what we find.'

Just then, there was a gentle knock at the door. Fisher heard it open.

'Mr and Mrs Morgan left before Miss Stirling was found,' Nightingale said, crossing the floor and retaking her seat. 'DS Wickham said he'll arrange for someone to let them know what's happened.'

'Good. Well I think I'm ready to meet Lucy's friends now. If you could give us their names please, Mr Cope?' As soon as they'd got the details, Fisher let Cope go. 'So, what did you make of him then, Beth?'

'He was full of himself when I was talking to him on the way here. Quietened down a bit once you started with the questions.'

'How old is he?'

'Oh God. I don't know. I'm rubbish at guessing ages.'

'Try.'

'Well, his skin looked very good. He hardly had any wrinkles.'

'Botox can be deceptive.'

'But his hands didn't look like an old person's.'

'Best guess?'

'Thirty-five?'

Fisher frowned.

'Sounded older.'

'Okay, forty then. I told you I was rubbish at guessing.'

'What was he dressed like?'

'Smart. What my nan would call dapper.'

That fitted with the whiff of expensive aftershave that still hung heavy in the air.

'Going back to his hands,' Fisher said, 'what were his fingernails like?'

'Better than mine. Neat and shiny. Looked like they'd been manicured.' After a beat, 'Why? Is that important?'

'Maybe our Mr Cope's the type not to get his hands dirty.'

'Does that mean you think it's unlikely he did it?'

'I wouldn't go that far.'

7.

After speaking with Jackson Cope, Fisher and Nightingale returned to the main hall. It was quieter now and Fisher surmised many of the guests had been interviewed and sent on their way.

'Any sign of Andy?' he asked.

'Looks like he's interviewing someone.'

'Is there anywhere we can wait that's not in the way?'

'There's an empty table by the bar.'

'Good. I could do with a stiff drink.'

'I don't think there's anyone serving.'

'I was joking,' Fisher said, though to be honest a little livener would have been very welcome.

Nightingale led the way to the table. Fisher had just eased the weight off his feet when she said, 'It looks like Andy's free now. I'll go get him.'

As Nightingale's footsteps grew faint, Fisher became aware of the murmurs of hushed conversations punctuated with the occasional scrape of a chair leg and solemn goodbyes. Soon, though, Nightingale's light tread returned, this time accompanied by a man's sure step.

'Guv,' Wickham said.

'How's it going?'

'Nothing so far. No one appears to have seen or heard anything. How did it go with the manager?'

'Same. Saw nothing and no ideas about a possible motive. He did give us the names of the people the vic was here with. I'd like to talk to them next if they're still around.'

'Here...' Nightingale said to a backdrop of rustling paper.

After a small pause, Wickham said, 'Ah. They've already been interviewed. Spoke to them myself. Though one of the names is different. This says Francesca Heath. The woman I talked to called herself Francesca La Salle. It's probably the same woman.'

'Make sure you check. Francesca's not that unusual a name.'

'Will do.'

'Any chance you'll be able to getting those interviews typed up and on the system first thing? I'd like to run through them as soon as.'

'I can give Beth my notes now, if you want?'

Fisher shook his head and gave a wry smile.

'Nice try, but even if she could read your scribble, she's going to be busy with her own notes.'

'Sorry,' Wickham said. 'No offence, Beth.'

'None taken,' she replied.

'So, did any of Lucy's friends have much to say?' Fisher asked.

'Not really. They all seemed equally shocked. No one had any idea about possible motives — no reported arguments, no grievances. There was one thing struck me as odd. I don't know if you know, but her boyfriend was Tom Morrelli, the singer. Well, he claims he went into the courtyard café for a smoke. Said he propped the fire door open with a bottle and either it got dislodged or someone moved it and he ended up locked out there for the best part of an hour. He only managed to get out after a waitress heard him banging on the door. By the time he rejoined the rest of the friends, Lucy was already missing. I did go and have a quick look and found a bottle on the floor by the door. I bagged it, just in case. It's possible someone could have accidentally knocked it and the door closed, though equally, someone could have deliberately moved it and locked him out.'

'What courtyard are we talking about?' Fisher asked.

'It's the open-air seating area for the café. It wasn't supposed to be open tonight.'

'You mentioned a fire door. Does that mean there's direct access to outside?'

'Access, yes, but not direct. There is a way out from the courtyard but it's an emergency exit only. The door on the external wall's alarmed. If Morrelli had gone through it, everyone would have known about it.'

'I haven't heard it go off.'

'That's because no one's gone through it.'

'Well shouldn't someone try it? What if the alarm's been disabled?'

'Sorry. I should've thought of that.'

'When we're done here, go back and test it. What was Morrelli doing, going in the courtyard, if it wasn't supposed to be open?'

'I told you: having a fag.'

'But presumably the gallery has got an area for smokers?'

'He said he doesn't like being around too many people.'

'He's a bloody rock star. Performs in front of thousands. Bloody convenient, getting trapped with no witnesses while his girlfriend's bludgeoned to death. Well, that's something for when we next talk to him. Okay, what about the other friends?'

'On the whole, they kept themselves amused while the vic was busy talking to guests. It wasn't until her sister wanted to leave and tried to find her that anyone realised she'd gone.'

'Has anybody mentioned seeing Miss Stirling outside of this room?' Fisher asked. 'On her way upstairs or anywhere near the studio?'

'Not as far as I know,' Wickham replied. 'The studio and upstairs in general were out of bounds tonight. Only the ground floor was supposed to be open to the public. There's a sign on the lift and at the bottom of the stairs that says staff only. The studio has also got a key card lock fitted.'

'Like anyone ever pays attention to no entry signs after hours. Especially rich folk whose already liberal attitudes are even more relaxed, courtesy of the buckets of free champagne they've drunk.'

'If you say so,' Wickham said. 'Can't say as I've been to too many celebrity bashes myself.'

'Trust me. It happens.'

'Ah there you are!' DCI Anita Fallon's shrill call cut across the hall. Fisher let the sigh die in his throat. Heels came marching towards them. 'I'm glad I caught you. Thought I might be too late.'

'For what?' Fisher asked.

'The next of kin. I'm coming with you. I assume you'll be leaving soon?'

'I was going to go in the morning. I want to get as much out of folk here before they disappear.'

'I've already arranged for one of the uniforms and a family liaison officer to go and let them know what's happened,' Wickham offered.

'Thank you. That's something at least,' she said, before her tone changed to one as sharp as a raptor's claw, 'DI Fisher, you are aware of who the next of kin is?'

'Some aunt. Eleanor somebody.'

'Eleanor Morgan, who only happens to be the wife of Rupert Morgan, QC.'

'Who?'

'The eminent prosecution lawyer.'

'So what do you want me to do? Haul them out of bed in the middle of the night and ask them to account for their movements?' Fisher knew he sounded tetchy, but she brought out the worst in him.

'Don't be facetious. I want them reassured that we'll do everything in our power to bring the perpetrator to account.'

'We really need to tell them that?'

and pretending to be hurt all the time. They get paid an awful lot of money to kick the ball, how can they make such a hash of it? Just a bunch of prima donnas if you ask me.'

'That's a bit harsh.'

'But true, don't you think?'

'Not really.' Fisher had always prided himself on his fancy rather than fouling footwork. 'But then I'm biased. I used to be one of them, back in the day. And as for prima donnas, given a striker kicks a ball upwards of eighty miles an hour, if they happen to mistake your shin for the ball, you bloody well know it, believe me.'

'Well, I hope you don't still resort to kicking people in the shin to get what you want.' She gave a little snort of a laugh and Fisher realised that was her attempt at a joke and laughed too. 'I didn't mean to pry, by the way. I though perhaps it was to do with a case you'd been working.'

'No case. Just a lifestyle that is well and truly in the past.'

When they stepped out of the lift, they found Morrelli waiting at his front door.

'Wanna drink?' he mumbled, as he showed them in. 'I'm on tequila, but I've got vodka, gin, whisky...'

'Not for us, thank you,' Fisher said. 'Mr Morrelli, we understand you lost your jacket earlier, at the gallery.'

Fisher heard a metallic rasping sound followed by a loud exhalation. His nose twitched as the acrid stench of cigarette smoke hit him. He waved a hand in front of his face.

'Huh? My jacket? Yeah.'

'What label is it?'

'Dunno. Can't remember. Lucy picked it out for me. I was going to wear one of the ones I normally wear for award ceremonies but she said it wasn't that sort of gig. Not smart enough.'

'What size then?'

'Prob'ly a forty regular. Or maybe a thirty-eight. It was a bit tight. I was going to take it back and get something else, to be honest.'

'You'll have the receipt then?

'Somewhere. What's all the interest in my jacket anyway? Shouldn't you be out looking for Lucy's killer?'

'I'd like to see that receipt, please Mr Morrelli,' Fisher pressed.

Five minutes later, after rifling through numerous drawers and shaking out a variety of bags, the singer finally found what they wanted.

'Here,' he said, padding across the room.

'Sir, it's a Fendi,' Nightingale said.

'Mr Morrelli, it would appear your jacket was found in the same room as Miss Stirling's body. Any idea how it might have got there?'

'What?' He sounded shocked enough. 'No. I told you, I left it by the bar. I only noticed it had gone when I went to leave.'

'Did you go up to Lucy's studio this evening?'

'No. Well, yes. But that was earlier. I helped fetch some things for her.'

'What time was that?'

'When we first got to the gallery. I didn't even know Lucy had gone up later. I thought she was still talking to guests.' After a short pause, he said, 'Maybe she took my jacket with her?'

'And why would she do that?'

'To keep it safe?'

'Rather than just give it to the cloakroom attendant?'

'Oh, yeah... I don't know then.'

'Why do you think Lucy went to the studio?'

'I don't know. I told you, I didn't know she had.'

'How was your relationship? Had you been together long?'

'Is that what this is about? You can't think I did it. Oh man.'

There was the sound of a metal screwcap being twisted.

'Mr Morrelli, I think you've had enough. Please put the bottle down.' He was relieved to hear a solid thump in reply. 'I'm simply trying to understand what happened. And in order to do that, I need to know more about Miss Stirling and her relationships. So, how were the two of you getting along?'

'Okay,' Tom said quietly. 'Lucy was fun. She had so much energy. We got together after her parents died. She was a very good person; kind and thoughtful. She was way too good for me, that's for sure.'

'Sounds like you cared a lot for her.'

'Hell yes. I mean even if I... well...' A heavy sigh. 'Never mind.'

'What?'

'Nothing. It doesn't matter. The answer is, yes, I cared for her.'

'And what about her? How would you describe her feelings for you?'

'I don't know. She cared for me too, I guess.'

'You don't sound too sure.'

'You never really know what someone's thinking do you?'

Fisher wondered where the declarations of undying love were.

'Do you know anyone called Patrick?'

'Patrick? I don't think so. Why?'

Fisher gave a subtle shake of his head, then said, 'I understand you went out to the courtyard for a cigarette. How did Lucy feel about you smoking?'

'She wasn't keen, but she was cool about it as long as I didn't do it near her.'

'And drugs?'

'Don't do 'em.'

Fisher gave an exaggerated sniff. He'd recognised the sweet smell of marijuana as soon as they'd entered the apartment.

'Okay,' Morrelli said. 'I might have the odd spliff but never around Lucy.'

'What about other stuff? Do much coke do you?'

'Never had it. Only do a bit of weed. And then, not often.'

'So how do you explain the traces of coke found in your jacket pocket?'

'Is this a wind up? Tonight's the first time I'd worn it. And I was planning on taking it back. There was nothing in my pockets. If you found the jacket near Lucy with the pockets stuffed with coke, someone's trying to frame me. Test me if you like.'

'Remind me again where you were around half eleven.'

'In the courtyard. I went out for a smoke and got locked out.'

'Mr Morrelli, in your statement,' Nightingale said, 'you claim to have been out there at least forty-five minutes, maybe longer. Why did it take you so long to attract someone's attention?'

'I had a few smokes before I even tried to leave.'

'Why go there?' Fisher asked. 'Why not go to the proper smoking area?'

'And have to listen to all those arty-farty, la-di-dah types banging on about their collections?'

'Types like Lucy, you mean?'

'Lucy was different. She wasn't stuck up. Unlike those so-called friends of hers.'

'How come you hardly saw each other all night?'

'It was her night. She had all those people to talk to. I was just killing time until she'd finished. Besides, I would have gone looking for her earlier if someone hadn't locked me out.'

'So when we check the statements of the waiting staff, someone should mention opening the door for you?'

'Why would they? What's to tell?'

'Come on... coming to the rescue of the famous Tom Morrelli?'

'That's true,' Tom said, his voice thick with smugness. 'I do tend to have that effect on people.'

Fisher remembered seeing Morrelli and his fellow band mates from Nevermind performing their debut single at the Brit Awards a couple of years before. Chiselled jaw, blond hair draped over eyes lined with long lashes. Fisher had been handsome once; not like the horror show he imagined he looked now with his mass of dark waves above a face that looked like a wax mask left out in the sun. Like Morrelli, he too now had a face most people would remember, but for all the wrong reasons.

'I thought we were going to take him in,' Nightingale said as the car accelerated away.

'On what basis? He's right. Someone could have planted the jacket in the kiln. Let's see what forensics make of the rest of his clothes first.'

In the boot were evidence bags containing the singer's clothes and shoes. He'd still been wearing them when they arrived.

'They looked pretty clean to me. Plus he seemed genuinely upset.'

'He could have rehearsed his response. Given the level of violence, it could have been a spur of the moment attack but equally it could have been the result of months of planning.'

'But what about the fact he was locked out? Surely it's only a matter of time before we find the waitress who let him out?'

'Who's to say he didn't go into the courtyard when he said he did, have a cigarette, better still, light two or three at the same time, then, while they're burning down — the stubs being evidence to support his account — he could have nipped upstairs, killed Lucy then returned to the courtyard, pulling the door closed behind him. What I want to know is, what's his motive?'

'Maybe he's lying about the coke? What if Lucy saw him with it and threatened to dump him?' Nightingale said. 'Or worse, report him to the police.'

'Would he care?'

'A lot of Nevermind's fans are probably kids. It might turn some of them off the band.'

'Probably turn more of them onto it. Adds to the cool image.'

'Suppose...' She didn't sound convinced. What Fisher wasn't sure about was whether that was because she was a young woman, open to the charms of a good-looking young man, or was she picking up on non-verbal clues that painted more of a picture than words alone ever could. And how the hell was he to know?

10.

A torrent of barks snatched Fisher from his dreams. Saturday morning and it felt like his head had only just hit the pillow. He pushed the bedclothes away and eased himself up onto an elbow. The doorbell sounded, setting off a fresh round of barking. He grabbed his trousers from the floor by the side of the bed and hastily pulled them on before carefully making his way downstairs.

'Morning.' It was Nightingale. 'Oh sorry. Shall I wait in the car?'

Fisher had an image of her hastily looking away from his naked torso.

'Don't be daft. Come in. Make yourself useful and stick the kettle on. I'll be with you in five minutes.'

Fifteen minutes later, Fisher joined her in the kitchen. He could hear Luna chowing down.

'You fed the dog?'

'I hope that was alright? She was sitting looking at her food bowl.'

'Saved me a job.'

'I would have got something for you, but I don't know what you have.'

'Don't worry about it. We haven't got time.'

'Actually, we're okay for time. I'm a little early. The roads were empty.'

'It's alright. I'll grab something later.'

'At least have some coffee. I already made it, though it's probably cold now.'

'Now that I won't say no to.' Fisher held out his hand and took hold of the smooth, warm ceramic. He drank the tepid liquid in two big gulps, returning the mug to the worktop by the sink.

'Are you supposed to be seeing your son this morning?' Nightingale asked as Fisher fastened Luna into her harness.

'How on earth did you know that?' He didn't realise she even knew he'd got a son.

'Alexa. You set a reminder to call a taxi and to text Josh to tell him what time to expect you. I assumed he's your son. Is it his birthday?'

'Yesterday. What are you, psychic?'

Nightingale snorted a little laugh.

'There's a present on the side.'

Fisher had wrapped it the previous evening, after the call to Josh.

'No flies on you, Sherlock.'

'If he lives nearby, we could drop it off. You might not get the chance later.'

Fisher attempted a smile.

'You sound like my wife. She's usually right, too. Grab the present. It's on the way. Shouldn't delay us too long.'

Stepping out of the house, Fisher sensed the sun was already climbing, the air warm on his unshaven face. He sank into the passenger seat. A huge yawn escaped him. What he'd give for a strong, hot black coffee. It had been a long time since he'd pulled an all-nighter; one of the few plus-points of having been consigned to his desk for the last nine months.

'Do you need to let him know you're on your way?' Nightingale said as they set off. 'It's only just gone seven. He'll still be in bed, won't he?'

'You're joking. He'll have been up since the crack of dawn playing computer games. He's always been an early bird.'

The seat next to Fisher dipped as his son rolled into him, embracing him in another hug before standing up. He felt his heart swell and for once he was grateful that his disability saved him from having to use the old 'must be something in my eye' line. Seconds later came the thump of feet rushing up the stairs.

Fisher rose to his feet, shoulders slumped. He suddenly felt very tired.

'Beth, perhaps you could help guide me out?'

They retraced their steps back to the front door. At the threshold, he sensed his wife poised to close the door. He followed Beth onto the step, then paused.

'Maybe it's time I talked to a solicitor?' he said.

The front door clicked shut behind him.

11.

Earlier that morning, while Fisher was sleeping as deeply as only the sleep-deprived can, Jackson Cope had left his house. He was later than planned due to a sluggish start following a broken night's sleep that left him with a foggy head even a cold shower had failed to shift. Nonetheless, it was still dark when he pulled into the gallery's staff car park. Entering through the back door, he closed it carefully, then stood with his head cocked, listening hard. When the only sound to greet his ears was the low juddering of the heating system firing up, he started down the stairs.

The basement was a capacious space; bright, white, humidity-controlled and temperature-regulated. Ordinarily it was home to all manner of miscellany used in the day-to-day running of the gallery: display stands, out-of-commission signs, storage crates, as well as stacks of chairs and folding tables used for events such as the previous evening's dinner. Today though, it was home to an array of canvases of all different sizes along with a plethora of sculptures and other artefacts, all ready for packing and transporting to their new owners. Cope hurriedly set out a collection of crates and placed each successful bidder's art work by the right sized crate, filling in a proforma dispatch note for each box. He worked quickly and efficiently. With the last proforma filled, he checked his watch. There was still half an hour to go before Barry, the gallery's stock supervisor, was due in. Cope looked at the rows of open crates, their consignments set neatly beside them... and then at the single empty crate that remained. He had intended on filling it first, when there was little chance of being disturbed, yet somehow, he'd ended up leaving it to last — some stupid act of self-sabotage, he wondered.

For a brief moment he stood immobile, wrestling with his conscience. Soon it would be too late. What would be the point of all those sleepless hours if he changed his mind now? No. He was going to stick to the plan. Acting swiftly, he tore off a blank dispatch note from the pad, scribbled down a name and address then slipped it into the clear plastic wallet taped to the spare crate's rough-hewn yellow wood. Next, he grabbed a trolley. Its wheel squeaked all the way to the service lift. As the lift rose, so did his heart rate. By the time it reached the first floor his breathing had grown shallow. By the second floor, beads of perspiration broke on his brow. He wiped them away with the palm of his hand while waiting impatiently for the lift doors to open. As soon as the trolley would fit, he pushed it through the gap. Outside Lucy's studio, blue and white barrier tape had been strung across the door, contrasting starkly with the corridor's white walls. Cope hesitated. It wasn't too late to change his mind, though it soon would be. It was now or never.

He rushed ahead into the room next to the studio and selected two of the canvases, hurriedly loading them on the trolley before running back in and grabbing a medium-size bronze that had caught his eye. He pushed the laden trolley with its squeaky wheel into the lift. Back in the basement, he took his cargo over to the spare crate and, as carefully as time would allow, secured it inside. With room for at least a couple more paintings, Cope checked his watch, swung the trolley around and returned to the lift, jabbing impatiently at the second-floor button.

By the time he alighted from the lift the morning light was spilling through the window at the end of the corridor. His eyes flitted to his watch again; he was fighting a rising panic. He started for the store room when a noise outside caused him to pause. He dashed to the window. On the horizon the sun was painting the roof tiles a riot of reds, but it was another red that caught Cope's eye — that of Barry's Micra.

Too late. He was out of time.

'Shit!'

He thrust the trolley into the room with the paintings then flew down the stairs two at a time. Back in the basement, he hurried to the part-filled crate, added a cocooning layer of Styrofoam beads, then began to nail the lid on, just as Barry entered, whistling a cheerful ditty.

'Morning Mr Cope. Didn't expect you to be in yet.' Barry's moon-shaped face beamed as he scanned the room. 'Looks like last night was a big success.'

Cope set the hammer down.

'Barry, about last night, there's something I need to tell you...' By the time he'd finished, the older man's face was as pale as it was round.

'What is the world coming to?' He shook his head dolefully.

'I know. It still hasn't sunk in,' Cope said. 'Best just to try and keep busy; take your mind off it.'

Barry nodded and reached for the hammer and a handful of nails.

'You can leave the lids off for now,' Cope said quickly. He noticed Barry's gaze slide to the crate he'd just sealed. 'I did that one then changed my mind. It makes more sense for the lids to go on last... in case I've forgotten something. I'm not firing on all cylinders this morning, given what's happened.'

Barry set the tools down and started the careful process of packing the crates. For a while the only sound was of the two men working. When they finished Cope sent Barry upstairs to the main hall, to begin the laborious task of dismantling the foldable tables and stacking the chairs, while he remained in the basement, ostensibly checking the contents of the crates before securing the lids himself. Shortly his mobile phone issued a quiet beep. He glanced down at the new text, already heading for the door.

12.

'Josh seems like a nice lad,' Nightingale said, as they pulled away from Fisher's old home.

'He is. Never given us any trouble. There's still time, I suppose.'

'I'm sure if he was going to go off the rails, he'd have shown signs by now. I always think lads who are into their sport and keep fit tend to be less prone to teenage angst than most anyway.'

Fisher was surprised at the observation. He knew Josh liked his football but...

'You could tell he keeps fit?'

'Sure. He looks quite athletic.'

'He didn't used to.' Fisher felt a shockwave hit him — how long before he didn't know his boy at all?

'Maybe having a girl on the scene has spurred him on?' After a short pause, she said, 'So when did you stop being a footballer?'

'A long time ago. Not that you can tell from my ripped physique, hey?' He attempted a laugh. Though the smile dissolved on his lips when he realised Nightingale wasn't going to argue with him. The truth was, even after his football career had ended, he'd worked hard to keep in shape. Right up until the attack. Since then, he kept promising himself he'd get an exercise bike. He just needed to organise it, that was all.

'How come you gave it up? If I had a job that paid in one month what most people take home in a year, I don't think anything would convince me to stop.'

'I think you'll find that's one week, not one month. And I didn't exactly have a choice. Simon Bankcroft saw to that.'

'*The* Simon Bankcroft?'

You didn't need to be a football fanatic to know the name of one of the top stars of the game.

'There is only one. Thank God. Plays as dirty today as he always did. Took my leg out from under me, smashing the knee cap and tearing pretty much every ligament and piece of cartilage there was.'

'Couldn't they operate and fix you up?'

'Could and did. Only it was never the same. Sadly, you don't make the team because of your sparkling personality.'

'So you joined the force?'

'Would you believe me if I said I wanted to make a difference?' The long pause said it all. He gave a snort of a laugh and went on, 'Let's just say my options were limited. But I was still fit, apart from the dodgy knee, had a few brain cells to my credit and I won't lie, I was attracted to something with a bit more job security than I was used to. Besides, they provided full training, and I always fancied myself as a bit of a Bosch.'

'A bit of a what?'

'Harry Bosch...? No? He's a detective created by writer Michael Connelly. But anyway, I must have missed the small print that said you have to deal with frigging idiots, like the bastard who threw acid in my face.'

After a moment's quiet, Nightingale said, 'Sorry.'

'Don't be. You didn't do it. Thankfully, that particular arsehole is serving a twelve-year stretch courtesy of Her Maj'.

They passed the rest of the journey in silence. At the station, Matt noticed the office was almost as quiet as it was dark. He was beginning to wonder where everyone was, then he heard her voice nearby and knew the reason for the subdued atmosphere. The Falcon was in the room.

'DI Fisher. Come, join me.' Fisher let Luna lead him over. As he approached, he heard the scrape of chair legs. The DCI said, 'There's a chair here, if you'd like to sit down.'

'Will you be sitting down?' he asked.

'I wasn't going to. I—'

'Then I'll stand too. There's nothing wrong with my legs.'

'Fine,' she said, sounding brusque. 'I had hoped you'd be in early, at least before the rest of the team. I wanted us to be clear on your role before the start of the briefing.'

There it was. She wanted to take him off the case. And after everything he'd told Josh less than an hour ago. Well, forget it. If that was her plan, she should have done it yesterday. He wasn't going to be made to look like a bullshitter to his own kid. He turned to face her and gave a shrug.

'I assumed it would be the same as usual. I run the investigation on the ground and report back to you.' He waited a beat before adding, 'That's how it usually works with the other DIs.' He flashed her a smile. 'I take it you're happy for me to start the briefing now?'

'Look, it's not the—'

Fisher jumped in, 'Still waiting on a few people, are we? That's okay. I'll give them another couple of minutes. So, how did you get on with the next of kin?'

After a long pause, Fisher heard her sigh before replying, 'It went well. They were understandably distraught. Eleanor Morgan in particular. I'd say they appreciated the visit.'

'When did they last see Lucy?'

'Last night. They were at the auction. Moral support.'

'I know it was before Lucy went missing, but what time exactly did they leave?'

'I don't know.'

'You didn't ask?'

'It was hardly appropriate. I was there to give reassurances, remember?'

'What about a will? Is there one?' Fisher pressed.

'Again, I didn't think it was fitting to start quizzing them there and then. They were in shock.'

'Well, somebody's going to have to do the asking. Lucy Stirling was a very wealthy woman by all accounts. Knowing who gains by her death is important.'

'Yes, but there's a time and a place for everything and last night was most definitely not it.'

'Fine. I'll go and see them today.'

'Just remember to tread carefully. I wasn't lying when I said Rupert Morgan is a good friend of the Commissioner. And besides, it's hardly likely Eleanor Morgan slipped away in between cocktails and bludgeoned her niece to death without anyone noticing.'

Fisher started to shake his head in disbelief, but quickly stopped himself, fearing she might take it that he was agreeing with her.

'I'll start the briefing now, shall I?' he said and before she could argue, spun around to face the room, deliberately over-rotating so as to present his back to her. 'Thank you everyone for giving up your Saturday...'

A hush settled over the room.

The briefing followed the standard routine and by the time it finished everyone knew as much as there was to know. As the gathered team dispersed, Fisher followed the DCI back to her office, where she wasted no time in telling him what she really thought.

'You're serious — you're actually going to try to take an active role in the investigation?'

'Why not? Like my legs, my lips and ears appear to be in perfect working order.'

'But why? Since your union rep got HR running scared quoting chapter and verse of the Disability Discrimination Act at them, we've already agreed you can work cold cases here from here in the office with no diminution to your rank or pay.'

'I didn't join the force to spend my days pushing paperwork. I wanted to be out, gathering evidence and catching criminals. That's what being a detective is. And based on the occupational health assessment HR provided me with, that's what I've been cleared to do... provided I've got suitable assistance. Ma'am, I would like DC Nightingale to assist me. She can make contemporaneous notes and be my eyes, so to speak.'

'Fine,' the Falcon agreed in a haughty voice. 'Why not take one of the more experienced detectives...someone like Andy Wickham? After all, I'm awash with resources.'

Fisher knew he'd got her beat and supressed a smile.

'That might be better for me,' he said, 'but not for the case. Wickham's capable of working his own leads. Nightingale's ideal. She's got the makings of a good detective but she's not there yet. It won't do her any harm to ride shotgun. She might even learn a thing or two.'

He waited a beat; when she didn't disagree, he continued, 'I'm planning on starting with the guests that were part of Lucy Stirling's party. I also want to go back to the gallery and have another look around.'

And then the real reason for her unease became apparent.

'This case...' she said. 'It's going to attract a lot of attention. You know that, don't you?'

'I dare say it will, seeing how the vic was an acclaimed artist, Olympic gold medallist, billionairess and love interest of a chart-topping rock star. All I can say is shame other murders don't appear to warrant the same degree of attention. After all, a life's a life.'

'And you think you're going to cope okay? With the attention could come a fair amount of criticism.'

'I can deal with the press. I've done it enough times before. But if you're referring to what might be said closer to home, with the powers that be, then I suppose I'll have to deal with that if and when it happens.'

Fisher waited, resisting filling in the silence. He knew that the press attention would be a great cause of concern for her. On the one hand, she'd be nervous of someone like him stealing her glory, but nowhere near as terrified as she'd be at the prospect of him bungling the investigation and bringing allegations of incompetence and bad management to her door. The problem was, she wasn't called the Falcon for nothing and the last thing he wanted was to have her beady eyes all over the case and his every move. He needed a sop to get her off his back.

'Look,' he said. 'Why don't you do the press interviews? I've never really enjoyed dishing out soundbites and it'll give me more time to focus on the investigation.'

'Hmm... that could work.' Fisher could virtually hear the upward curve in her lips. But then she was back to normal and her cool, aloof tone returned, 'But that's not my only concern. Managing the press is one thing, managing the investigation is another. As Senior Investigating Officer I'm responsible for making sure all of the right resources are deployed in the right way.'

Here we go, when she starts quoting exact lines from the Police Management Handbook, you know this is no spur of the moment conversation.

'I know you don't want to hear it,' she went on, 'but I'm seriously concerned about whether you're going to be able to actively investigate this yourself. I mean, look at interviewing a suspect. You know how important non-verbal cues are; without them you're in danger of believing every piece of nonsense that gets thrown at you.'

'I appreciate that,' he said. 'But tone of voice and evasive sentence structure is something I'm becoming particularly attuned to. For example, if I were to comment on yours right now, I'd say you are looking for any reason to take me off the case.'

'Nonsense.'

'You've just called into doubt my ability to carry out my duties as a detective without a single ounce of evidence.' When she didn't reply, Fisher couldn't resist a little push. 'So, how am I doing so far, as far as non-verbal assessment goes?'

'I would be failing in my duty, if I didn't check that you're fit to lead on such a complex and high-profile investigation as this.'

Fisher didn't need tone of voice, body language or anything else to recognise bullshit when he heard it. He knew she saw the case as her ticket to getting more pips on her shoulder and she didn't want him or anyone else screwing it up.

She switched to a softer tone, sweet and sugary but as false as saccharin, 'Despite what you think, it's not me I'm worried about. You've always been such a team player. I know how much you'd hate to let the others down.'

And there it was — the sucker-punch.

'I don't intend to let anyone down,' he snapped. 'Now, if you've finished with your little pep talk, I'd like to get on. I've got a killer to catch.'

13.

While Fisher was playing career tennis with the Falcon, Nightingale decided to make herself useful and went to see Colin Clough, the administrative assistant appointed as evidence holder. It was his job to secure and record all of the material obtained during the investigation.

Colin was head bent in concentration, scribbling on a large A4 pad.

'Won't be a minute,' he said, not looking up.

Nightingale watched as he consulted a typed list of names from the previous night's auction-dinner. The guest numbers looked a bit low; unlike the ticket prices.

'Is that for real? A thousand pounds for a table. Just for dinner and an auction.'

'Bargain... you could seat eight on a table. Single tickets went for a hundred and fifty quid a piece.' He gave a cheeky wink. 'How the other half lives, eh? So, how can I help?'

'I need copies of some statements.' She gave him the names of Lucy's friends and her sister. 'DI Fisher plans on interviewing them this morning.'

Aside from individual accounts of their evening, the statements also contained the witnesses' contact details. Colin put the list on the table in front of him, then started to look through the papers.

'How come the guest list is so small?' Nightingale asked, commenting on the discrepancy between the names in front of her and the number of seats in the main hall of the gallery the night before.

'It's not really a guest list, just a record of ticket sales. I'm having to use the statements to compile a list of people who actually attended the event. Unfortunately, it looks like quite a few guests had left by the time we got there.'

While Colin flicked through the statements, Nightingale skimmed the typed sheet. One name in particular caught her eye.

'Beth!' Fisher yelled from the front of the room.

'You go,' Colin said, 'I'll bring them over.'

He came up with the goods as Fisher and Nightingale were heading for the door. On the journey to the first address, Fisher seemed disinclined to talk and the small car was claustrophobically quiet.

'Is everything okay?' Nightingale asked.

'What?'

'I just wondered if you were okay.'

'I'm fine.'

'How come you sent Kami and Aaron to the post-mortem? I would have thought you'd have gone yourself.'

'And waste half a day listening to what is largely silence? I'd rather wait for the report.'

'Oh.'

'You sound disappointed.'

'It's just I've never been to a post-mortem before.'

'You're not missing much. It's not like in the films. It's tedious watching a dead body having all its organs taken out and weighed and bits cut off or scraped out and smeared onto glass plates, only for everything to be put back. But if you really wanted to go, you should have said. I could have sent you instead of Kami.'

'No. It's okay. As much as I'd like to see one, I'd rather do the interviews with you.'

'Good, because I'm relying on you. I'll need you to watch and listen and make copious notes. You might think you'll remember everything but after a couple of days, your brain will be so full of different people's accounts of what they saw, what they did, who they spoke to, you won't know which way is up.'

Shortly Nightingale announced their imminent arrival at an address on the outskirts of town. Fisher lurched forward in his seat as she brought the car to a stop. She unclipped her seatbelt and pulled at the door handle.

'Hold your horses. Before you go rushing off, let's take a minute to look at what we know about our witness, starting with what she had to say for herself last night.'

Nightingale reached over to the back seat for her bag and retrieved the sheaf of statements. After flicking through them to find the one she was looking for, she began to read, 'Carla Porter, was the vic's sister—'

'Blood sister, who wasn't adopted,' Fisher said, as a reminder to himself.

'Here she's just down as Lucy's sister. According to what Ms Porter told Andy, she hardly saw Lucy, who had spent all night talking with the guests. Porter said she didn't know anyone else there and spent most of the night on her own at the bar. Around eleven, someone spilled red wine down her top; she tried to rinse out what she could in the toilets, but soon afterwards decided to go home. The thing was, Porter had gone to the gallery in a limo with Lucy and had expected to go home the same way, so she hadn't got any money for a cab. When she tried to find Lucy and couldn't, she got hold of Jackson Cope, the gallery manager, who offered to look.'

'Does she say when she last saw Lucy?'

'She says she saw her across the room on and off throughout the evening but can't say exactly when the last time was.'

'Does she mention Morrelli or any of the other friends?'

'Morrelli left the bar shortly after Lucy, to go for a cigarette. She didn't see him again until after Lucy had disappeared. Same as with the others. Looks like they all went off and did their own thing, then met back around eleven-thirty, around the time Lucy's body was discovered.'

'Okay, now we can go.'

***

'I'm sorry, I'm still in my pyjamas,' Carla Porter said when she greeted Fisher and Nightingale at the door to her house. She sounded sniffly. 'I should be at work but I couldn't face it.'

'I think given the circumstances...' Nightingale said, in a kindly voice.

'Where do you work?' Fisher asked. He hadn't expected any of the people they'd planned on seeing having to work on a Saturday.

'Aldi. On the checkout. On the weekends, anyway. In the week I've got a couple of cleaning jobs plus I do a few nights behind the bar in the local pub. Keeps me out of trouble.' She gave a half-hearted laugh, followed by a heavy session of nose blowing. 'Anyway, you'd better come in.'

'Are you okay with the dog coming inside?'

Fisher imagined her looking at Luna, registering the harness, then looking back at his shade-covered eyes.

'Yes. Of course.' They followed her in. 'I'll just go get dressed.' Her voice sounded close, giving Fisher the impression of a rather cramped lounge.

'Please don't get changed on our account. Makes no difference to me.' Fisher tapped the side of his glasses.

'Oh, okay. If you don't mind. Here... sit down.' Fisher heard what sounded like a pile of magazines being dropped onto the floor. 'Sorry about the mess. Could you pass me that ashtray? Are my fags over there as well?'

A minute later came the strike of a match. The acrid stench of sulphur accosted Fisher's nostrils. He wished people wouldn't smoke. The smell lingered on Luna's coat for hours.

'I still can't believe it,' Porter went on. 'I almost convinced myself it was all a bad dream, but now, seeing you both sitting there...' A new bout of sniffing started.

'Last night you said you couldn't think of anyone who might have done it. Have you had any ideas since?'

'No.' The answer came quick and sharp. 'It doesn't make any sense. Everyone loved Lucy.' Her voice caught in her throat. 'Absolutely everyone.'

'No rows or disagreements with anyone recently?'

'No. Lucy never fell out with anyone. She didn't need to. People did what she told them to do... I mean asked... did what she *asked* them to do. She used to have a lot of good ideas, so people just ended up doing what she said. It's not like she was bossy, or anything. I didn't mean that.'

'That's okay. I understand,' Fisher said. 'I know you gave a statement last night but could you take us through it again? You never know, something new might spring to mind.'

She did, but it didn't.

'It sounds like you didn't really enjoy the evening very much. I mean, aside from what happened to Lucy.' Fisher attempted a sympathetic smile. He'd never been that big on black-tie dos. Unlike Mandy, who had loved life as a WAG.

'Don't get me wrong. It was really nice of her to invite me but... well, I suppose I'm more a pie and a pint sort of person. I went because Lucy wanted me to go and I wanted to make her happy. Plus, I'd never been in a limo before, so that was fun. It's just... I don't know, I'm not exactly one of them, am I? They've all been to posh schools and university. I didn't even make it to grammar. They know so much about so many things. I always think if they ask me a question, whatever I say will sound stupid. Lucy said I was silly to think that, but... well, she was nice like that.'

'Talking of Lucy's friends, do you know anyone called Patrick?'

'Patrick?' she said with an uptick of surprise. 'No.'

'Lucy never mentioned Patrick or introduced you to someone of that name?'

'No. I'm sure she didn't. Who is he?'

'It's just a name that's cropped up. Probably nothing. So, who was older, you or Lucy?'

'Me. I was three when she was born. She was Jessica back then. She was there one day and gone the next. Mum told me Jessica's dad had come and taken her away. It was years before I found out the truth.

'How did you find out?'

'When Mum died, I still thought Jessica had gone to live with her dad. I put notices in all the papers about the funeral. I wanted to make sure she knew about it. I really hoped I'd see her there. I always wondered how she was doing. If she was okay, you know? When she didn't show, it really upset me and I said something to my aunt. That was when she told me Jessica had been adopted. Turns out Mum didn't know who the father was. Same as with me. Aunty Jean said Mum couldn't cope with two kids and no decent salary — she only ever had cleaning and bar work. Like me, I suppose, only I ain't got no kids.'

'When did your mum die?' Fisher asked.

'Ten years ago.'

'You were what... seventeen, eighteen? It must have been tough, being so young.'

'Eighteen.' There was a moment's quiet, then she said, 'Mum used to drink a lot. Did drugs too. I'd kind of got used to looking after myself by then.'

'How did she die?'

'Had too much of both one day.'

'Is that when you got in touch with Lucy — when your mum died?'

'No. That was only this year.'

'You waited all that time?'

84

'I didn't know Lucy was Jessica until after Christmas. When Aunty Jean told me about the adoption, she swore blind she didn't know anything about the family who had adopted her. Turns out she was lying. I was round hers in the New Year when the news came on about Mr and Mrs Stirling getting killed in a helicopter crash somewhere foreign and she said "your poor sister". When I asked her what she meant, she made out I'd misheard. But I knew I hadn't. The newspapers said they had a daughter, Lucy. I googled her. As soon as I saw pictures of her, I could see the resemblance — to Mum, I mean. I waited for her, outside the gallery one day, told her I was her sister. She was like me, alone with no family. I thought she might want to be friends.'

***

'Sad isn't it?' Nightingale said, as they made their way to the next appointment.

'Huh?'

'Sisters separated at such a young age. I understand why women do it, especially when they're on their own, but in this case it's hard to see who was better off as a result. Carla living in relative poverty with a mother who loved her, or Lucy adopted by a billionaire and his wife who probably gave her everything she ever wanted apart from the one thing they couldn't — a real mother's love.'

'It was only sad for Lucy if she knew she'd been adopted. And even then, growing up in the lap of luxury must have gone some way to compensate.'

As soon as he said it, Fisher's thoughts jumped to Josh. Would he, one day, think of another man as Dad, happy to do so because of the size of his bank balance? The very thought of it made his heart heavy.

He forced it out of his mind and said, 'So, anyway, what did you make of Porter?'

'She seemed pretty normal. It must have been difficult being thrust into a totally different social circle. It's like getting invited to a party by someone you think you have something in common with, only when you get there you don't know anyone else and everyone's talking about things they've done or having some clever conversation on a topic you don't know anything about, making you feel like a stupid, ugly misfit.'

There was a coating of emotion on Nightingale's voice and Fisher sensed she was no longer talking about Carla Porter.

She went on, 'And then, after being separated all those years, just when they were getting to know one another, this happens.'

'Maybe it's because Porter came on the scene that it happened. Maybe she was the catalyst. What if Lucy was thinking of changing her will and planned on leaving her sister something or maybe everything? That might put the cat amongst certain pigeons.'

'You mean Lucy's aunt?'

'Who knows? If there's an existing will, it might have upset someone else. So, does she look much like Lucy?'

'Not especially. I can sort of see a resemblance, but that might be because I know they're sisters. Lucy was quite striking. Do you remember her from before your accident?'

'Not really. Diving wasn't my thing.'

'You didn't see that hair advert she did?'

'I can't remember it. Even if I saw it, it's not the sort of thing I tended to notice.'

'Well, she looked amazing. Long blonde hair and pale blue, almost grey eyes. She could have passed for Scandinavian. Carla on the other hand's got brown hair and...' After a moment's pause, 'I don't know what colour eyes she's got.'

Before Fisher could quiz her any further, they were interrupted by his phone buzzing in his jacket pocket.

'Rupert Morgan's expecting you in half an hour,' DCI Fallon said the second he hit answer.

'Whoa, hang on. I've already arranged to see him this afternoon.'

'He's got somewhere else to be later and has asked for your meeting to be brought forward.'

'But I'm almost—'

'Save it. Whatever you were about to do can wait. I told him you'd be on your way.'

She terminated the call. For a split second, Fisher thought about calling her back and telling her where Morgan could stick his meeting, then he reminded himself, this might be more of her game playing. He thought back to her comment about Morgan being an old friend of the Commissioner's. Last night the Falcon had insisted on being the one to ply the Morgans with reassurance. Now there were difficult questions to be asked — such as whether Rupert Morgan or his wife had an alibi — she was happy for him to be the one to do the asking. Was this her attempt at loading the gun, hoping the eminent Mr Morgan would be the one to pull the trigger? If it was, then the last thing he was going to do was make it easy for her.

14.

'Blimey, this is a bit of alright,' Nightingale said, as the car crunched its way up the long gravel drive of the country residence of Mr Rupert Morgan QC.

'What's it like?'

'Huge. A proper mansion. Even bigger than yours. It could have been used in Downton. There's a two-storey garage — I think it's a garage — it's actually bigger than my mum and dad's house.'

'It just goes to show, the law might be an ass, but it's a bloody high paying ass,' Fisher said. Not quite as high paying as football, he thought, but wisely kept to himself.

The reception they received was almost as grand as the house itself, being met at the door by a young-sounding woman who escorted them to the drawing room and offered them drinks. She left them to await the arrival of their hosts.

A door opened and footsteps started across the floor.

'Detective Inspector Fisher. Rupert Morgan QC.' Fisher noted the hard burr in the lawyer's voice, telling of his Scottish roots.

Fisher held out his hand for a brief moment but Morgan continued past.

'This is DC Nightingale,' Fisher said, gesturing in Nightingale's general direction. He listened for a second footfall, but heard only silence. 'I take it your wife will be joining us?'

'Eleanor's in bed, asleep. She's taken some sleeping pills. It's all been rather too much for her.'

'I had hoped to question you both together,' Fisher said.

'Well you'll have to make do with me.' In his mind's eye, Fisher could see a hooked eyebrow over a hooded eye looking down a haughty nose.

'If I can start with last night. I understand you and your wife left the gallery before Lucy's body was discovered.'

'That is correct. My wife wasn't feeling well.'

'What time was that?'

'Around half past eleven.'

'So, not long before Lucy was found.'

Morgan cleared his throat.

'I wasn't aware of when that was. The young chap who came to break the news didn't give any details.'

'Was it just yourself and your wife who went last night?'

'No. My firm sponsored a table. My daughter Caroline and her husband and my son Henry were with us. Charles Peterson, one of the partners, and his wife and daughter also joined us.'

'And did you all leave at the same time?'

'Yes. Caroline and Justin had left the children with a babysitter and were keen to get back. The Petersons dropped Henry in town on their way home. None of them were aware of what happened until I phoned them this morning.'

'And how did you and your wife get home?'

'I drove.'

'Did you come straight home?'

'Yes. I dropped Eleanor at the door, before parking the car in the garage. She went to bed while I retired to my study to read for a while.'

'Good book?' Fisher asked, waiting to hear any hint of a pause that might suggest the story was fabricated.

But Morgan's reply came quickly enough.

'*The Bondage of the Will*. Martin Luther.' He sounded even haughtier than before. 'Mr Luther makes some complex theistic arguments. I can recommend it.'

Fisher gave a single nod.

'Thanks. I'll stick to my Michael Connellys all the same. So, back to last night. Did you speak to Lucy at all?'

'When we first arrived. She came over to our table to say hello. I tried looking for her when we were leaving, but she wasn't in the main hall, so we left without saying goodnight.'

'And how did she seem when you spoke to her? Did she say anything to you that, with the benefit of hindsight, might be important?'

'Not at all. She was excited about the auction, naturally. Determined to raise as much money for the appeal as possible, seeing that it was in memory of her parents.'

Fisher could hear Morgan moving around, then something rattled. A desk drawer perhaps?

'These are the details of the family solicitor. She already knows what's happened. I called her first thing. I said you'd be in touch.'

Fisher made out the sound of a piece of paper being folded, then the zip on Nightingale's bag.

'I look forward to talking with her,' he said. 'Obviously, we're keen to know whether Lucy made a will or not.'

'As far as I know, she hadn't, despite my constant entreating. Death always seems too far in the future to someone so young.'

'If that is the case, would you know who stands to inherit?'

'My wife, of course. As Lucy's only living relative, she's the sole beneficiary.'

'What about Lucy's sister?'

'Legally speaking, Miss Porter is no longer recognised as Lucy's sister and as such has no inheritance rights.'

'Did Lucy know that?'

'Of course.'

This new train of thought prompted another question, 'How long had Lucy known she was adopted?'

Morgan cleared his throat. Judging from the gruff sound the question displeased him.

The silence stretched and Fisher was about to push for more, when the legal man continued, 'Since that so-called sister came a-begging earlier this year.'

'A-begging?'

'Look at the girl's background. She will have taken one look at Lucy and seen a potential gold mine.'

'And how did Lucy react?'

'With compassion and kindness. She had a more generous spirit than me. I would have told the urchin to sling her hook.' Morgan went on, 'You know, far be it from me to tell you how to do your job, but if I were you, I'd go and talk to that so-called sister. Uneducated girl like her may well have believed she'd be in the running for Lucy's money when she died.'

'Is there anyone else you'd like to finger for the murder, while we're here? How about Lucy's boyfriend, Tom Morrelli?'

'That waste of space? He hasn't got enough fire in his belly to raise his voice, let alone his fists. You know, I was very pleased to hear DCI Fallon's going to be throwing everything at this case. I want the bastard who did this caught, and quickly.'

'Of course. It goes without saying. We always do everything in our power to catch a murderer, regardless of who the victim is.'

'Well, if you need more resources, let me know. Myself and Lord Davis happen to be very old pals.' So, it was true, Morgan did have the ear of the Police Commissioner. 'So, if that's everything? I trust you can see yourselves out.' Fisher heard the strike of footsteps in the direction of the door, but then Morgan stopped walking. 'You know, Detective, I hope for your sake that you've got more gumption than you've shown, because from what I've seen so far, I'm not impressed.'

15.

They had been on the road ten minutes since leaving the Morgans' and were on their way to the next address, that of Oliver and Francesca Heath, who Fisher was trying to call.

'Still no answer?' Nightingale said.

'No.' He returned the phone to his pocket. He'd already left one message. No point leaving another.

'Do you still want to go or shall we try the other guy?'

'How far away are we?'

'Not far. A mile or so.'

'Let's stick with the plan. They might be in but not answering.'

Shortly, they were standing outside the home of Mr and Mrs Heath, having familiarised themselves of the couple's accounts of the previous evening in the car beforehand. Nightingale pressed the bell. A shrill ring sounded in the hall beyond.

'What's the house like?' Fisher asked. 'I remember this being quite a nice part of town.'

'It's really nice. Sort of cottagey; lovely sash windows. They've gravelled the front over and put pots out. No garage though. Still, saying that, I wouldn't say no.'

'Is it big?'

'Not particularly.'

'Try again,' Fisher said, nodding towards the door.

Nightingale left her finger on the bell longer this time, which seemed to do the trick as they were soon rewarded with the sound of a latch turning.

A husky female voice said, 'Hello?'

After brief introductions, Francesca Heath showed them in to a fresh and floral-smelling room that, even with Fisher's severely limited vision, appeared darker than usual.

'Would it be possible to open the curtains?' Nightingale said. 'Unless, of course, they're because of...'

'Oh, you mean because of Lucy's death? No, nothing so quaint I'm afraid. I had a bit of a headache earlier. I'm fine now.' Curtain rings clattered over a wooden pole and Fisher's darkness warmed subtly. 'If you were hoping to talk to Ollie, I'm afraid you're out of luck. He's at the pool. He'll be there for another hour at least.'

'The pool?' Fisher said.

'He's a dive coach. I'm supposed to be there too, training, only after last night... I'm afraid I had a little too much to drink.'

'So, Mrs Heath... Actually, is it Mrs Heath or Ms La Salle? Only we seem to have both down for you.'

'Heath is my married name; Ollie insists on using it. I prefer to use my maiden name these days. I plan on going into fashion modelling when I quit diving. I think La Salle has a much more exotic ring to it.'

'You're a diver?' Fisher said.

'Yes. Medalled bronze in Rio, though I'm hoping to do better next time.'

'My apologies. I'm afraid I don't know many Olympic divers.'

'No one ever does. Apart from Tom Daley and Lucy.' After the briefest of pauses, she added, 'Obviously that will all change if I get gold in Tokyo... or should I say, when I get gold.' She punctuated the sentence with a small snort. 'Got to think positive.'

'Best of luck. I understand Lucy had given it up.'

'Supposedly.'

Something about her tone caught Fisher's attention.

'Does that mean she was returning to it?'

'I don't know. Just something someone said.'

'Okay, well Mrs Heath, we've read the statement you gave last night. It looks like the last time you saw Lucy was when she joined you and some friends at the bar immediately after the auction ended.'

'Yes. Then she went off to talk to some guests. The rest of us hung around for a bit, maybe ten, fifteen minutes, then I joined some girlfriends... they're supermodels.'

Fisher guessed La Salle was in her early twenties and wondered how many years the average career of a catwalk model ran to, before dismissing the thought as irrelevant.

'And you were with these girlfriends for the rest of the night?'

'Yes. Well, I think so. It's all a bit fuzzy.'

'You didn't spend much time with your husband then?'

'No. Ollie was busy keeping Felix company, seeing how Lucy was otherwise occupied.'

'Felix?'

'Felix Lee. He's a friend. Well, not so much my friend. To be honest he gets on my nerves if I spend too much time with him. It's like being around a fourteen-year-old schoolboy with his silly jokes and catty comments. He doesn't know when to stop. For some reason Ollie finds him amusing.'

'Comments about Lucy?' Fisher asked.

'What? Oh no. He wouldn't dare. Doesn't stop him having a go at just about everybody else though. Tom was last night's target.'

'Oh?'

'It was all so banal. Felix couldn't resist dragging up some of Tom's past after Carla got Shane Harman's autograph on an old napkin. He thought it would be funny to suggest Tom should get Georgia Bellucci's on a pillowcase.'

Fisher gave her comment some thought before confessing, 'I'm sorry. I don't understand.'

'Tom and Georgia used to be an item. She ditched him for Harman. It was just Felix's way of having a dig. He never really liked sharing Lucy with Tom.'

'How did Lucy react to that?'

'I don't think she was there then. I can't imagine she would have been bothered in any case. Felix was always like that. Besides, not much fazed her.'

'Like finding out she had a sister?'

'What? Oh, Carla. Yes. I never could quite get used to the fact they were related. But yes, Lucy tried to make her feel welcome.'

'Did that upset anyone — Lucy deciding to bring her into your group of friends?'

'It didn't make any difference. I barely noticed her, to be honest.'

'So, had you and Lucy known each other a long time?'

'Years. We were both on the swim team at school. It was very handy having a friend with her own Olympic pool and personal coach. If it had been down to me, I doubt I'd have got very far. Lucy would make me feel guilty if I wanted to skip training. She was one of those people who, when she made her mind up to do something, there was no stopping her.'

'It sounds like she was very headstrong.'

'Oh absolutely.'

'Could that have had something to do with what happened last night?'

'In what way?'

'I don't know, I'm just hypothesising. Do you have any idea why your friend was killed?'

'I assumed she walked in on a robbery. I remember someone saying it would be a good time to do it, seeing how everyone was too busy enjoying themselves to notice.'

'There were no signs of a robbery,' Fisher said. 'The front door was locked once the auction started. Anyone wanting to come in would have had to ring the bell. The cloakroom attendant confirmed nobody did.'

'Maybe the cloakroom attendant was in on it.'

It had already occurred to Fisher to check Molly O'Leary was who she claimed to be. She hadn't worked at the gallery long and they were taking her word for a hell of a lot. The reference to Molly also reminded him of another line of enquiry.

'Patrick?' she said in response. 'No, I can't recall Lucy ever mentioning anyone called Patrick. Was he there last night?'

'That's what we're trying to ascertain.'

'Well I don't know any Patricks.'

'What about Tom Morrelli — how well did he and Lucy get on?'

'He was her boyfriend.'

'Was it a happy relationship?'

'What does happy look like?' Fisher imagined a shrug accompanying the comment.

'Well, did they argue much?'

Fran gave a little tinkle of a laugh.

'Argue? With Lucy. Don't be silly. No one argued with Lucy. There was no point. You couldn't win.'

16.

Voices and the sound of splashing water echoed somewhere ahead. Fisher thought fleetingly of childhood summers spent in Italy, where he and his brother played in pools hewn into rock that had loomed above them like a prehistoric cathedral. So much more enjoyable without the spiky smell of chlorine that hit him as he made his way through the reception area towards the café, where the receptionist suggested they wait for Oliver Heath. In the background children chattered and chomped noisily on bags of crisps and chocolate bars.

Nightingale steered him to an empty table.

'May as well get a drink while we wait,' he said, pulling a note out of his pocket, possibly a fiver. He hadn't quite mastered the art of feeling the difference. 'Grab us a coffee and whatever you want.' The note slipped from his grasp.

'Actually, this might be Heath now,' Nightingale said. 'There's a guy just come in I'm sure was at the gallery last night.' After a second, 'Maybe not, he's gone straight to the counter. Didn't even look over.'

As Fisher sank into a chair and settled Luna by his feet, Nightingale went over to get the drinks. Shortly she returned, the sound of a second tread falling into step with hers.

'DI Fisher, this is Felix Lee. Mr Lee was at the gallery last night. He was another of Miss Stirling's friends.'

'Not just one of her friends, darling, her *best* friend,' he said. 'I don't mind telling you, I almost cried myself to sleep last night. I only hope I don't look too ghastly.'

'Had you and Lucy been friends for long?' Fisher asked.

'Oh, like forever. Ever since my twenty-second birthday. I'd hired a private room at Carwash. You know the place? Very retro, and of course everyone's legs look divine in flares. Well, anyway, Ollie had just started going out with Fran, though it was all hush-hush because he was part of the Olympic training team and coaches weren't supposed to fraternise with the athletes. But it was perfect, as it meant I could invite Lucy. I'd been badgering Ollie to introduce us for ages. I love collecting celebrities and Lucy was on her way up. Plus, I thought she could keep little Frannie company.'

'A private room at Carwash must have cost a pretty penny,' Fisher said.

'Oh absolutely. It was exorbitantly expensive. Which is why I loved it. No riff raff. I mean, what is the point parading up and down catwalks for Valentino or Dior or whoever else is willing to throw good money at you, if you can't spend it on having the best birthday bash?'

'You're a model?' Fisher said.

'One of the best, darling.'

'So how come you're here this morning? Part of your fitness regime?'

'Hahaha.' Felix Lee stuttered out a peculiar laugh. 'Swim? In all that chlorine? I don't think so. No. I came to see Ollie and Fran. Thought I might be able to talk them into going for a spot of lunch. Friends united in grief, as it were. Only Fran is apparently wallowing in her pit and Ollie hasn't finished with his water babies. Hence, I'm sitting here with you, sipping this dreadful coffee, while Ollie's is growing cold.'

'Well, you've saved us a trip,' Fisher said. 'You were next on our list.'

'I was? Should I be flattered?'

'We're talking to all of Lucy's friends who were at the gallery last night.'

'I'm not sure there's anything else I can tell you. I told everything I know to the PC Plod who took my statement last night.'

'Sometimes, after a night's sleep, people can remember things they'd previously forgotten or dismissed as unimportant.'

'Not me. I'm not just a pretty face. I happen to have excellent recall.'

'Well, perhaps you'll be able to help us with some details that didn't appear in your statement?'

'Such as?'

'Were you aware Tom Morrelli lost his jacket?'

According to Tom's statement, Lee had helped look for the missing article.

'Yes. What about it?'

'It wasn't mentioned in your statement.'

'Why would it be? Don't tell me amidst this tragedy, Tom is still bleating on about it. He either forgot where he left it or one of the bar staff moved it when they were clearing up. But who cares? It's hardly important given what's happened.'

'You don't think someone could have deliberately taken it?'

'What on earth for? Okay, it was Fendi, but it was off the peg. Most of the guests there were worth millions. They are so not going to be interested in a jacket worth a few hundred pounds.'

'Presumably not everybody there was loaded.' Though as he said it, Fisher wondered how true it was.

'You must be thinking of the delightful Miss Porter. You're right, of course. If it was anything other than a man's jacket I would agree. She has a habit of making things disappear.'

'Such as?'

'My Montblanc fountain pen went missing not long after Lucy started dragging the poor wench around with us. Then Fran lost something. I can't remember what exactly. I shouldn't be surprised if she took that as well. You can virtually smell the envy emanating from her.'

'Did you share your suspicions with Lucy?'

'Of course, but naturally she didn't like the idea that her darling sister was a common thief. Preferred to believe I'd simply misplaced the pen. But as I've already pointed out, I have an excellent faculty for recall.'

'What about Tom Morrelli? What can you tell us about him and Lucy?'

'It was a paparazzi's dream. I don't know if anyone's told you, but Tom is to die for. Straight or gay, who wouldn't want to jump into bed with him? And Lucy was one of the nation's sweethearts.'

'I meant about their relationship.'

'What's to say? He's a rock star who likes late nights and partying. Lucy was a health-nut whose idea of a wild night out was stopping off for a virgin cosmopolitan at Disrepute after a West End show. Chalk and cheese. They only got together because Lucy hated going home to an empty house after her parents died. She started going to showbiz parties, drinking more than usual, mixing with a different crowd. She snapped out of it after a few weeks and went back to normal. Only with Tom in tow.'

'Yet they were still together. Can't have been that bad a match?'

'Hmm.'

Lee seemed reluctant to elaborate. Fisher changed the subject.

'Do you know anyone by the name of Patrick? We understand Lucy might have been meeting him around the time she was killed.'

'Patrick? Patrick who?' Lee asked, his interest reinvigorated.

'I was hoping you could tell me.'

'Oh.' He sounded disappointed. 'No. No idea. But you can take it from me, he wasn't some secret love interest. Lucy wasn't like that. If she had her eye on someone else, she would have already ended it with Tom.' A hand settled gently on Fisher's arm; he shifted uncomfortably. 'Now Tom on the other hand—'

'Hi. Sorry I've been so long,' came a well-educated voice, carried on the back of fast approaching footsteps. 'I'm Oliver Heath.'

The hand lifted off Fisher's arm. He heard the shuffling of chairs and muted introductions.

'Mr Heath, please join us,' Fisher said. 'We were just talking about Miss Stirling.'

'Talk to anybody about Lucy and you'll hear the same things,' Heath said, after taking a seat. 'She was a wonderful human being. Generous, kind, compassionate. I don't know anybody who didn't like her.'

'Yet somebody killed her.'

'Doesn't mean they meant to. Maybe she was in the wrong place at the wrong time.'

'What would someone be doing in her studio?'

'A robbery gone wrong. Isn't that what they say on TV? Maybe an unsuccessful bidder fancied helping themselves to one of her pieces.'

'That might make more sense if something was missing when she was found.'

'Perhaps whoever did it didn't realise she didn't keep her finished work in the studio. She might have interrupted them while they were looking for it?'

'Where did she keep it?'

'In the room next door.'

'How do you know that?'

'I told him,' Lee jumped in. 'I was there earlier in the evening before the auction started. Lucy asked me and Tom to fetch her pieces for her. Tom got the sculpture from her studio, while I got the paintings from the store.'

Fisher nodded.

'I see. Why do you think Lucy went to the studio so late in the evening?'

'That's what we were all asking ourselves last night.' Ollie had resumed the answering. 'It makes no sense. She would have wanted to circulate, keep the guests entertained.'

'Might she have gone there for a bit of privacy?' Fisher asked.

'For what reason?' Lee jumped in again.

'What about drugs?'

'Lucy, do drugs?' Lee threw the word back at him and stuttered another laugh, as though it was the most ridiculous thing he'd ever heard. 'Lucy hated drugs.'

'Maybe she wasn't doing them. Maybe she accompanied someone else. Know anyone there last night partial to a line of coke?'

'Hahaha.' There was that annoying laugh again. 'A sniffer dog at last night's bash would have been spinning like a tornado. The place was full of showbiz luvvies with nostril hairs that look like they've got a permanent case of dandruff.'

'Does that include Tom?' Fisher asked.

This time it was Heath's turn to reply, 'Tom doesn't do drugs.'

'He already admitted to smoking marijuana when we visited him.'

'That's hardly the same as cocaine. Believe me, Tom wouldn't want his good looks to suffer.'

'So, what's your view of Tom and Lucy's relationship, Mr Heath? Mr Lee has already given us his.'

A pause, then, 'I wouldn't take too much notice of anything Felix has told you, Inspector. I keep telling him, his love of gossip will get him in serious trouble one day.'

Fisher experienced a kick of excitement.

'Which particular piece of gossip would this be?'

'No gossip,' Felix Lee said sharply. Fisher wondered whether the reply was accompanied by an exchange of glances. 'I simply told the Inspector I didn't think Luce and Tom would last. That's all,' Lee said with a pointed emphasis on the last two words.

'Oh,' Heath said with palpable relief. 'Yes, well we all thought that.'

'Are you sure that's all?'

The fact his question was met by silence, left Fisher convinced there was something the two friends weren't telling. Aware that pressing the point would get him nowhere, he brought the conversation back to the enigmatic Patrick and for a while the two friends bounced ideas around, trying to rouse some common memory, but to no avail.

Fisher curbed a sigh. They were getting nowhere.

'I think we're done with the questions, for today, gentlemen. Thank you for your time.' He pushed his chair out and stood up.

'Sir...' Nightingale said, sounding uncertain. 'While you've been talking, I've been reading through Mr Heath and Mr Lee's statements.'

'And...?'

'There appears to be a discrepancy between their two accounts.'

He resumed his seat.

'Is there now?'

'Yes.' There was a brief rustle of paper, then Nightingale said in a clear voice, 'Mr Heath, you said that after Miss Stirling left the group, Mr Morrelli was the next to leave, followed by your wife. You and Mr Lee then went to view the exhibition in a side room before stepping outside for some fresh air. On returning, Mr Lee stopped to talk to someone while you returned to the bar.'

'Yes. That's what happened.'

'Mr Lee... Does that fit with your recollection?' Fisher asked.

'I think so, yes,' Lee said.

'But that isn't what your statement says,' Nightingale said. 'It says after the two of you had finished viewing the exhibition, you went to speak with one of the guests — a music video director —

who you approached in the hope of obtaining work. It doesn't mention anything about going outside.'

'Doesn't it?'

'Your perfect recall had the night off, did it?' Fisher said, with no hint of humour.

'I probably didn't think it important enough to mention. The same way I didn't say anything about looking for Tom's jacket.'

'I assume the cloakroom attendant will have seen you go out and return?' Fisher said.

'No,' Heath said. 'We went out the back way.'

Fisher's scalp prickled.

'The back way?'

'The service door, for deliveries,' Heath said. 'We went straight out after viewing the exhibition; that door was closer.'

'Plus, there was less chance of getting hounded by the paps that way,' Lee added. 'Everybody's entitled to a bit of privacy sometimes.'

It was possible. Back in the day, when Fisher was a household name, there were times he'd have done anything to be able to walk down the street without being recognised. He grudgingly accepted their account... for now. But it had made him aware of a different problem, one he would need to deal with.

'Back to the office?' Nightingale said as she climbed into the driver's seat after having secured Luna in the back. The engine fired into life.

'Turn that off a second. We need to talk,' Fisher replied. Nightingale cut the engine. 'Anything strike you back there?'

'Yeah. I got the distinct impression Lee was going to tell us something; something about Lucy and Tom. I wondered whether Lucy had had enough of Tom and maybe this Patrick was his replacement?' Before Fisher could reply, she let out a shocked, 'Oh! What if Tom found out? He could have sent Lucy a note pretending to be from Patrick, luring her into the studio, then when he confronted her about it, he lost his temper and grabbed the first thing to hand. That could explain why we still haven't found evidence of any Patrick having been there.'

'Anything else?' he pressed.

After a short silence, Nightingale said, 'I don't think so.'

'What about their movements?'

'You mean the fact they both said something different? I thought I should raise it, since they were both there. Was that the wrong thing to do?'

Fisher shook his head.

'No. That was the right thing to do. Thank you. But I was talking about them having gone out the back way. The back way I didn't even know existed. I'm surprised you didn't mention it.'

'I didn't know about it,' she said, sounding defensive.

'There were no fire exit signs pointing to the back of the building?'

'I didn't notice any.'

'A service entrance might mean a service lift, which would mean another way up to the second floor. You're supposed to be my eyes, Beth. How is this ever going to work if you don't use yours?'

'But we spent most of the night either upstairs in the studio or shut in that room interviewing. Even when we were in the main hall, we stayed at the same table. I didn't exactly have a chance to look around.'

Was that a slight wobble in her voice? He knew she was doing her best but, for the first time, he couldn't help but wonder if he'd made a mistake choosing such an inexperienced officer to assist him. Maybe the Falcon was right. The thought irritated him, like sunburn — made worse by the fact it was of his own making. The problem was, if he'd asked one of the others, they'd have been pissed off at being landed with what they'd see as largely driving duties. At least Beth didn't complain... and she was keen and willing to learn. And in a moment of enlightenment, it dawned on him that although she might be inexperienced now, if she stayed that way, he would be the one to blame, not her.

He flicked a finger in the direction of the ignition.

'Start it up and head for the gallery. We're going to take a proper look around this time.'

17.

It was approaching lunch time by the time they pulled into the gallery car park. Nightingale commented on a closed sign propped in the middle of the entrance. The car rolled gently as she manoeuvred around it.

'I'll run up and see if there's anyone around.' Fisher twisted in his seat, making a fuss of Luna, while he waited. Shortly Nightingale was back. 'The front door's locked but there's a note saying deliveries to the rear.' She started the engine. Minutes later the car came to a stop for a second time. 'Looks like we're in luck. The door's been propped open with a cone.'

After retrieving Luna from the back seat, they headed over.

'Hello! Anyone there?' Nightingale shouted after guiding Fisher inside. 'There are stairs going down on the right and up on the left, and a lift dead ahead.'

Fisher strained, listening for the slightest sound. Picking up a noise from somewhere to his right, he bellowed, 'Hello...?'

Footsteps rang out on the steps below.

'Detectives!' It was Jackson Cope. 'You should have called to say you were coming. I'd have had someone meet you at the front.' Fisher could hear the strained breath of a man who sounded as though he had rushed to meet them. 'How can I help?'

'We'd like to take a look around,' Fisher said. 'Get a feel for the layout. If you've got time...?'

'I err... It's just I've got pick-ups scheduled all day today.' After a long pause that Fisher chose not to fill, Cope said, 'I suppose I can fit a short tour in. Let me just lock up downstairs.'

Fisher heard something scrape across the floor then a solid click as the external door closed. Cope moved towards the stairs.

'I'd prefer to take the lift, if you don't mind,' Fisher said.

Cope paused. 'You want to see the basement? There's nothing down there. It's only used for storage. At the moment it's full of crates. It'll only take me a second to lock the door.'

'May as well take a look, now that we're here.' Fisher started towards the lift, letting himself be guided by Luna.

Cope rushed past, his footsteps ringing hollow on the lift's metal floor, followed by the sound of a button being thumbed.

'No need to hurry. I've got the doors.'

Once they were all inside the metal box, Cope jabbed the button repeatedly. The doors gave a quiet rattle as they closed and the lift dropped, smooth and silently.

The lift slowed. Fisher softened his knees for the inevitable loss in momentum. After the doors opened, Nightingale guided him forwards. As they entered the room, a blast of cool, dry air rushed to greet them.

'How did the auction go?' Fisher asked.

'It was an enormous success. We made almost double what we'd hoped for, even managing to sell a couple of pieces that featured as part of the side exhibition, adding further to the coffers. All of these crates here—'

'There's about twenty of them,' Nightingale murmured to Fisher.

'They all contain items auctioned last night. Quite a few contain more than one piece. Like I said, it was a very successful evening. Lucy...' his voice stalled for a moment. 'Sorry.' He cleared his throat. 'It's just that Lucy would have been immensely proud.'

'You must have had an early start,' Fisher said.

'Yes. I had little choice. The delivery drivers were already booked. I need the space back. I've got a new exhibition coming in.'

'How did people get an invite for last night?' Fisher asked.

'Tickets were available here at the gallery as well as on our website.'

'Was it mainly art collectors and the like?'

'There were a lot of collectors, yes, but we also had musicians, film and media folk, entrepreneurs plus a few celebrity sportspeople.'

'A lot of folk with a lot of money to burn,' Fisher said.

'They would need to have, at a hundred and fifty quid a ticket,' Nightingale muttered.

Fisher's eyebrows inched up.

'A very reasonable sum, given it included a three-course dinner and complimentary champagne,' Cope said, sounding haughty. 'So, are we done here?'

'Nightingale?' Fisher said.

'Yes. I think so.'

'So, where would you like to go next?' Cope asked. 'We could start in the main hall?'

'Sounds as good a place as any,' Fisher said.

Cope took them back up to the ground floor, through the kitchen and into the body of the gallery.

'This is where the auction was held. As soon as we finish clearing everything away from last night, it'll be set up for the new exhibition.' He led them across the room. 'The room on the right hosts our more permanent exhibits. Many of them are available to purchase by private negotiation.'

Nightingale took a quick look before Cope guided them through to the reception area, where he pointed out the cloakroom, lift and stairwell. Next, it was the café and nearby customer toilets.

'And this is the courtyard garden where patrons can enjoy a spot of alfresco dining. Weather permitting, of course.'

Fisher heard what sounded like heavy doors being pushed open. He stepped forward, the temperature dropping noticeably. The slightly damp, green-smelling space conjured up an image of lush-looking foliage. A subtle burbling sound could be heard nearby.

'A fountain?'

'A cascade. A specially commissioned piece by Jempson. His work with natural stone is world renowned.'

Fisher nodded.

'So this is the courtyard where the fire exit leads out onto the street?'

'Yes. Which is wired up to our alarm system. Our fully operational alarm system, as the test in the early hours proved.' From the acid tone of his voice, he hadn't quite forgiven the decision to check it so late.

'Someone claimed to have been locked out here last night,' Fisher said. 'Is that possible?'

'Nobody should have been out here,' Cope said. 'The door was closed and there's a sign that clearly says no admittance.'

'Maybe they couldn't read,' Fisher said drily.

Nightingale's shoes clipped across the stone floor.

'There's an empty pint glass and what looks like the foil from a cigarette box. It contains ash and several cigarette butts.'

Fisher heard the rustle of an evidence bag.

'So, assuming they weren't lying about being here, would they have been locked out?'

'Yes,' Cope said. 'It's a magnetic fire door. When the courtyard is open, the lock is disabled and the doors are held open. As it is now. Otherwise it locks on closing.'

'Nightingale, could the door be wedged open with a bottle?'

She walked past. 'I'd say so, yes.'

Fisher gave a nod.

'I think we're done here.' They started to leave but after only a couple of steps he stopped. 'Any way of accessing the upper floors?'

Nightingale walked past him, back into the courtyard; he imagined her eyes scouring the walls for a possible way up. She gave a confident, 'No.'

With nothing else to see on the ground floor, the tour continued on to the first floor, where offices for the gallery's small administrative team spurred off a long corridor.

'All these doors would have been locked and only accessible with a staff key card,' Cope assured them.

They continued on to the second and top floor where, apart from Lucy's studio, the only other room was a store.

'Lucy kept her finished pieces in here.' A door clicked open.

Fisher picked up the scent of apples as Nightingale brushed past.

'Some of these don't look finished.'

'Lucy was working on those around the time of Helen and Gordon's accident. Well, just before,' Cope explained. 'I dare say she would have got around to finishing them at some point.'

With nothing more to see, they returned to the ground floor, taking the service lift.

'Your receptionist didn't mention this lift when we spoke to her,' Fisher said

'Or the adjacent stairs,' Nightingale added.

'Which receptionist? We have several.'

'The one working the cloakroom last night. Molly O'Leary.'

'Molly hasn't been with us long. It's possible she's never been to this side of the building. You can only access it through the kitchen, where there's a sign on the door that says Authorised Personnel Only.'

'Which she could go through if she wanted?'

'Yes. Not that she had any need to.'

'Do you take up references for your staff?'

'Of course. We take security very seriously and have a very rigorous vetting process. Have to, for our insurers. Some of the works we exhibit are worth substantial sums.'

'We'll need to take a look at your staff files.' Before Cope could object, Fisher went on, 'Obviously the rear stairs and service lift open the investigation up to a much wider range of people. It means anyone could have come in through the back entrance, slipped upstairs and met Lucy in the studio without anyone being aware.'

'That's not the case at all,' Cope said. 'The back door is an automatically locking fire door, like the one in the courtyard, only the alarm isn't usually enabled until the building is shut up for the evening. It doesn't open from the outside without a specifically programmed swipe card, which only a handful of people have. My card opens it. Lucy's did. And then there's Barry, our stock supervisor. I did give the catering manager a card to use when he arrived Friday evening. He returned it when he left. I can't think of anyone else off the top of my head.'

'To be clear then, if someone slipped out through the back door, say to go for a cigarette, they wouldn't have been able to get back in the same way?'

'Not without a card.'

'Not even if someone propped the door open, like you did earlier?'

'I only did that because we'd just had an order picked up and it needed several trips. The catering crew were under strict instructions to keep the door closed when it wasn't in use. I was up and down to the basement all night. I would have noticed if it was open. If you don't believe me you could check out the CCTV footage I went to the trouble of providing earlier. The camera at the back covers the service door. You should be able to see whether the door was open or not.'

Fisher clenched his jaws, biting down on his frustration. It wasn't so much that no one had told him about any CCTV cameras, it was the fact he hadn't thought to ask.

'We will. Don't worry.' He pulled a business card out of his pocket and held it out. 'I'd also like details of who has cards and what access that gives them.' The card slipped from his fingers. 'Going back to what you just said about being this end of the building a lot. Did you see anyone using the rear stairs or service lift?'

'No. And I wouldn't have expected to either. Like I said, the only way to this side of the building on the ground floor is through the kitchen and the sign clearly says no admittance. Any member of the public venturing into the kitchen would have immediately been sent out.'

Not according to Messrs Lee and Heath. But then something else occurred to Fisher.

'The kitchen staff... presumably there was a lot of coming and going between the main hall and the kitchen all night. It would have been relatively easy for one of them to slip up to the second floor, wouldn't it?'

'It's possible, but why? What possible reason would any of them have to want to kill Lucy?'

What reason indeed? Fisher knew that to find the reason was to find their killer.

18.

'How did Cope seem to you?' Fisher asked. 'I thought he sounded on edge when we first got there.' They had left the gallery and were in the car on their way back to the station.

'I thought he was alright,' Nightingale said. 'A bit stressed maybe. Not surprising seeing as we turned up unannounced, plus he was busy.' After a brief pause, she added, 'Looks like both Heath and Lee were lying though — about going out for a walk. From what Cope said, they wouldn't have been able to get back in.'

'I can't see how he can be so sure it wasn't propped open at some point. The caterers would have been ferrying stuff out to their vans long after the auction finished. They wouldn't have wanted to keep opening and closing the bloody door. And I bet any smokers amongst them would have wedged it open and slipped out. Just because Cope didn't see it open, doesn't mean it didn't happen.'

'I could go through the catering staff's statements when we get back, see if anyone says anything about the back door being open?'

'Would they have mentioned it? They knew it was supposed to be kept closed. I think we might have more luck talking to Heath and Lee again. See what they say about the door being locked.'

Back at the office, Fisher sent Nightingale to type up the day's interviews and to get her hands on a copy of the gallery's CCTV footage, as well as that from the roadside cameras en route to the

Morgans' residence. The Falcon might think the legal man's professional standing extended him certain privileges but, call him old-fashioned, Fisher preferred hard evidence. At his desk, he sat quietly in his own personal darkness for a while, listening to a room full of clattering keyboards and muted conversations. The air was thick with the smell of coffee and warm bodies. A room full of people; everyone doing their bit. He needed to make sure he did his. But how? Was asking the right questions ever going to be enough? But before he had time to give thought to an answer, he became aware of approaching footsteps, one heavy and one dainty tread.

'Nothing we didn't already know,' boomed the deep, resonant voice of Detective Constable Aaron West, a giant of a man. One of two officers Fisher had tasked with attending the post-mortem.

'Nothing at all?' Fisher asked.

'The pathologist did comment on the level of violence.' DS Kami Aptil's light voice sounded like a tinkling bell by comparison. 'She said the killer continued to strike long after the fatal blow, despite the fact the victim would have been lying on the floor, non-responsive with her head clearly split open.'

So either they were dealing with one angry killer or someone determined to make sure there would be no miraculous recovery.

'What about defence wounds?'

'None.' Aptil again. 'The injuries to her head suggest she was low to the ground, squatting or kneeling, facing away from her attacker when the first blow hit. I spoke to the lab and they said that pretty much fitted with the blood spatter analysis.'

How had the attacker got Lucy into such a subservient pose? Why hadn't she simply run away or called for help? Did her killer have another weapon trained on her — a gun or knife maybe? If so, why not use it?

'Okay, well, one more piece in the jigsaw I suppose.'

After the two detectives left, Fisher slipped his headphones on. He planned on listening to everything they'd turned up so far. It wasn't that he thought others wouldn't spot the anomalies or see the connections that he could, rather it was because he knew the spider at the centre of the web was in the best position to see how all the strands tied together.

First came the guest statements. Most were anodyne accounts: dinner and drinks with friends for some; a tense evening's bidding for others; then a drunken dance afterwards, courtesy of the free-flowing alcohol that Fisher presumed was intended to help boost the bids. Most references to Lucy were limited to general observations: a gracious host who worked the room, spreading charm and charisma. No one claimed to have seen her leave the hall on the way to her studio, nor could anyone offer any reason why she had. When Fisher's head nodded forward for a second time — the robotic voice of the computerised speech sending him to sleep — he sat up, set his bent arms out to the side like fledgling wings and enjoyed a yawn so wide it threatened to dislocate his jaw. Something touched his arm; he gave a start and pulled his headphones off his ears.

'Yes?'

'It's Beth. I thought I'd better let you know it's coming up to half past five.'

Gone were the sounds of a busy office. Fisher realised most people must have already left, heading home to enjoy what little remained of their Saturday.

'Sorry. I lost track of time. We can go now if you want. I can carry on with this at home.'

Fifteen minutes later, as the car accelerated away from the station, he said, 'So, how'd you get on?'

'Okay. The statements are all written up. I've also made a start on the CCTV footage. I found Rupert Morgan's Range Rover heading away from the gallery at the time he said. I managed to follow it as far as the ring road. I'll take a look at the A road that heads out his way tomorrow. That'll be as far as we can go. There are no cameras after that.'

'Do what you can.'

'Will do. Oh, I also took a quick look at the CCTV from the gallery. I thought I might see Lee and Heath slip out. No such luck. The catering vans were parked so close to the back of the building they blocked the camera. So I rang Felix Lee and asked him how he got in, seeing how the back door was locked. It turns out Lucy gave him a key card earlier in the evening when he fetched her pieces for the auction. He said he'd planned on giving it back but forgot.'

'If he had Lucy's card then how did she get into the studio?'

'It wasn't her card. It was a spare. It had guest written on it.'

'How many bloody cards are there? Get onto Cope first thing, find out where that list is that he's pulling together. If there are spares here, there and everywhere, what's the point of having any frigging security arrangements?'

Yet another dead end.

Fisher heaved out a sigh; carried on the back of it, a large chunk of his dwindling reserve of optimism.

***

At home later that night, with the crust of his takeaway pizza in the box on the coffee table ready for the birds in the morning and Luna asleep at his feet, Fisher reached for the chilled bottle of lager in the cool box by his chair. He took a long pull, savouring the cold clean taste.

For a moment, all he wanted to do was embrace the darkness and let the laidback vibe of the Zero 7 track playing in the background wash over him. But... there was work to do. He set the bottle down and opened the laptop resting on his knees. He lowered the volume of the music, turned the computer on, then, using voice commands, navigated his way through the file directory.

So far, he'd played all of the statements given by dazed, tired guests on the night, destined to remember the evening for all the wrong reasons. Next were the guests who had left before the crime had been discovered, whose statements had been garnered over the course of the day. Most of the names meant nothing to him. Others were as familiar as his own: TV personalities, pop stars, soap stars and — Fisher gave a wry smile — even a well-known footballer. And then came a name that had him sitting up in his seat, an uncomfortable tightness in his chest: Amanda Fisher.

What the hell was she doing there? Maybe it was a different Amanda Fisher?

With his voice catching in his throat, he instructed the computer to play her statement. After her name came the address: his old home. She had arrived by taxi, with a Frazer Marchant. A 'friend'. Fisher remembered the whiff of expensive cologne. Toffee-nosed prick.

She and Frazer had shared a table with six strangers, and had remained there throughout dinner and the auction that followed, only having left their seats for the occasional toilet break. Afterwards they had stayed, drinking and dancing, until eleven-thirty when they'd left by taxi. There was little of interest, at least as far as the case was concerned.

Despite the fact the statement had been taken by a uniformed officer, Fisher could virtually hear his wife speaking; her tone of voice and the little nuances that she punctuated her speech with, all captured in that short narrative.

For a moment, he sat motionless, confused by the dull pang of loss that suddenly afflicted him. He thought he was over all that.

What was he like, this Frazer? Obviously loaded, having spent three hundred quid on a night out to look at some pictures. He'd need to be if he was to keep Mandy in the style to which she'd grown accustomed. She'd have been in her element amidst the celebrities, the rich and the highbrow.

He cast his mind back, to earlier, happier days when they'd first started seeing each other. He couldn't recall her having been so decadent or self-indulgent back then. Then, when he was still unsigned, she'd fallen in love with the cheeky lad who made her laugh. Or so she'd said.

When did she fall out of love? More to the point, when did he stop making her laugh? Was it when the boot had crunched into his knee, destroying his only assets and stripping him of the only thing he knew how to do? Or was it when he was lying in the hospital bed, bandages over his eyes, unable to cry despite being told he would never regain his sight? There hadn't been much laughter then, that was true.

How much did the posh twat in his Jag, with his gold-plated tickets, make her laugh? Fisher's thoughts skipped to the conversation with his son; the birthday trip to the match. The box... the VIP treatment. How long before Josh started to feel the same sense of entitlement?

His anger began to simmer. He pushed the laptop away and reached for his beer. A few greedy gulps later and the bottle was empty. He grabbed another from the cooler. Ten minutes later, his anger was easing. He forced the memory of Mandy and her new man out of his mind, reached for his laptop and opened the next file.

Forty minutes later, he was done. There'd been no major revelations, no half-hidden clues, but there was also no Frazer Marchant. Likely as not, whoever had been tasked with getting his statement had yet to catch up with this man who liked to flash the cash, seeing as he'd probably been with Josh at the match for a large part of the day. Well, if they were still trying by the following lunch time, Fisher would enjoy giving them the address of his wife. Or should that be, soon to be ex-wife?

19.

Fisher had been enjoying a deep dream-filled slumber. In it he'd been fishing, casting a line into a large hole. Only instead of fish, it was gargantuan, vicious-looking rats with teeth like planks that he was reeling in. One by one he slipped them off the hook and one by one they scurried away. Then one rat stayed and started to sing a familiar tune. Then the rat disappeared, though the melody remained. Fisher stirred as the dream world dissolved. Still the music continued to play. Slowly, realisation hit — it was his phone, some cheesy ringtone to guarantee he'd never confuse his phone for anyone else's. He patted a hand on the bedside cabinet; found the phone. Fingers fumbled to find the keys in his haste. In the background the silence seemed impossibly loud. Not even the song of a solitary blackbird came from the window to herald in the new day. No call in the early hours was ever good news. His already arid mouth grew even more dry, his stomach lurched and his heart began to race.

'Hello?' His voice was gruff, strained with tension.

'Detective Inspector Fisher?' It was a woman. Refined-sounding. 'This is Olivia Rees-Bowers, Lucy Stirling's solicitor. I apologise for the unsociable hour but your message said it was urgent.'

Fisher's anxiety evaporated like ether on warm flesh, leaving him with a residual chill. He pushed himself up to lean against his pillow and rubbed a hand over his face.

'No, that's perfectly fine. I'm glad you called. What time is it?'

'It must be five-thirty in the UK. I'm currently on holiday in Mexico. Terrible news about Lucy. I couldn't believe it when Rupert told me. Still can't.' There was a pause, though that could have been down to the fact she was calling from the other side of the Atlantic. 'So how can I help you?'

'At this stage my main interest is whether Lucy had made a will.'

'If she had, she didn't use our firm. It's possible she went elsewhere or even did it herself — there are a lot of online resources around these days — but I think both are highly improbable seeing she had us on a retainer. There would have been no additional charge to prepare a will for her, which due to the complexity of her business holdings would have been quite an undertaking. Plus, Lucy knew me. I helped her with the probate application after Helen and Gordon died. She knew she could trust me. I don't see why she'd have gone anywhere else.'

'Did she ever talk about writing a will?'

'I discussed it with her once. I advised her to do it as soon as her inheritance came through. She said she'd give it some thought. I daresay that's as far as she got, like so many people of her age.'

Fisher's guilt slinked down to his guts. Must make a bloody will! He was considerably older than Lucy and had yet to get around to it. If anything should happen to him, as it stood, Mandy would get everything. Something else to add to the list.

'And if there is no will?'

'As the sole heir, her aunt, Mrs Eleanor Morgan, gets everything.'

'How much is everything?'

'I can't tell you that. Even if you could give me the requisite approval, it will take some time to work out. Apart from her cash and property assets there are shares in countless companies and subsidiaries, as well as other investments.'

'Ballpark?'

'Let's just say, once you get into the billions, the exact figure becomes less significant.'

Fisher let out a low whistle.

'People talk about her being a billionairess but I thought that was a figure of speech. That's one hell of a motive.'

'Surely you're not suggesting Eleanor Morgan killed Lucy for the money?'

'A lot of people will kill for a damn sight less.'

'Perhaps in the world you occupy.'

'In anybody's world. Believe me.'

'Then I hope, for her sake, Mrs Morgan has got a cast-iron alibi.'

That would be one of the first things he planned on asking, when he finally got to meet her.

'Do you know the Morgans?' he asked.

'Rupert, professionally. I've met Eleanor a few times, at dinners and charity events. I find it inconceivable either of them could have had anything to do with murder, let alone Lucy's murder. For one thing, they simply don't need the money. Rupert is a wealthy man in his own right. And apart from her roles on various boards, all of which I expect pay handsomely, Eleanor, along with her sister Helen, inherited a vast fortune when their parents died.'

Fisher didn't bother to disabuse her of the naïve notion that money would be no motive for the well-to-do. In his opinion, the rich were rich for one reason only — their desire for wealth. Like squirrels hoarding nuts, the wealthy seemed hardwired to want to amass even bigger fortunes, even when the cheeks of their bank balances were already bulging. Instead, he thanked Ms Rees-Bowers and left her to her holidaying before clambering to his feet to start the slow process of preparing for the new day, too awake to contemplate even a few more minutes of snatched sleep. As a result, he was dressed, breakfasted and ready to go by the time Nightingale arrived.

The streets were still quiet and Fisher took the opportunity to share the news.

'You really think it was the Morgans then?' Nightingale sounded as dubious as the solicitor had.

'Apart from the money, what other reason was there to kill her? According to everyone, Lucy was a modern-day Mary Poppins, practically perfect in every way.'

'Maybe Heath was right and it was an opportunistic thief. Or what if everyone's wrong about Morrelli? What if he nipped up to the studio for a quick line of coke? He'd been there earlier and could have left the door unlocked. What if Lucy read him the riot act and he lost it and lashed out?'

To her credit, Nightingale didn't seem to be letting the rock star's good looks influence her thinking. Fisher paused to think about it for a minute.

'Why wouldn't he have gone to the gents and used the top of the toilet cistern, like everyone else? She definitely wouldn't catch him there.'

'What about the fact his jacket was found in the studio?'

'Planted. Anyone with half a brain would know that hitting someone over the head is going to make a mess. The last thing they'd want is to get blood and brain matter all over their own outfit. Easy enough to grab a jacket off the back of a chair to keep their own clothes clean, then leave the jacket in the kiln, ready for the jacket's owner to come under the spotlight.'

'That could explain why Morrelli got locked in the courtyard — to stop him looking for his jacket and from realising Lucy was missing.'

'Unless Morrelli set it up so that's what we'd think.'

Nightingale sighed. He shared her frustration.

Walking into the office, the smell of strong coffee and the mouth-watering aroma of bacon smacked Fisher in the face. He could feel the saliva start to flow, despite having already eaten.

'Bacon butty, sir?' someone asked.

His stomach growled, urging him to indulge, but the morning's briefing called.

'Leave one on the side for me. I'll have it later.'

Later wasn't long; after updating the room with his and Nightingale's activities the previous day, concluding with his conversation with Lucy's solicitor, the rest of the team's feedback was disappointingly scant. Afterwards, Nightingale went off to continue studying the CCTV footage and Fisher returned to his desk. He threw a chew down for Luna, then called Wickham over.

'Andy, take a seat.' Fisher gesturing towards the side of his desk where a chair normally resided. 'Lucy's apartment: talk me through what you found again.'

'Like I said in the briefing, there was nothing of any interest.'

'Your sandwich, boss.'

Fisher heard the clink of a plate being placed in front of him and reached out, his fingers making contact with the soft dough. Turning back to Wickham, 'Humour me. Talk me through the search,' he said, before taking a bite.

'Okay... Well, the place was tidy. She seemed pretty organised. It looks like she did most things online. We found her passport, driving licence, birth certificate and some papers to do with her adoption in a desk in her lounge. Everything's been bagged up and brought back, including a laptop and a notepad containing passwords and account details. No will though.'

Fisher swallowed a mouthful of sandwich and asked, 'What about neighbours?'

'All said the same thing: lovely lady, polite, always said hello and never any trouble. No late-night parties, no raised voices, no arguments.'

'Any grumbles at all?'

'Nope.'

'Okay, well fingers crossed you have more luck at her parents' place.' It had already been agreed Wickham would extend the search of Lucy's properties by heading over there that morning.

'Don't hold your breath. The woman I spoke to said Lucy rarely stayed there. Seems she preferred the apartment in town rather than a hundred-acre estate in the middle of nowhere.'

'You never know, one of the staff might know something. Lucy grew up there... And don't forget to ask about Patrick,' Fisher called as Wickham started back to his own desk.

Fisher was just finishing his sandwich when Nightingale came over.

'I've gone through all the footage,' she said. 'It looks like Morgan took the back roads after leaving the ring road. Interestingly, there's a lay-by just after the last camera. From there, it's possible, if you cross to the estate opposite, to get to the gallery on foot. It's quite a short cut. If you know your way through, I reckon it would only take ten, fifteen minutes, depending on how fast you run. As far as we know, the Morgans left just before half-eleven and Cope found Lucy's body at what... ten to midnight? It's tight, but not impossible.'

Fisher shook his head.

'It's one thing getting back to the gallery but getting inside without being seen and luring Lucy up to her studio is another thing entirely.'

'Morgan could have phoned Lucy, asked her to meet him in the studio. That might be why her phone was broken. He didn't want us looking to see who her recent contacts were.'

'But he'd know we'll be accessing her records.' As he said it, Fisher made a mental note to catch up with the officer who had been charged with going through Lucy's call history.

He was still thinking through the timings when Wickham approached.

'I'm going to head out to the Stirlings' place now. I can go get that statement from Mrs Morgan while I'm out that way, if you like?'

As the person with the strongest motive, Mrs Morgan was very much a person of interest. Fisher had said as much in the morning

125

briefing, when he'd told the team how he intended on returning to the Morgans' home to get her account later that morning.

'That's okay. It's a nice day for a run into the countryside.'

'I don't mind,' Wickham pressed. 'It'd make sense. I'll be virtually passing.'

Fisher reached for his coat on the back of his chair. He stood up and slipped an arm in his sleeve.

'Like I said, got it covered.'

20.

At the Morgans' residence, Fisher and Nightingale were shown into the house by the same woman as the previous day. Only today it was a different room. This one was laced with a heavy floral scent, which grew stronger with the arrival of Mrs Eleanor Morgan. She greeted her guests with the cool air of the comfortably rich, offering them a seat, which they took, and drinks, which they declined, before taking a seat on a chair opposite.

'Feeling better today, Mrs Morgan?' Fisher asked.

'What? Oh, my migraine? Yes. I'm fine now, thank you.'

After giving his condolences, Fisher explained the reason for their visit.

'I thought you covered all of that with Rupert yesterday,' Eleanor Morgan replied.

'It's possible you know things your husband doesn't.'

'Doubtful... but ask anyway.'

'Did you speak to Lucy during the evening?'

'When we first arrived, she came over to our table. We spoke for a few minutes; wished her luck with the auction, that sort of thing.'

'And that was the only time?'

'Yes. When we were leaving, Rupert went to look for her while I was in the ladies — I needed somewhere quiet to sit until the tablets kicked in. He wanted to let her know we were off, only he couldn't find her. Obviously, now we know why.'

'And were you alright on the journey home? You didn't need to stop at all?'

'Why would we stop?'

'When my wife gets a migraine car travel makes her nauseous.'

'Oh I see. Thankfully the tablets I take are very effective. Look Inspector, I'm sure you haven't come all this way just to enquire about my health.'

'You're right. I digress. Please, tell me about Lucy.'

'Where do I start? She was one of a kind. Which is what makes what happened to her all the more terrible. I can't begin to comprehend why someone should have done what they did.'

'Were you close?'

'Yes. Very. Lucy reminded me so much of my sister. It was a blessing to have her around after Helen died.'

'She certainly seemed to have a lot going for her. It's remarkable how much she managed to achieve, for someone so young.'

'As I said, she was just like Helen: very driven. If she had her eye on something, you could guarantee she'd get it. Take the auction, for example. Its success was entirely down to Lucy's efforts. It was only a matter of time before she took over the running of the gallery and I'm sure she'd have done as good a job as Helen did. They were like two peas out of the same pod.' Every so often, Eleanor Morgan would punctuate her comments with deep breaths and intermittent sniffs, but from what Fisher could tell, her upper lip was far too stiff to ever really wobble and he found it hard to get a sense of her level of grief.

'You talk about their similarity, yet Lucy was adopted.'

Eleanor Morgan attempted to clear her throat, which up until then had appeared perfectly clear. 'Yes. Though you would never have known. She had grown so completely into Helen's mould. You know the saying the apple doesn't fall far from the tree? I used to think that was true and I'll admit, I expected there to be difficulties somewhere down the line. Thankfully I couldn't have been more wrong. It's hard to believe she came from the same stock as that Porter girl.'

'Did Lucy ever talk about being adopted?'

'No. Of course after her sister first made contact, Lucy asked me if it was true, but that was the only time.'

'What did you tell her?'

'The truth. What else could I say?'

'Was she upset?'

'Upset? No. What possible reason could she have to be upset?'

'Some people find the thought of their birth mother giving them up distressing.'

'Not Lucy. She knew she was extremely well loved and very much wanted by my sister and brother-in-law.' There was a pause, then, 'I can't believe I'd even think it, let alone say it, but I'm glad Helen isn't here to have to bury her. It would have destroyed her. She doted on that girl. It's no wonder she flourished, the amount of love they lavished on her.'

'Their deaths must have hit her very hard.'

'Of course. It hit us all very hard,' she said quietly and then, more robustly, 'but Lucy dealt with it with great stoicism. After the initial shock, she coped admirably.'

'It must have been tough, not only having to deal with the loss of both parents but then to have to step into their shoes and take over a huge business empire. How on earth did she manage?'

'It wasn't as onerous as you might think. The different organisations under the company umbrella are all managed by paid directors. Gordon — Lucy's father — used to chair the board of non-executive directors. Although Lucy took that on, she relied heavily on the other board members for advice. Apart from that, the only other role she intended to take on was the day-to-day running of the gallery.'

'Was that common knowledge — that she was planning on taking over managing the gallery?'

'It depends what you mean by common knowledge. Mr Cope knew. He said he supported the idea, but he didn't exactly make it easy for her. He's one of those officious controlling types who likes to keep things to himself. I dare say the fact it meant he'd be out of a job was little incentive either. Though to be honest, I had started to wonder just how much Lucy really wanted it. As I said, once she made her mind up about something there was no stopping her, yet she appeared happy to let Mr Cope run the place while she played with her art.'

Fisher thought someone who could sell a painting for several thousand pounds was doing a lot more than playing.

While he pondered the information, Mrs Morgan asked a question of her own: 'Inspector, I realise that, things being as they are, Lucy's assets are frozen until the perpetrator is caught or the case closed. I wondered... do you have any idea when that is likely to be?'

Fisher was stunned by her directness. He thought of the Falcon. No doubt she'd want him to promise fast results, whereas he preferred to under-promise and over-deliver. Given the circumstances, which would probably end up with him getting kicked off the case if he said the wrong thing, he settled for the truth.

'It's impossible to say at this stage. It's still very early in the investigation. So far there are no clear suspects.'

'But surely it was the work of some mad man? One of those stalkers you hear so much about.'

Fisher sat forward.

'Did Lucy ever mention being stalked or say anything about being worried, perhaps about someone paying her too much attention?'

'No, but she was an extremely attractive woman.'

'What about the name Patrick? Does that have any significance?'

After a moment's pause, she replied. 'No, but I know she received a lot of correspondence from the public. Perhaps Lucy kept some of the letters? I would have thought that would be a good place to start.'

Fisher made a mental note to check with DS Wickham, who had made no mention of finding any fan mail in the victim's flat, and said, 'Thank you. I'll look into that. Of course, while we will be keeping an open mind, I'm sure, given your husband's profession, you are aware most murders are committed by someone known to the victim. I'm hoping that—'

'I hope you're not implying that I had anything to do with it?' Eleanor Morgan interrupted, with a voice as cold and sharp as a steel blade.

'Not at all,' he said, thinking, perhaps the lady doth protest too much? 'I was just wondering... how well do you know Lucy's friends?'

'Surely you don't suspect any of them? They're all Cambridge-educated and from very good families.'

'You don't think murderers can come from an affluent background?'

'Don't be ridiculous, of course I didn't mean that. It's only... well, what motive would any of them have?'

'What about Tom Morrelli?' Fisher asked. 'He's quite new to Lucy's circle of friends, isn't he?'

'Relatively, I suppose, yes. They met earlier this year. I've always found him to be extremely polite whenever we've met.'

'Did they have a strong relationship?'

'Strong relationship? They were young. It's all about having fun at that age, isn't it?'

'Well did you see it lasting?' Fisher wasn't going to let her off the hook that easily.

'I don't know. They didn't strike me as a naturally compatible couple. I saw him as a welcome distraction for Lucy after Helen and Gordon died, but she'd since come through the other side and I believe was ready to stand on her own two feet again.'

'So Tom had served his purpose and was no longer needed?'

'Life is tough, Inspector. Love is even tougher.'

***

The gravel crunched underfoot as they made their way across the drive back to the car.

'Given she's got a billion plus reasons to have wanted Lucy dead, the fact we can't screw them down on the details of their whereabouts in the minutes leading up to the murder bothers me,' Fisher said. 'With her supposedly holed up in the ladies' and him wandering around looking for Lucy, either of them could have slipped upstairs and done it. I tell you what, though, they're surprisingly calm if they did do it.' Fisher blew out a thin stream of air. So far they had yet to rule a single suspect out. 'What about you? Any alarm bells ringing?'

'Not alarm bells but, well, there were a couple of things that struck me as odd. I thought, if the killer put Morrelli's jacket in the kiln hoping to implicate him, I would have expected them to bad-mouth him as well, maybe make up a few arguments between him and Lucy. But they didn't. Mrs Morgan actually called him polite. Also, if Mr Morgan did it, without his wife knowing, what was the motive if he doesn't stand to gain anything personally?'

'Presumably he'll benefit from whatever she gets. Don't forget, Rupert Morgan told us he'd encouraged Lucy to make a will. What if he found out she'd decided to take his advice and was contemplating making one that had a detrimental impact on his wife's inheritance? When we get back, remind me to put a request in for details of the Morgans' finances. Maybe something's happened and they need the money?'

The car alarm blipped. Fisher stopped walking. After positioning himself next to the open passenger door, he handed Nightingale Luna's harness. He climbed into the passenger seat and strapped himself in. While he waited, his mind started to wander. He thought about Mandy, his wife. Would he have ever killed for her benefit? Possibly. No. Probably. But not for money. It would have had to have been something much more serious, life-threatening even. With a pang of sadness, he admitted to himself that now, even if he was physically able to do such a thing, he wouldn't. When had that changed?

He thought back to when he'd first left hospital, returning to the house — their home, as it had been then. He'd been shocked at the transformation in Mandy. Before, she'd always been charming, fun loving and easy going... nurturing, not so much. Then, after he'd lost his sight that all changed and she took it upon herself to look after him in a way he didn't know she was capable of. So, despite the skin grafts, the pain and the constant stench of sickness, under her care Fisher found his anger slowly subsiding and for a while it appeared the acid attack had somehow resurrected his dying marriage, because it had certainly been on a downwards trajectory before. Had been ever since he'd traded his football boots for a warrant card, when Mandy — desperate to hold on to the celebrity lifestyle she loved so much — had set herself up as a party organiser. At the time, he'd simply been glad she had something to do that she enjoyed, not least because it gave her less time to moan about his choice of career direction. Only, as it turned out, she never did stop resenting his decision to subject them to a life of mediocrity and continued to foster a dream of him becoming a football coach, manager or TV pundit. So, while he was enduring long, dark days of soul searching, wondering what the future held for him as a blind detective, Mandy was rebuilding her dream of an alternative future.

'We should screw the force for every penny they've got,' she'd said, as he was trying to find his way around a new bleak, black world. 'You were at work when it happened. They had a duty of care. Then we can sell your story to the nationals. It'll make you a household name again. You could become a presenter, get your own show.'

Mandy's argument for wanting him to pursue a celebrity lifestyle was so they'd never need worry about money again. But what did 'need' look like? The only cutbacks she'd ever had to make was not buying a new designer handbag every time she bought a pair of shoes. When had the woman he'd married turned into this materialistic, hard-nosed stranger?

And now, it appeared she'd found someone who liked the finer things in life as much as she did. Once again, his thoughts turned to Josh and he wondered what type of man his boy would become, being brought up in a household where cash was king. His jaw clenched. The idea rankled like a bad smell.

The driver's door opened, rousing Fisher from his thoughts. Nightingale climbed in and started the engine. Grabbing the handle above his head, he leaned to one side and reached into his trouser pocket for his mobile. With his screen reader switched on, he quickly found what he was looking for and hit the call button.

It was answered after two rings.

'DS Pearce.'

Jimmy Pearce was a good solid detective, one of a number tasked with chasing down guest statements.

'Jimmy. It's Matt Fisher. You caught up with one of the guests, guy called Frazer Marchant, yet? Oh, you are? Okay, forget I called... No. It's only, if you were having problems getting hold of him, I had another address for you to try.'

'Was that the same guy who was at your wife's house yesterday?' Nightingale asked after Fisher hung up.

'Yes. How did you know that?'

'I saw the name Frazer on the guest list and wondered if it was him.'

'And you didn't think to say anything?'

'I wanted to check it was the same guy first but... well, then we left the office and I didn't get the chance. I would have told you as soon as I was sure.'

He'd hoped Nightingale would be his eyes, help point him in the right direction. It wasn't going to work if she didn't tell him what she saw that he couldn't.

'Still... you should have said something.' He twisted in his seat to face her and gave a tight smile. 'Next time, eh?'

21.

'We're coming up to the lay-by just off the ring road now,' Nightingale said. They'd driven straight from the Morgans', retracing the route to the gallery the couple claimed to have taken the night of Lucy's murder. '...And here's the gallery,' she said, shortly. Fisher felt the car slow and heard the familiar tick-tock of the indicator. Nightingale continued, 'According to the milometer it's just under a mile and a half to here from the lay-by. But like I said, there's a route through the housing estate, if you know your way around.'

'Still, he'd have to run. Does Morgan look fit enough to cover that sort of distance at a reasonable pace?' Fisher had a picture of the prominent lawyer with the stout, fleshy look of a man with a penchant for long lunches and fine wines.

'I'd say so. He's tall, slim, looks like he keeps himself fit.'

'Still...'

The logistics of it nagged at Fisher. Would Morgan have had time to make his way back, get to the studio, kill Lucy and slip back out unnoticed?

'Let's go in, seeing as we're here,' he said. 'There's something I want to check.'

Luna guided him up the steps into the reception area. He heard Nightingale hurry ahead to open the door.

'Good afternoon Inspector,' came a woman's warm Irish brogue. 'How are you today?'

'Miss O'Leary. Hello again. I'm fine, thank you.'

'Call me Molly. Is it okay if I stroke your dog?'

'Sure.'

Unlike some guide dog owners, Fisher didn't ordinarily mind people petting the dog while she was working, provided they were in a safe place and sensible about it. He smiled as her tail smacked into the side of his leg with the regularity of a metronome. She was clearly enjoying the attention.

'When we spoke the other night,' he said. 'I asked whether anyone had left and then come back. You said no one had. Have I remembered that right?'

'Well I didn't see anyone come back but I suppose it's always possible someone could have.'

She must have stood up, for when she spoke, Fisher picked up a whiff of mint on her breath.

'But I thought you said the door was locked,' he said. 'If someone came back, wouldn't they have needed you to open it for them?'

'That's true, for most of the night, but towards the end, when a lot of people were leaving, I suppose someone could have slipped in as someone else was going out. I wouldn't have seen them if I was in the back, fetching coats.'

'Sir, presumably if anyone had let someone in, they'd have mentioned it in their statement, wouldn't they?' Nightingale said.

Fisher chewed on his lip. Not necessarily, he thought. Not if they knew the person; took them to be a well-respected, trusted kind of person who claimed to have simply forgotten something.

He gave a nod.

'Well, that was all we came for. Thank you again for your help Miss O'Leary.' Ready to leave, he took his cue from the sound of Nightingale's footsteps, and orientated himself towards the door. But then he paused and turned back. 'Actually, is Mr Cope around? I'd like a word.'

'He's in the basement,' O'Leary replied. 'I'll call and let him know you're here.'

'That's alright,' Fisher said. 'We can find our way.'

'You need a swipe card to get beyond the kitchen. I'll just—'

'Actually, I don't think you do... need a swipe card, that is.'

'Are you sure? I always thought—'

'Pretty sure.' Fisher smiled, hoping it was in her direction. 'I'll be back eating my words if I'm wrong.' He recalled the position of the door to the main hall and turned towards it.

Luna began walking, Fisher close to her side. Nightingale explained who they were as they travelled through the kitchen. The sounds of chopping, frying and washing-up mapped their progress through the long room. Soon, they were out the other side and stepping into the lift. Fisher felt the floor sink almost imperceptibly under his feet. He softened his knees. Barely a bump and the doors started to open.

They stepped out. Cope's familiar Australian twang could be heard arguing somewhere ahead. Fisher reached out and set a hand lightly on Nightingale's arm, stopping her from advancing any further. He put a finger to his lips, then stood hunched forward, listening hard. When it became clear the dispute related to some mundane matter, he straightened up and moved towards the basement door, shouting the gallery manager's name. The hurried slap of leather on concrete was soon heading their way.

'Detectives. I thought you were finished here.'

'We were expecting some information from you... staff access details?'

'Yes. Sorry. I can do that for you later today, as soon as I've—'

'I'd rather you do it now, if you don't mind,' Fisher said. 'As we're here.'

'Of course. If you'd like to wait in reception, I'll bring it over. It shouldn't take long.'

'That's okay. We can wait here.'

'Mr Cope, are you going to tell them about Miss Stirling's missing things?' a male voice Fisher didn't recognise said.

Fisher's ears pricked up.

'What missing things?'

'Some of Miss Stirling's work — two canvases and a bronze. I was just saying to Mr Cope, I saw them myself Friday morning. Now they're not there.'

'And where were they when you saw them last, Mr...?' Fisher asked.

'Keane. Barry Keane. I'm the stock supervisor here. They were in the store Friday morning. I saw them when I put the paintings for the auction by the door, like Miss Stirling asked me to. When I went in this morning, they'd gone.'

'Is that the room next to the studio?' Fisher asked, recalling the layout from when Cope had shown them around.

'That's right,' Keane replied. 'I was in there earlier, looking for my sack barrow. Miss Stirling sometimes borrowed it.'

'You don't seem overly worried about the missing pieces, Mr Cope?' Fisher said.

'That's because, unlike Barry here, I don't want to set hares racing before I've had a chance to check they're actually missing,' Cope said, sounding exasperated. 'I imagine all that's happened is Lucy had a move around and they're hidden behind something. If it's that important, I'll go and check now. I was going to do it when we'd finished down here anyway.'

Fisher imagined all sorts of fiery glances being sent in Barry's direction.

'If something's been taken, it could have a bearing on what happened on Friday night. Nightingale, run out to the car, get some barrier tape and seal the store room door. Then get on to the SCSI, Carrie somebody.'

'Carrie Finch.'

'That's her. Call her and tell her we need to extend the crime scene. I want someone out here asap.' As Nightingale hurried off,

139

Fisher said to the two men, 'Once the room has been forensically tested, we'll need you both to take a look, see if the missing pieces have simply been moved. In the meantime, Mr Cope, perhaps you could go get that information I asked for?'

Cope left without argument. Ten minutes later, he was back.

'I've put everything you asked for on this USB.'

Fisher held out his hand and felt a small thumb-sized object being pressed into his palm. He heard the door swing open.

'All done,' Nightingale said.

With nothing more to do there, they left the two men in the basement and started for the exit. As they were crossing the main hall, a woman's faltering voice said, 'Excuse me...?'

'Miss Porter,' Nightingale said, sounding surprised. 'I'm sorry. I almost didn't recognise you. You're looking a lot brighter than you did the other morning.'

'Yeah, well, I figured I couldn't stay in my pyjamas forever, could I?'

Nightingale gave a polite laugh and said, 'No. Well I'm glad you're feeling better. So, how can we help?'

'I hope you don't mind but I saw you and thought... well, I wondered if there was any news of who did it?'

'Still early days but we're making good progress.'

'Well, I hope you get them soon.'

'Oh we will, don't worry,' Fisher said. 'So, Miss Porter, what brings you here?'

'I came to look at some of Lucy's paintings that are on display. I miss her. I know it probably sounds stupid but I thought it might make me feel closer to her. You know, I haven't even got any photos. I should have taken some when I had the chance, but you don't think do you? She had enough people sticking cameras in her face as it was, didn't need me doing it as well.' She sniffed out a laugh. 'It's funny, I never did get my head around the fact Lucy Stirling was my sister. I'd never met anyone famous before.'

Fisher recalled his mother telling anyone who would listen how her son was *the* Matt Fisher, the famous footballer.

'Perhaps Lucy's aunt will let you have a painting?' Nightingale said.

'I won't hold my breath.'

'Why do you say that?' Fisher asked.

'She doesn't like me. She and her husband think I only got in touch with Lucy so I could sponge off her. You know they told Lucy not to give me anything despite the fact I never asked her for anything?'

'Did Lucy tell you that?'

'She didn't have to. I overheard them. They stuck their noses in all the time. And it wasn't just me. Ask Tom. They stopped Lucy giving him money even though he really needs it.'

22.

Tom Morrelli made some effort to live up to the mean and moody image his record label promoted. He grumbled the entire journey from his apartment to the station and twice tried to light a cigarette, until Fisher took them off him. Carla Porter's comments had only added to the nagging feeling Fisher already had about the rock star. Now, he and Nightingale were sitting in an interview room with Morrelli opposite. The whining had dried up. Perhaps the significance of being asked to submit to a voluntary interview was sinking in.

Fisher kicked off the questioning. 'Tell us about the money you asked Lucy for.'

Tom shifted noisily in his seat.

'It's not what you think. It was just a loan. I promised to pay it all back. With interest.'

'What was it for?'

'The band's next tour. We've all been living the life of paupers, trying to save enough cash to pay for it. Everything was organised. Then when it came time to pay the deposits on the venues, we found out our trusted accountant wasn't to be trusted after all. Every fucking penny gone. Now we're running around trying to scrape enough money together while he's sunning himself on some frigging beach in South America.

'So you asked Lucy to cover it?'

'Hardly. We all threw our own money in first. But that still left us short, so we agreed to see if family and friends would pitch in. I asked Lucy if she'd loan me some. A loan,' he stressed. 'That was all.'

'How did it make you feel when she said no?'

'She didn't say no at first. She agreed. Then her aunt convinced her to change her mind.' Fisher could hear the anger simmering in his voice. 'Said we should just report it to the police and wait till we get our money back. I'd already told Lucy we'd reported it and even if we do manage to get any of it back, it'll be too late. The venues need paying now. We'll have to cancel the whole tour if we can't find the cash. How the hell do we explain that to our fans?'

'That must have caused a few rows with Lucy?'

Morrelli gave a flat snort.

'You didn't row with Lucy. There was no point. If she'd made her mind up about something, that was it. I just couldn't understand why she wouldn't help, seeing as she'd get it back.

'How much money are we talking about?'

'Seventy-five K.'

Fisher whistled softly, but before he could resume his questioning they were interrupted by a knock at the door.

'DI Fisher...?' It was DS Kami Aptil.

Fisher clattered his way around the table, letting Luna lead. He stepped out of the room and pulled the door closed behind him.

'What've you got?'

'Miss Stirling used her mobile banking app not long before she died to transfer seventy-five thousand pounds from one of her accounts into Tom Morrelli's.'

'Seriously? You can transfer that sort of sum with online banking?'

'She had what her bank calls a premier account. She could do up to a hundred K.'

Fisher gave a soft whistle.

'Well, let's see him talk his way out of this one.'

Back in the interview room, Fisher took his seat. His stomach lurched in response to a sudden stab of self-doubt. Ordinarily he'd be scouring the suspect's face for any signs of guilt or unease when dropping a bombshell like he was about to. Now all he had to go on was the smallest of sounds, like the suspect shifting in his seat or a subtle vocal change. Would it be enough? Why did he have to be so pig headed? He'd had the chance to bring Wickham into the interview with him; an experienced officer, he'd have known what to look for. So much for putting the victim first. Well, it was too late now.

Fisher cleared his throat.

'So, Mr Morrelli, you were telling us about your row with Miss Stirling after she refused to give you the loan. What happened next?'

'Nothing happened and I already said there was no row.' Morrelli sounded sulky. 'I told Lucy I understood. Even though I didn't. I just didn't want to ruin the night for her.'

'You didn't discuss the matter again?'

'No. I was going to raise it again over the weekend.'

'Have you checked your bank balance recently?' Fisher listened hard.

'No. Why?'

'A transfer of seventy-five thousand pounds from one of Miss Stirling's accounts was made around the time of her death.'

'What?' The word exploded from him. 'What are you saying? She loaned me the money after all? I swear I didn't know... She must have changed her mind. Oh, God...' His voice caught in his throat.

Fisher responded quickly, 'Is that a pang of guilt I hear, Mr Morrelli?'

'What?'

Fisher was desperate to see the other man's face. To scrutinise his reaction.

'You sounded guilty. I wondered why.'

'I don't know... I suppose because... well, I won't ever have the chance to say thank you.' Too many gaps for Fisher's liking. It wasn't a convincing explanation.

'Did you know Miss Stirling's password for her banking app?'

'What? No. You're not really suggesting I transferred it, are you? I wouldn't do that. Seriously, you've got to believe me.'

'You said yourself, you needed the money, otherwise the band might not survive. What happened, Tom? Lucy saying no forced your hand?'

'This is madness. I told you, I couldn't have killed her. I was locked in the courtyard the whole time.'

'So you keep saying, but we have no evidence of that.'

'What about the waitress who let me out? Talk to her. She'll tell you.'

'She might be able to tell us when she let you out of the courtyard, but not how long you'd been there for. What's to say you didn't go in when you said you did, stay long enough for a couple of fags before nipping out, killing Lucy then going back and locking the door on yourself?'

'Oh man, this can't be happening.' Tom sounded like someone lost at sea whose life raft just sprang a leak.

Fisher pressed on. He still had a lot of unanswered questions.

'Did you go to the studio often, Mr Morrelli?'

'Not often, no. I met Lucy there a few times, when we were going into town.'

'Did you ever watch her operate the kiln?'

'The kiln? No. Yes. Well... maybe. She might have put something in it and turned it on while I was standing there. That's all. Why?'

'Do you have any idea how hot a kiln gets?'

'Bloody hot, I expect. That's the point of them, isn't it?'

'If I said it was a thousand degrees, would that surprise you?'

'Not really.'

'Any idea what a pre-heat setting does?'

'I don't know what any of the settings do. I've never used the thing.'

'You never noticed the pre-heat button on the front?'

'I already said no. Look, what's this all about?'

But Fisher had heard enough. After arranging for Tom to be escorted back to a cell, he and Nightingale returned to the office.

'Give the lab a call,' Fisher said, heading for his desk. 'Find out when we can expect the results from the shirt and trousers he was wearing on Friday.'

'Will do. Oh, it looks like Andy's on his way over.'

Nightingale and Wickham exchanged hellos as their paths crossed.

'You got five minutes? Wickham asked.

Fisher extended a hand towards the chair at the side of his desk.

'Heard you brought Morrelli in.' Chair legs scraped across the floor. 'Is it him? Is the case solved?'

Fisher paused. He wasn't ready to back his hunches just yet.

'Not quite. So, how did you get on at the Stirlings' place?'

'Found a lot of paperwork, some going back years, personal and business, including copies of their wills naming Lucy as sole benefactor.'

'Any sign of a will for Lucy?'

'No. I told you before, the housekeeper said even after her parents died, Lucy preferred being in town. If there is a will, it was unlikely to be at her parents' place.'

Fisher nodded.

'So, did the housekeeper have much to say about Lucy's family or friends?' he asked.

'She knows Rupert and Eleanor Morgan of old. Has a lot of respect for them. Said they know how to keep a clear line between staff and members of the household, like that's a good thing. I asked about Francesca La Salle and her husband. She says La Salle and Lucy had been friends for years. The Stirlings built an Olympic sized pool for Lucy to train in. Lucy and La Salle regularly swam together as teenagers. At some point it sounds like there was some sort of falling out after La Salle turned up late and found Oliver Heath, now her husband, with Lucy in the pool, giving her a coaching session. La Salle accused him of favouring Lucy and stormed out. She never trained there again. Heath continued as Lucy's coach and so was a regular there. Nice enough lad, was all the housekeeper had to say about him. Seems he's good pals with Felix Lee, who she sounded less keen on. Says Lee used to flounce around the place, draping himself over the furniture like he was part of the décor. Called him a proper little popinjay. Never heard that one before, had to look it up.'

Fisher smiled.

'And Carla Porter?'

'Mixed messages. I couldn't tell if she thought Porter was the salt of the earth or casing the joint. Apparently, Porter took a lot of interest in things. The housekeeper put it down to her just being interested in everything, coming from such a different background.'

'And Morrelli?'

'She was very complimentary. A lovely young man with very nice manners. Turns out he had a promising career as a doctor. He'd been studying medicine at Cambridge, following in daddy's footsteps, when he met his fellow bandmates, quit his studies to concentrate on carving out a career in music. Much to his father's disapproval.'

'Cambridge, huh?'

Lucy and the others had also graduated from Cambridge. Was that relevant?

'Someone training to be a doctor certainly wouldn't be fazed by the sight of blood and brains,' Wickham said.

Fisher nodded, 'True. Though it's not like Lucy died at the hand of an experienced surgeon. Anyone could have wielded the bronze weight that had made such short work of her skull. I don't suppose during any of the searches you came across any evidence of a stalker? Maybe a cache of letters from a besotted fan?'

'No. There were some letters but nothing that stood out. Why's that?'

Just then, somewhere behind him, a door opened forcibly enough to hit the wall with a bang. Stomping footsteps advanced. Fisher didn't need to see to know the Falcon was on the warpath.

'What's this about Tom Morrelli being in custody? Why wasn't I informed?'

'I brought him in to question him on a new development,' Fisher replied. 'It seems—'

'You know the media are all over this case.' He could hear her pacing. 'I'm the one who has to take their questions. I'm the one the Commissioner is looking to, to manage the force's reputation. Me. Not you. On that basis, if there's a development, you fucking tell me about it. A-s-a-fucking-p.'

Fisher clamped his lips together and started to count to ten.

He'd got to three, when a loud bang on his desk caused him to jump.

'DI Fisher, will you answer me!'

It was as if someone had hit a mute button. The office fell silent. Luna scrabbled to her feet and gave a low growl, anxious and protective. Fisher put a hand to her head and stroked her, coaxing her to calm down before responding to the DCI.

'Threatening me isn't going to achieve anything.' He kept his voice steady and measured.

'Oh for God's sake. All I did was bang the desk and I wouldn't have needed to do that, if you'd answered.'

'Answered what? All I heard was *you* not *me*. And as for not informing you, I planned on letting you know as soon as we'd finished interviewing him, but you weren't in your office. I would have tried your mobile only DS Wickham wanted to update me on the search of the Stirlings' place.'

Fisher waited, determined not to be the one to try to thaw the frosty silence that had fallen between them. Eventually the Falcon buckled.

'What are these new developments?' she said snappier than a terrier.

Fisher explained about Morrelli's financial difficulties and the transfer of cash out of Lucy's account around the time she died.

'And you still haven't arrested him?'

'I'm just waiting on the lab results on the clothes he was wearing Friday night. As soon as—'

'As soon as nothing,' she snapped. 'You've got means, opportunity and now motive. Everything points to him. What more do you want, a fucking signed confession? I'm happy we've got enough. I'll organise the press conference. Wickham, get down to the charging suite and make the arrest.'

'But ma'am—' Fisher interjected. It was his arrest. But Wickham was already noisily pushing his chair away.

'Don't let us trouble you DI Fisher,' the Falcon said, her voice thick with catty glee. 'You carry on doing what you can to strengthen the case. DS Wickham is perfectly capable of dealing with the suspect.'

Wickham took the cue and his confident stride could be heard heading towards the door. Before Fisher could say anything else, the sound of the Falcon's heels clipping across the floor cut the conversation dead. Overwhelmed by silence, the dark world Fisher now lived in seemed even blacker. He reached out a hand and let it move gently through the air, his fingers finding the reassuring silky soft touch of Luna's head.

'Just you and me now girl. Just you and me.'

23.

'He took it surprisingly well,' Wickham said.

He was back in the chair at the side of Fisher's desk after making the arrest. Fisher had been surprised when he'd heard Wickham return to the office, having had visions of the buzz-cut, athletic and firm-jawed sergeant sweet-talking his way onto the press podium next to the Falcon. Instead, there he was, giving Fisher the lowdown.

He went on, 'There was some effing and blinding to start with, pleading his innocence, but it was a bit half-hearted. I think he realises he's in a tough spot given everything we've got against him. The only thing he got worked up about was his right to a phone call. Didn't like it when I suggested he might have to wait. In the end I left him with the custody sergeant to organise one.'

Matt sank back in his seat. It looked like the Falcon had called it right. Innocent men normally put up more of a fight. Clearly the rest of the office thought the same, as the calls of 'Great job!' and the sound of an occasional clap on the back accompanied Wickham's return to his own desk.

So, that was that.

At least his weekends would be his own again. Maybe he should give Josh a ring, arrange to see him, though he wasn't sure what he'd suggest doing. What could a thirty-four-year-old blind man and a fourteen-year-old boy realistically do together? He was still pondering the question when he picked up Beth's faint scent.

'Sir?' she said haltingly.

'I take it you heard the news?'

'Just. What happened? I thought you wanted to wait for the lab results.'

'I did.' He held back. Didn't want to admit — even to himself — that it had taken the Falcon to overcome his crisis of confidence. He heaved a sigh. Beth would find out anyway. 'It was the DCI's decision. She sent Andy down to make the arrest. Doesn't mean we can rest on our laurels though. There's still a lot to do to make the case against him watertight.'

'I'm not sure you're going to like what I've got to tell you then.'

If Fisher's hopes sank any further, they'd be antipodean.

'Take a seat.'

Chair legs scraped the floor nearby.

'The lab called,' she said. 'They've finished testing Morrelli's clothes. There's no blood, DNA or anything else to tie him to the scene.'

Fisher groaned.

'Nothing? Not even on his shirt?'

'No. They did find traces of lipstick, though it wasn't a match for the one Lucy was wearing.'

'Could be anyone's. A misplaced friendly kiss, a smear from the touch of a friend or a fan. Means nothing.'

'He must have had something else covering his legs and chest,' Nightingale said. 'We already know the back of the lapels on his jacket came up clean, so he can't have used them to cover the front of his shirt with. What about those plastic apron-type things you sometimes see sculptors wearing? Maybe Lucy had some disposable ones in the studio. He could have put one of those over his front and one around his waist then stuck them in the kiln afterwards with his jacket. Maybe they melted?'

'It doesn't sound very likely. The CSI said the kiln was only warm. But leave no stone unturned: call the lab. Tell them what you're thinking. See what they say.'

'Will do.'

'In fact, go and give them a ring now. The CSIs might not have started the store room yet. Get them to check the whole place for anything like that. A bit of thin polythene can be screwed up into quite a small ball.' As Nightingale rose from her chair, another thought struck him. 'What if he was naked?' He imagined Nightingale's shocked expression. 'Think about it. Out of everybody there, he's the only one who could have got away with meeting Lucy for a secret assignation with no clothes on. He could have rinsed himself in the sink then got back into his clothes.'

'Why would he leave his jacket on?' Nightingale asked.

'Less blood to have to wash off him?'

'Shit. If that's the case, how the hell do we ever prove it?'

24.

Jackson Cope led the two white-suited crime scene investigators to the store next to Lucy's studio. They made it clear his continued presence wasn't required. He flashed them both an obsequious smile before retreating to his ground floor office, where he watched through the glass as a handful of uniformed officers started a detailed search of the gallery, peering behind radiators and opening up display cupboards. He didn't know what they were looking for. Didn't want to ask, in case it made him look guilty. The only concession he made was when they'd asked him to unlock the basement. Watching from the open door, the first stirrings of fear tiptoed up his spine as they started to drop what appeared to be a random collection of items into evidence bags. He had to ask then. Not that they told him anything. Thankfully, due to his hard work and diligence, all the crates had already been dispatched. He thought of the repercussions had they still been there.

It was only when he'd needed the gents and walked in to find another white-suited scientist leaning over a cistern lid on one of the toilets that he started to panic. The CSI shooed him out before festooning the doorway with more blue and white tape. Cope returned to his office and reached for his phone.

25.

Despite his misgivings, Fisher resolved not to look for problems where none existed and, going with the mood of the room, joined the team for a celebratory pint after work. A decision that was most certainly influenced by the absence of the Falcon, who was enjoying the limelight in front of the TV cameras as she shared the good news with the nation. And she must have done a good job, as Fisher had been home less than twenty minutes when the phone rang.

'I just saw the news. You did it! You solved the case.'

The surge of pride Fisher felt at that moment washed away any doubts he might have had.

'Told you your old man still had it in him.'

'I never said you hadn't. I just... You know what I meant.'

'It's okay. I'm joking.'

'I couldn't believe it when they said Tom Morrelli had been arrested. I thought he was like, really dope.'

'Dope?'

'Like cool. So, do you think the band will carry on without him? If they do, it won't be anywhere near as good. He's like the best lead singer ever.'

'I didn't know you went in for that sort of music.'

'Yeah. Nevermind are pretty sick. I've downloaded all of their albums.'

'Well, you might want to start looking for something else to listen to. But anyway, the good news is, it means I'm not going to have to work next weekend. How do you fancy doing something together? Seeing as I missed your birthday.'

'That'd be awesome.'

'You haven't got any plans already, like seeing that girl of yours?'

'I can always see her another time. I don't mind.'

And it really didn't sound like he minded. It had been a long time since Fisher had felt so happy; happy enough to brush aside the apprehension his next question gave rise to.

'So, any ideas what you'd like to do?'

They hadn't actually 'done' anything together since the accident. Fisher wasn't exactly sure what he could do anymore. But if he could turn up to work each day *and* catch a killer, then there wasn't much he couldn't do. Was there?

'How about ice skating?' Fisher was still wondering if he'd heard right, when Josh burst out laughing. 'Got you back. How about we go down to Ramsgate? You always said fish and chips taste best at the seaside.'

Fisher smiled. He did always say that. It was true, too.

'That's a great idea. Only problem is, I can't exactly drive us there. And, I don't really want to bother your mother.'

'Can't we get a taxi?'

Fisher shuddered at the prospect of the cost of the hundred-mile round trip, but if that's what Josh wanted...

'Now why didn't I think of that? You'll need to okay it with your mum first.'

'She won't mind. She's going away for the weekend with Frazer. I'm supposed to be going to Nan's. Hey, I could stay with you.'

'Let me talk to your mother first. See what she says.'

It turned out Mandy wasn't at home. Her Pilates class didn't finish until nine when it would be too late for a call of that nature.

Instead, Fisher and Josh said their goodbyes, agreeing to talk nearer the time, after Fisher and his wife had had the necessary chat.

With the phone growing cold in his hand, Fisher found himself hoping she'd be as difficult as she usually was and refuse to let Josh stay over. He didn't want to let his son down, but he could barely look after himself — how the hell could he be responsible for a fourteen-year-old? On the other hand, it sounded like Josh was a lot more grown up than he remembered... perhaps it would be fun? At least he had until the following day to mull it over.

26.

The following morning, Nightingale picked Fisher and Luna up at home as usual. Though for once Fisher settled Luna into the car himself, taking the time to make a fuss of her before climbing in the passenger seat. He was relaxed, smiling even.

'Has there been a new development?' Nightingale asked, as the car accelerated away.

Fisher turned towards her; scars pulled taut as he frowned.

'Development?'

'You seem a lot happier today. I though perhaps something had happened.'

Fisher was immediately reminded of his unease at Morrelli's arrest. He pushed it aside.

'My good mood has nothing to do with the case. Well, not directly, though I am looking forward to not having to work the weekend. Me and Josh are having a day out. I'm taking him to the coast for fish and chips.' He still couldn't believe Mandy had been so amenable. In fact, she'd been so conciliatory he hadn't even bothered to raise the thing about Josh staying over, not wanting to sour her mood. There'd be time enough for that another day, when he was more ready for it.

He was still smiling when he got to the office, contemplating what he could do to make the most of his and Josh's time together. He started towards his desk when Nightingale set a hand lightly on his arm.

'Something's wrong,' she whispered.

Fisher stopped. She was right. The day after an arrest, the office should have been buzzing. Not today. Today, you could hear a pin drop.

'DI Fisher. In here. Now!' DCI Fallon shouted in a voice that could freeze fire.

Her office door slammed shut. His mouth grew dry.

'What's going on?' he said, loud enough to appeal to the room. 'Anybody?'

Wickham came to his rescue.

'Apparently someone came in first thing with important information about Lucy Stirling's murder. The DCI was the only one in, so she dealt with it. That's all I know.'

The click of a door opening was quickly followed by the Falcon's high-pitched yell, 'DI Fisher! Did you not hear me the first time?'

Fisher started to make his way over. As he walked, his good mood fell away. He stepped over it and left it at the door as he entered her office.

The Falcon wasted no time in telling him how the case against Morrelli had all but evaporated as the result of a single phone call. It turned out his claim of being locked out, trapped in the small courtyard café, was true. Though he had lied. Not about where he'd been, but about *who* he'd been with. He wasn't alone, as originally claimed. He had in fact been with his old flame Georgia Bellucci, rekindling the smouldering embers of their past relationship. Being something of a gentleman, Morrelli had opted for silence, not wanting to risk Ms Bellucci's husband finding out. Shane Harman, it seems, had been too busy signing autographs to notice his wife's absence at the time.

'They could be in it together?' Fisher said, though with little conviction, once the Falcon had finished. 'She could be covering for him. What if they didn't have their little get together in the courtyard? What if they were upstairs in the studio and Lucy found them there?'

'And maybe Georgia Bellucci knelt on the floor in front of him to protect his legs from getting blood and Christ-knows what else on his trousers?' The Falcon snarled. 'You've made me look a right bloody fool.'

She was being unfair. It hadn't all been down to him. He wasn't even the one to make the arrest. But he was too full of disappointment and self-reproach to argue. Yet despite his angst, he wasn't quite ready to give up.

'There are a couple of other leads,' he said, trying to inject some hope into a hopeless conversation. 'You never know, they might turn something up.'

'Then I suggest you have everything crossed they're solid-gold leads.' She was speaking calmly, coldly even. He could hear the strain in her voice. 'Because you've got exactly one week to put this right.'

'What do you mean?'

'If the right person isn't safely locked in a cell four floors below my feet by next Monday then you're off the case. I've already started the ball rolling to bring in another DI.'

'You can't—'

'I can and I will,' she said not giving him time to finish. 'Given how little time you have, I suggest you don't waste it standing here arguing.'

Fisher walked back in to a silent office. No banter, no rattle of keys by an army of two-fingered typists. Did they already know his cards were marked? Like a man in a trance, he let Luna guide him back to his desk.

What was he going to do? They were back to square one. Maybe he should just give up now? What did he care if she gave the case to someone else? He'd been so desperate to prove the bastard who stole his sight hadn't stolen his life, that he could still do it, but he'd been wrong. Obviously.

He flopped down onto his chair and felt the weight of Luna's head on his lap. He lifted a hand and gave her a half-hearted stroke.

Slowly a familiar anger began to stir. Why should he give in? He was better than that and he had a week to prove it. It would mean working the weekend, but... He groaned. Josh and fish and chips on Saturday. There was no way he'd be able to take the weekend off now. Not if he had any chance of making enough progress to avoid being kicked off the case. Oh, Mandy would love that — yet another opportunity to point out what a loser he was. And then there was Josh. He really had sounded proud when he'd thought his old dad had got it all figured out. Why the hell did he let him think he'd made the arrest? He couldn't win. Either Josh finds out he lied and took the credit for someone else's actions, or he carries on with the charade, leaving Josh to think he nailed the wrong guy. Couldn't be much worse. Mandy was right. What sort of father was he?

'Thought you might like a cup of tea,' Nightingale said. He hadn't noticed her approach. He heard the clunk of something being placed on his desk, then the scrape of chair legs on the floor nearby. She went on, 'I just got a call from the team at the gallery. They've finished the follow up. They managed to get a number of clear prints in the store room next to Lucy's studio. It looks like at least five different people have been in there recently. Lucy's prints were the most widespread. Two other sets were found on several paintings and sculptures and another two were confined to an area near the door. No matches to anything on the national fingerprint database.'

'What about Morrelli?'

They had taken Tom Morrelli's prints when they arrested him.

'No matches.'

'And the gallery staff?'

'I don't think we've got their prints.'

'Why the hell not?' Fisher huffed. 'I don't know, if you want something doing properly...' A minute later he banged the receiver back onto the phone having arranged for an officer to go out to the gallery later that morning.

'What would you like me to do now?' Nightingale asked.

'I don't know,' he snapped, just as his mobile started to ring. 'I need to take this. Just go back to whatever you were doing.'

He reached for his phone, which was somewhere in front of him. Only he'd forgotten about the tea. His fingers hit the hard ceramic, sending hot liquid spilling over the desk.

'Shit!' He jumped up and heard Luna scramble to her feet and out of the path of the scalding stream.

'Here, you take this.' Nightingale pressed his mobile into his hand. 'I'll sort that out.'

He heard her rush off as he pressed the phone to his ear.

'Hello?'

'Matt. It's Amanda. About Saturday...'

A jolt of optimism surged through him. Maybe he wouldn't need to disappoint Josh after all. Maybe she was going to do it for him?

'Let me guess, you've changed your mind?' he said, trying not to sound too happy about it. In the background, he heard Nightingale return and start wiping the desk.

'What?' Amanda said. 'No. Not at all. The opposite in fact. Josh mentioned about stopping over Saturday night. I'll be honest, I wasn't entirely happy with the idea, but I can see how much it would mean to him and I suppose it would be good for the pair of you to spend some time together.'

Guilt gripped Fisher's gut. He bit back a groan.

'Ordinarily I'd jump at the chance, but... well, actually something's cropped up. I'm going to have to take a rain check. I was about to call.'

'You're not serious?'

'I wish I wasn't but I'm going to have to work. I can do the following weekend... Probably.'

'And there was me thinking you were actually prepared to put your son first for a change. I should have known. It's always the same with you, isn't it, Matt Fisher? The job always comes first.'

Fisher didn't have it in him to argue. Not this time. She was right.

'You do realise he's going to be devastated.'

That's it, give that knife a good old twist. Like it doesn't hurt enough already.

'I'll make it up to him.' It sounded lame even to his own ears.

'Goodbye Matt.'

She hung up and for a brief moment he stood listening to dead air. His heart was thumping. He was angry. At Amanda. At himself. At just about everything and everyone...

Suddenly his legs felt as heavy as his heart. Needing to sit down, he reached for his chair and hit something solid. It was Nightingale.

'Sorry sir. Let me help you. Here...' She set out a hand and gently directed him to his seat.

'Beth, just leave it,' he snapped.

'I'll get out of your way once I've—'

'Just go!'

Fisher felt Luna brush up against him. Her cold, wet snout pressed into his hand and he had a sudden compulsion to bury his head in her soft fur and sob.

'Matt?' It was Wickham.

He took a deep breath, cleared his throat and said, 'What is it?'

'I wondered if there's anything you want me working on in particular, given, you know... the circumstances?'

Fisher's anxiety got him in its cold grip.

'Circumstances?'

'The Falcon just told me — you know, the Monday deadline.'

'About me making the transfer window, after all?'

'Look, no one wants you to go. The last thing any of us need is some career-hungry DI being parachuted in and taking the credit for everything we've done. So, what do you want me to do?'

But Fisher had already stopped listening. It was like his worse fears were coming to fruition. All he felt was hurt and resentment.

'You never know, it might work out quite nicely for you,' he said through tight lips. 'You must have been wondering when I was going to fuck off so you could have my job.'

Fisher expected to hear the thump of feet stomping away; instead the woody, spiced mix of Wickham's aftershave caught in his throat.

'Don't be such an arsehole,' Wickham said, close to Fisher's ear and low enough to avoid being overheard. 'We all want the same thing. No one's gunning for you... Well, the Falcon might be, but none of the team are, so I'll forget you said that.'

Wickham must have stood back up, as the aromatic smell grew faint. Fisher knew he should accept the reassurance, be grateful even, but he was still smarting as Wickham walked away. He couldn't help it.

Slowly the sounds of the office drifted back into his awareness — the sounds of a room-full of busy people — and for the first time in his career he didn't know what to do.

27.

Jackson Cope listened to the uniformed officer, a gangly twenty-something who looked alarmingly like a schoolboy in fancy dress. He was explaining how all the staff were required to provide a fingerprint sample for elimination purposes — voluntarily, of course, at this stage. As the officer talked, Jackson's brain raced. What had they found? They must have found something, otherwise what where they going to check the prints against?

For a moment, the part of Jackson used to getting his own way contemplated a churlish response, citing human rights or workload or the impracticality of getting everyone to come in. Then the officer suggested perhaps he should go first, by way of setting a positive example. It would be easy enough to explain how his prints got pretty much anywhere, so why did the blood drain from his face and sweat begin to prickle his scalp? He looked at the officer, who stared back, waiting for a reply.

Jackson pulled on a tight smile.

'Of course. When are you thinking of doing it?'

'No time like the present.' The officer turned and beckoned to another uniform hovering by the door.

This one, a dark-haired young man with dark circles under his eyes to match, entered toting a small leather case.

'Is there somewhere I can set this up? It doesn't need much room, just a free surface that's out of the way.'

Jackson took them to his office and watched them unpack the scanner. His hands grew clammy. He moved them to his side, about to wipe them on his trousers, but stopped himself. What would generate more suspicion — sweaty palms or trying to hide his sweaty palms by wiping them on his trousers?

The officers didn't appear to notice. They smiled and thanked him, once the deed was done, and sent him away to corral the rest of the gallery's employees. He'd already agreed to phone staff not in work that day to ask them to come in, or attend a nearby police station, if preferred. And he would too... just as soon as he'd made another call.

28.

In the middle of the busy office, surrounded by his colleagues, Fisher felt very alone. Duly deserved, by his reckoning, too. He reached for his headphones. If nothing else, they would discourage people from attempting to talk to him. He opened the file containing the guest statements. Ignoring the dross — anodyne accounts of people who didn't know Lucy and who he deemed least likely to have killed her — he returned to the accounts given by her friends and family, looking once more for any discrepancies or nuggets of information that might lead him to the person who found their way onto the second floor and wielded the fatal blows.

There was no discrepancy. No nugget. But there was something he had forgotten about.

'Couldn't we have just phoned?' Nightingale said. They were in her car, on the way to Felix Lee's home in a very fashionable, bohemian part of town.

'I want you to watch him, scrutinise his facial expressions while I ask the questions.'

'Looks like he's doing all right for himself,' Nightingale said as the car drew to a stop. 'It's got a gated car park. Maybe he's a thief, like the pink panther, only he nicks art, not diamonds.'

'I thought he lived in a flat?'

'It's an old converted warehouse or brewery. It looks well smart.'

The car moved forward slowly a short distance, before coming to a stop. Nightingale immediately jumped out and unhooked Luna from the rear seat. All three of them made their way into the apartment block.

'He's on the third floor,' Nightingale said, as the lift doors clanged shut.

Moments later, as they stepped into the corridor, a door clicked open in front of them.

'Oh...' Even from that single syllable Fisher recognised the sound of Felix Lee audibly switching excitement for disappointment.

'Expecting somebody, Mr Lee?' Fisher said.

'No. But one can but hope.'

'Can we come in? This shouldn't take long.'

Lee must have moved away from the door to admit them as Fisher felt Nightingale's hand on his elbow, propelling him in the right direction. He needed it too, as soon the quiet tread of bare feet on a wooden floor was drowned by their own footsteps. After they stopped, Fisher picked up another sound — a push of air and a soft creak of leather as their host made himself comfortable.

'To what do I owe the pleasure?' Lee asked.

Fisher reorientated his focus several feet lower, down towards Lee's seated position, and said, 'A number of items may have been taken from the gallery around the time Miss Stirling was murdered. Two paintings and a sculpture. They were in the small room used as a store, next to Lucy's studio. We found a number of fingerprints...'

'And you came straight to my door. Quelle surprise! I take it you want my dabs — that is the right term, isn't it?' Fisher could hear the smirk on his face.

'You don't seem overly alarmed, Mr Lee.'

'Why should I be? I already told you I was there on Friday night. I helped fetch Lucy's pictures for the auction.'

'That's right. You and...?'

'Tom.'

'Yet we didn't find Tom's prints in the store.'

'The sculpture was in the studio. Tom fetched that while I got the paintings from the store.'

Just then, the door to the hallway opened. A voice called out, 'Hi. Can't stay long. Fran's just nipped...' The voice faded as though someone had turned down the volume.

'Mr Heath,' Fisher said, recognising the voice.

'Hello.' His previous confidence seemed to have abandoned him.

'I'll be free in a minute,' Felix Lee said. 'The detectives are done here, I think.'

'For now. Don't forget to drop by the station to have your fingerprints taken. As soon as possible, if you don't mind.'

'Why? I've already admitted I was there,' Lee said, sounding as sullen as a teenager told to tidy his room.

'Fingerprints? You can't suspect Felix. I already told you, he was with me,' Oliver Heath said with a worried edge to his voice.

'Two paintings and a sculpture are missing from the gallery, taken from the second-floor room that Lucy used as a store. We're asking people who have recently been in that room to submit their fingerprints so we can eliminate them from our enquiries.'

'I went there to fetch Lucy's auction pieces, remember?' Lee said.

There was far too much emphasis placed on the word *remember* for Fisher's liking. He could virtually see the warning look that would have accompanied his words. Something was going on.

'Have you ever been into Lucy's store, Mr Heath?' he asked.

The room fell silent apart from the ticking of a clock. Fisher realised just how much in the dark he really was, not being able to see those little tells — a swallow, or a hand drifting up to scratch a nose or cover a mouth, or an attempt to cover up an intake of breath. Though when the answer was as long as this one in coming, he didn't need to see anything to know he was on to something.

'It seems your memory fails you, Mr Heath,' he said. 'Thankfully, fingerprints are more reliable. If you could let us have yours too. To rule you out of our enquiries, of course.'

Oliver Heath's memory must have made a miraculous reappearance as he started, 'Actually, I think I may have—'

But Fisher had already moved on, 'Mr Lee, with regards to the missing pieces, when you were in the store Friday evening, can you remember what was on the shelf to the left of the door?'

'Well... I remember seeing some bronzes,' he said eventually. 'Two, I think. And quite a few paintings, but then the room was full of them.'

'But specifically in the area near to the door?' Fisher pressed.

'There were probably six... maybe ten paintings there,' Lee replied. 'Some of the bigger ones were on the floor, leaning against the wall. I remember thinking it was a stupid place to leave them. I could have easily knocked them by accident.'

'Can you recall any details? Something we could use to identify specific pieces by.'

'I remember one of the bronzes was a male diver. It was quite exquisite. Lucy had a great eye for the human form. I meant to mention it to you,' he said, obviously talking to Heath. 'Thought it might make a nice present.'

Fisher's gut gave a small squeeze, a nudge to say he'd been right to trust it. The figure of the diver was amongst the items reported missing; now he knew it had definitely been in the store early Friday evening.

'I want descriptions of the missing items circulated straight away,' Fisher said as Nightingale drove them back to the station. 'Get onto the gallery, see if you can get hold of Barry, the stock supervisor, ask him if there are any photos. If there aren't, see if he can remember enough to make it worthwhile sitting him down with one of the police artists. Once we've got something, we'll

169

need to do some phoning around, call a few galleries, see if they can help pull together a list of dealers who a fence might try to sell the stuff through. If we can track down the stolen items, there's a chance we could be onto our killer.'

'I'll get straight on to it,' she said. 'By the way, what was the deal with getting Oliver Heath's prints?'

'Gut instinct. I didn't like the way he stalled. It was a simple question, so why not a simple answer? But even if for some reason he'd been there and we find some of the prints are his, it doesn't necessarily follow he's our man. Any art thief worth their salt would have worn gloves.' After a brief silence, he said, 'I think it's also worth taking another look at the CCTV from the rear of the gallery. Get the techies to blow the images up; we really could do with getting a better view between the catering vans.'

'Will do.' After a short pause, she said, 'I wonder how big the paintings were? If they were quite small, they could have been taken out in someone's bag or hidden inside a folded coat. I remember seeing on the news once, this couple actually managed to nick a guitar by sticking it under the woman's coat. They walked straight out with it.'

'Let's not rule anything out. Maybe we need another word with the receptionist. See if she noticed anyone with a particularly large bag, or someone who wanted their coat before they actually left.'

'What if they didn't check their bag or coat in?'

'She might have still noticed. I would have thought she'd have asked if they wanted to check it in. Tell you what, let's go to the gallery now. You can go talk to that Barry, find out if there are any photos of the missing pieces and I'll quiz Miss O'Leary,' Fisher said, only just managing to stop himself referring to her as the lovely O'Leary.

29.

Molly O'Leary greeted them with the same soft, melodic voice Fisher knew he'd never fail to recognise. She quickly got hold of Barry Keane, the stock supervisor. Nightingale went off to find out what he could tell her about Lucy's missing pieces, while Fisher stayed to quiz Molly.

'We'll have the neighbours talking if we keep meeting like this,' she said as soon as they were alone. Fisher couldn't help but laugh. She went on, 'Actually, I'm glad you came. I was thinking of calling you.'

'Oh?'

'It's about Friday night. I didn't see it myself, so I wasn't sure if I should say anything. It might just be a bit of gossip. But... well, I overheard one of the barmen saying how he'd walked in on someone snorting coke in the gents. I know it's probably quite common in the music industry but I was still surprised someone actually had the nerve to do it here.'

'It was a musician?' Fisher asked. Tom Morrelli and Shane Harman were the only famous musicians at Friday night's event. If Tom was lying about the coke, what else had he lied about?

'Yeah... at least I think it was. The guy said something about it being very rock and roll... I guess I just assumed. Maybe I'm wrong?'

'Don't worry about it. I'll ask the barman. What's his name?'

'I don't know. He was with the catering team. To be honest, I couldn't even tell you what he looked like.'

'It doesn't matter. We'll find out. On a different point, you know I asked whether anyone came back for some reason after the auction ended?'

'Yes.'

'I just wondered whether anyone turned up to collect a package?'

'No. I would have got Mr Cope to see to them if they had.'

'What about anyone taking something out with them?'

'You mean that they didn't check in?'

'Yes. Maybe a painting they bought in the auction?'

'No, but I would have stopped them anyway. I wasn't told anyone would be taking anything out with them — I would have asked Mr Cope if it was okay.'

Fisher nodded, then came the question that had brought him: 'Were there any guests who insisted on keeping their coats or handbags with them?'

'A few women wanted to keep their bags on them, mainly clutch bags, you know, for lipsticks and tissues. I don't recall anyone taking a coat through with them.'

'Anyone with anything bigger than a clutch bag?'

'Yeah, three or four women had normal handbags.' Molly managed to furnish him with descriptions of three women as well as one name: Carla Porter. 'It wasn't a massive thing. Just a normal handbag, similar to mine. Here...'

Fisher heard something heavy being placed on the counter in front of him. He tentatively reached out a hand and made contact with a pliable fabric, not dissimilar to leather but smoother and more plasticky. He took in the bag's dimensions. It was big but not as ridiculously big as some he'd seen hooked onto the arm of a celebrity in the past; large enough perhaps to fit in a make-up bag, a purse, umbrella and perhaps a folded jumper.

'Did you ask her if she wanted to check it in?'

172

'Yes. I asked all the guests. She said she'd prefer to keep it on her. Probably didn't want to have to carry her fags around all night.'

'How do you know she smokes?'

Before she could reply, the door to the main hall banged open. Nightingale's heels resonated on the hard floor as she made her way over. She wasn't alone.

'Hello Inspector,' came a familiar Australian twang. 'I came to see if you needed anything.'

'Good morning Mr Cope. If you could give me one minute. Miss O'Leary, you were saying...'

When an answer wasn't immediately forthcoming, he wondered if he'd somehow put her in a tight spot.

'I don't know,' she said, eventually. 'Maybe I could smell it on her?'

'Okay, thanks. Beth, did you get the size of the missing pieces?'

'The smaller canvas is twenty centimetres square, the larger one is forty by fifty centimetres. The sculpture is thirty centimetres tall. Barry showed me one that's similar. It's pretty heavy.'

'Not exactly easy to spirit away in the bottom of a handbag or under a folded jacket then?'

'No.'

'Okay, thanks. Now, Mr Cope...'

'Yes?'

'Were you aware people were engaging in illicit drug taking Friday night?'

'What?' The word burst out.

'Cocaine. In the gents. You didn't get any complaints?'

'No. It wasn't that sort of event and we're not that sort of place.'

For a moment, Fisher was tempted to tell him what he could do with his indignation. He knew that a surreptitious line or two was all too common an occurrence at celebrity bashes, even high-brow ones like Friday's, but it was fruitless to argue, at least until he had all the facts. Instead, he gave Cope a curt nod, then turned towards where Molly O'Leary had been standing.

'Thank you for your help, Miss O'Leary. If you do happen to remember any more about what we were discussing, please let me know.'

After making their way outside, they were at the bottom of the long flight of steps when Molly called for them to stop.

'Thanks for waiting,' she said, joining them on the pavement a little out of breath. 'I'm sorry but I didn't exactly tell you the truth back there. It's just, I didn't want Mr Cope to hear. You see, I know Lucy's sister smokes because she tried to have a fag in the staff toilets at the back of the cloakroom.'

'What was she doing in the staff toilets? I thought the gallery has a smoking area?'

'It has. But she didn't go in there for a smoke. Someone had spilled red wine down her top and she wanted to rinse it out. I felt sorry for her. She said the customer toilets were really busy and didn't fancy having to stand half-naked for everyone to gawk at. I could tell she was having a miserable time, which is why I let her through. If I'd known she'd be stupid enough to have a cigarette while she was in there, I wouldn't have been so generous. Thankfully, I had to go and use the loo. She'd hung her shirt over the back of a chair under the hand-dryer, and was standing on the toilet with her head out of the window about to light up. If she'd set the detectors off the whole place would have had to be evacuated. Could have got me sacked.'

30.

'When you take another look at the CCTV footage from the back, check out the coverage from the front at the same time.' Fisher said as they sped across town. 'Give yourself a margin of about half an hour before Molly saw Lucy go upstairs until the time the first patrol car arrives. Look for anyone who turns up or anyone leaving with anything that looks out of place.' Just then his phone began to ring. He pulled it out of his pocket. 'Yes?'

'It's Andy. I got your message. What's up?' Fisher had tried calling Wickham as they left the gallery, only getting his voicemail.

'I need you to do some ringing around. One of the barmen was overheard talking about seeing someone snorting coke in the gent's Friday night. There was a suggestion it was someone famous, possibly a musician. I want to know if it was Morrelli. The coke in his pocket didn't get there by itself and if Morrelli put it there, it means he lied to us and begs the question has Georgina Bellucci also lied to give him an alibi? And if it wasn't Morrelli, who was it, and did they have anything to do with planting coke in Tom's jacket before it was stuffed into the kiln?'

'I'll get onto it straight away.'

Fisher returned his phone to his pocket. For the first time he felt a glimmer of hope. He had barely crossed the threshold to the office when it was cruelly quashed.

'DI Fisher, DCI Fallon asked to see you as soon as you're back,' someone shouted over.

He walked to the Falcon's office, knocked and walked straight in.

'You wanted to see me ma'am?'

'Yes. Glad you can grace us with your presence.'

'I'm sorry. I've been out following up a lead. Have I missed something?'

'What's this about a theft at the gallery?'

'What?' Fisher was confused. How the hell did she know? He'd intended on briefing her as soon as he'd got in.

'One of the gallery staff came by earlier to get their fingerprints taken. Imagine my reaction when the desk sergeant calls me to ask which case it should be logged against?'

He didn't need too much imagination to decipher that cold, clipped tone. He had nobody but himself to blame.

'I'm sorry. You're right. I should have—'

But she hadn't finished. 'Of course, I knew nothing about it, seeing as you hadn't bothered to brief me. Imagine the humiliation that caused, having to admit to not having a clue what they were talking about.'

Fisher couldn't help himself.

'Humiliation? Humiliation is when you find out you've spent the whole day with your jacket inside out; or your tie sticking out of your fly like some limp dick; or you've missed half of your chin when shaving and look like something that the cat dragged in; or you've wrapped your teenage son's present in paper for a baby.'

'Don't you dare use your disability to belittle me,' she snarled. Fisher waited for the onslaught that never came. Instead, she took a deep breath in. When she next spoke, she appeared to have regained control. 'I refuse to make this about you. So... the thefts at the gallery. What do we know?' Fisher gave her what they had so far. 'And you didn't think it worth mentioning until now?' she said. 'It's obvious what happened. Thieves go in, ransack the place. Lucy comes along, catches them at it. They grab the first thing they see. Before you know it, she's lying dead on the floor and we've got a murder investigation on our hands.'

'There was no ransacking. Like I said, all that's missing is a couple of paintings and a sculpture and, in my defence, the manager initially suggested they had probably just been moved. There was a lot of upheaval on the run-up to the auction.'

'Andy, get in touch with the CSI team, I want them—'

'Andy?'

'Matt.' Wickham's tone was a dry as his cough.

So, that was how it was, was it?

Fisher drew himself tall.

'That's all been taken care of,' he said. 'Hence the request for people's prints. Five sets of prints were found. We have already matched three of them to Lucy, the gallery manager and the stock supervisor, leaving two unidentified.' He paused. He knew he was going to have to tell her about Lee and Heath. Though the need to tell her anything stuck in his craw. He noisily cleared his throat, then said, 'I suspect one set will come back to Felix Lee. He admits to having been in the store earlier that evening and said he saw at least one of the missing pieces while he was there. I also asked another of Miss Stirling's friends, a Mr Oliver Heath, for his prints.'

'He'd been there too?' the Falcon asked.

'No... Well, he said he couldn't remember whether he had or not. Just something about his account jarred.'

'As always you're being very thorough...'

'Thank—'

'But thoroughness is the preserve of academics and scientists. It isn't getting us results, is it? We now know, on the evening of her murder, items were stolen, taken from the room next to Lucy Stirling's studio. It's not too much of a leap to see what happened. She went to the studio for some reason and came across the thieves. I dare say she confronted them and... well, the outcome speaks for itself. On top of which, you have two men who you suspect forensics will be able to place in the room where the art was taken, and instead of bringing them in and getting their fingerprints as a matter of urgency, you're twiddling your thumbs waiting for them to pop by whenever they damn well please.'

'That's not—'

But she wasn't finished. 'I want them brought in and printed asap. In fact, get them in an interview room. Separate them. If the thief killed Lucy, it's because they panicked. If they panicked once, they might again if we give them a hard enough time.'

Fisher rubbed his forehead. He could feel a headache brewing.

'Fine. I can bring them in. If that's what you want. But finding their fingerprints in the room next to the murder scene means nothing. Felix Lee already admits to having been there that night. I've got Beth working on the CCTV from the gallery. Whoever took the items had to have a way of getting them out of the building. Why don't we—'

'If *I* want them brought in?' Her tone had the same effect as nails down a blackboard. 'Is that how it's going to be? Every time a decision's needed, I've got to be the one to make it? I thought you wanted to lead the investigation.'

Fisher clenched and unclenched his teeth, the throbbing in his head getting stronger.

'I don't want to take the decision because I don't agree with it. Yes, the missing items represent a strong lead, but the guy has already said he was in the store. Aside from that, it's one hell of a leap from someone nicking a few pictures to forcing the victim down on the floor and bashing her head in. And why was she kneeling?' he added, unable to keep the exasperation from his voice. 'If she'd walked in on them, surely she'd have run off and called for help.'

'Not necessarily,' Wickham jumped in. 'Not if it was one of her friends. Isn't it more likely she'd have confronted them?'

'How did they get her on her knees?' Fisher pressed.

'Maybe she threatened to call the police?' Wickham replied. 'She grabs her phone, they knock it out of her hand, she bends to pick it up. Before the killer could stop themselves, they grab the sculpture and smack her over the head.' Adding, 'Her phone was found near to the body.'

'And so that clinches it then?' Fisher snapped.

'That sounds a bloody good fit from where I'm standing,' the Falcon said.

Fisher hadn't given up yet.

'But why strike her repeatedly? And how do you explain the puddle of dirty water over her?'

'Detective Fisher, are you deliberately being difficult?'

'No. I'm just trying to make sure we don't have a repeat of the last fuck-up, but it's obvious you've made your mind up. I'll go straight out and bring them in. Have another go at interviewing them.'

'Actually, I think it's better if DS Wickham does that,' she said, in her usual aloof tone. 'Andy, take one of the other sergeants in with you, someone who's not afraid to ask the difficult questions. We need to put some pressure on these so-called friends of the victim.'

Fisher pulled his chin up and puffed out his chest.

'Ma'am. With respect, I should be the one doing the interviews. I've spoken with both suspects already. I'm best placed to tell if their accounts change.'

'With respect? You call my last decision a fuck-up and then have the audacity to say "with respect". So far, all you've done is come up with excuse after excuse. If you didn't prevaricate so much, both men would already be in custody and we wouldn't be having this conversation.' She paused, perhaps to give her simmering anger time to drop low enough to not boil over. 'No. It's time for a fresh pair of eyes.'

Fisher knew with Wickham in the room, the Falcon wasn't going to back down. In fact, she'd dig her claws in even harder. Well let her. He could be just as bloody-minded.

Luna stirred at his feet, in reaction to the excess tension on her harness. Fisher took a steadying breath and relaxed his grip. He needed to win control back.

'Ma'am. I can understand—'

A sharp rap on the door caused him to pause. The handle turned.

'Ma'am, your visitor has arrived.'

'Thank you.' The door clicked shut. 'Well, I think we're done here. DS Wickham, don't forget to keep me appraised of the outcome of the interviews with the two suspects.'

'Ma'am.'

Wickham left the room. Fisher didn't move. He was desperately trying to get a grip of his raging emotions.

'DI Fisher, I said we're done here.'

He wanted to tell her she was wrong. On so many counts. But what more could he say? She would be deaf to whatever argument he used. He could hear her bustling about behind her desk, doing her damndest to pretend he wasn't there, then the click of the door opening. The sounds of a busy office grew louder. He bent down, ruffled Luna around her ears, took a deep breath, then turned and set a course back to his desk.

Wickham was waiting just outside the Falcon's office. He fell into step with Fisher as he left the room.

'I want you to know, none of this was my idea.'

'It didn't need to be,' Fisher growled. 'All you had to do was light the blue touch paper and stand back.'

'What's that supposed to mean? ...Oh, what's the point? Think what you want to think.'

Fisher chewed down on the hard words he wanted to say. Words designed to hurt; to spread the pain. Instead, with a stony face and a flat voice, he said, 'What are you waiting for? Go on, be a good boy and do what the Falcon told you to, bring the bad guys in.'

'You know you can be a real arse sometimes,' Wickham said, before walking off.

31.

Fisher sat contemplating the recent developments, wondering if the Falcon was right. Had self-doubt stopped him from taking more decisive action? He'd sensed Heath and Lee were hiding something on more than one occasion. So why hadn't he brought them in for questioning?

The truth was, he just couldn't see them killing anyone for a couple of paintings and a lump of bronze. Especially not so violently. He drummed his fingers on the desk. Part of him wanted it to be true, if only so the case could be closed and life could return to normal. Only, there would be no normal ever again; if that happened everyone would know he couldn't cut it. He'd been the first to interview the two men, yet it had taken a decision by the Falcon to bring them in. He'd have no choice but to resign. To quit.

He'd been so sure he still had what it takes. And maybe he did, with the right support. Wickham... so eager to come up with suggestions. Please Miss... what if Lucy found them taking the stuff... what if she was picking up her phone... what if he went and boiled his head?

'Sir?'

Fisher started. He'd been too preoccupied to notice Nightingale approach.

'What is it?'

'I've gone through the CCTV footage. I can't see anyone other than taxi drivers turn up at the front, and no sign of anyone taking stuff out that looks like it could be the missing art. The lab blew some shots up from the back. There's a lot of coming and going but everyone looks like they're part of the catering team; either in chefs' whites or waiters' outfits. And from what I can tell they only go from the back door to the catering vans, so unless the stolen items were stashed in one of the vans...'

'And the two friends?'

'No sign of them.'

'So, they were lying. Okay, well, thanks.' He slouched back in his seat. It looked like the Falcon was right, after all.

But Nightingale wasn't finished.

'There is one other thing... I'm not sure if it's relevant,' she said hesitantly. 'I had an idea... I wondered if someone had hidden the paintings and sculpture inside the gallery and went back for them later — I thought maybe someone who worked at the gallery — so I let the CCTV run a bit longer. After the caterers had gone, no one left by that door until after Cope made the triple-nine call and we'd arrived. Over the next few hours, a few people left that way — staff, I imagine. None of them were carrying anything that looked remotely like a painting. Then, nothing happened until Cope arrived at six the next morning. Barry, the stock manager, came in just before seven, but then at seven-forty, someone else turned up. I thought I recognised the car when I saw it pull in, then I clocked the number plate and saw who got out and, well...' She stalled.

Fisher inched forward in his seat.

'For God's sake, who was it?'

'It was the man who was at your house Saturday morning — Frazer Marchant. He got a couple of cases out of his boot. Flight cases I think they're called; like a normal suitcase but metal. Anyway, he took them inside. Fifteen minutes later he came back out, put the cases back in the boot and drove off.'

183

'Did the cases look any heavier or lighter when he came out?'

'I couldn't tell. He wasn't like dragging them or anything.'

Fisher's heart was thumping. He remembered the strong hit of aftershave after the door had opened. The voice calling to his wife — *his* wife — as this Frazer passed on the way to his car. He must have gone straight to the gallery. But why? Could his wife's new beau be up to no good? How he'd love to show that smug bastard—

'Sir...?'

'What?'

'I said, do you want me to follow it up? I could call him and ask him what he was doing.'

'And let him know we've seen him? You may as well just call and offer to give him an alibi and be done with it.'

'What then?' When Fisher didn't reply, Nightingale said, 'I could call Mr Cope at the gallery and ask him?'

'Just leave it. I'll sort it.' His mind was in overdrive as he thought of the various possibilities.

'What shall I do now?'

'What? I don't know. Do whatever you...' He almost said, whatever you damn well please, but stopped himself just in time. He took a calming breath. This wasn't her fault.

'Look, DS Jordon is running down contacts in the art world,' he said. 'Why don't you go and see if she needs a hand.'

'You don't need me to—?'

'No. I just need some time to think.'

With his jaw clenched tight, Fisher slipped his headphones on and navigated through his files until he found what he was looking for. He input the number for Frazer Marchant into his mobile and for a moment sat with his finger hovering over the call button.

What was he going to say? Hey, arsehole, did you nick some valuable paintings and a sculpture just after dealing Lucy Stirling a fatal blow, then hide them somewhere to pick up the following morning?

184

He set the phone back onto the desk and pushed it away.

It seemed ridiculous just thinking about it. It was hardly likely the man was going to kill Lucy, stash the stolen items, then calmly turn up the next morning for them. But what other reason was there for being there Saturday morning? He should have let Beth make the call. She could have asked the questions without it sounding personal. With a pang of guilt, Fisher realised it was personal. He let his hand drop to the desk and reached for the phone.

After three rings: 'Frazer Marchant.'

'Hello Mr Marchant, this is Detective Inspector Fisher of—'

'Matt Fisher? *The* Matt Fisher? Hi. Sorry about the other morning. I was in a bit of a hurry. It didn't occur to me who you were until afterwards.' Marchant didn't exactly sound like he was quaking in his boots.

'I'm calling in relation to a serious crime that took place in the gallery on Friday night.'

'I've already given one of your lot a statement.'

'This is about something that wasn't in your statement.'

'Oh?'

'Can you tell me what you were doing at the gallery on Saturday morning?'

'Oh that,' he said, sounding disinterested. 'That was the next day. I thought the statement only covered the time until we left the gallery Friday night.'

'Just answer the question.'

'No mystery. I went to collect the canvases I bought in the auction — two of them, by a little-known artist I foresee making it big someday soon. Shame I didn't predict what was going to happen to Lucy Stirling. If I had, I'd have been a damn sight more bullish about bidding for her pieces. They'll be worth a fortune now.'

'I might remind you that on Friday night that young woman lost her life by violent means.'

'I'm sorry,' Marchant said quickly. 'I didn't know her and well... I'm so used to working in a world of artists who are long-dead. Please... my apologies.'

'I was under the impression the gallery was delivering the auctioned items, yet you went to pick yours up yourself. Why?' Fisher knew he sounded churlish.

'I intend to sell the paintings for a profit, which means keeping costs to a minimum. I live quite close — well, I mean, Amanda lives quite close. It was no effort to go and pick them up and save on delivery.'

'Who did you deal with when you got there?'

'The manager. Mr Cope. I messaged to let him know I was there and he let me in.'

'Did you see anyone else while you were there?'

'No. Not on the Saturday, at least. Friday night I had the pleasure of meeting one of your former teammates, the wonderful Jim Vine. Amanda introduced us. His interest in contemporary art came as quite a surprise, for a footballer, I mean.' He gave a guffaw that Fisher was sure must have been put on. 'I was telling young Josh about it. I didn't realise he was something of a hero of his.' Was he winding him up? 'Well, if that's everything Inspector...?'

Thrown a curve ball by the mention of Josh, Fisher was too stunned to speak and before he knew it, the only thing he could hear was the sound of his own breathing. Marchant, it seemed, had terminated the call. Fisher slammed his phone down. Bastard! He quickly tracked down another number, picked the phone back up and waited.

Jackson Cope sounded out of breath and irritable when he eventually answered. He kept his responses concise to the point of curt and although Fisher sensed an undercurrent of nerves, everything he said tallied with Marchant's account.

Damn it! Fisher would have enjoyed booting the tosser out of his son's life. He replayed the conversation in his mind, wondering if he'd somehow imagined Cope's unease.

It was some hours later, after everyone else had left, when Fisher heard Wickham come in. He was grumbling about something or other. Fisher heard him say goodbye to whoever he'd been talking to, followed by the tap of heels growing quiet.

'Where's Beth?' Wickham's voice sounded unusually loud in the empty room.

'I sent her home. So, how'd the interviews go?'

'They're sticking to their story.'

'You tell them there's no sign of them going out the back way on the camera?'

'What do you think?'

'And?'

'They just said we must have missed them amongst all the catering staff.'

'And their fingerprints?'

'A perfect match for two of the sets. Plus, there were also some of Lee's in the studio. According to him, he regularly visited Lucy there.'

'So that's all the prints accounted for: Lucy, Jackson Cope, Barry the stock guy, Lee and Heath.'

'Yep. Either one of them took the stuff or the thieves wore gloves,' Wickham said.

'What reason did Heath give for his prints being there?'

'Said he'd helped Lucy get something not long ago. He's lying. I'm sure of it.'

Whilst Wickham was talking, Fisher strained his ears, trying to figure out whether the Falcon was in her office, or worse, standing somewhere nearby, listening to their conversation. There was only one way to find out.

'Are we on our own?' he asked.

'Yes.'

'I take it you've told the DCI the outcome?'

'Yes, and she wasn't happy. It didn't help that Francesca La Salle, Heath's wife, contacted Rupert Morgan, who then phoned the Falcon and had a go. Wanted to know when she was going to start interviewing proper criminals. Suffice to say, the air turned blue after she'd put the phone down.'

'So, what are you going to do now?' Fisher asked.

'I was going to go back to working the leads I was looking at before. Unless there's something else you want me to do?'

Fisher considered asking him to do some digging into a certain Frazer Marchant. Only if there was any dirt to be found, he wanted to be the one to find it. He shook his head.

'No. Carry on as you were.'

He heard Wickham start to move away, then stop.

'Oh, Kami caught me earlier. She phoned around the bar staff. You wanted to know who'd been snorting coke in the toilets. Turns out it was Shane Harman. Apparently, he made no attempt to cover it up. I did wonder if Harman knows about Morrelli and his wife,' he went on. 'If he knew the pair were squirrelled away in the courtyard, he could have planted some coke in Tom's pocket out of spite.'

'To get him in trouble?' Fisher said. 'Bit of a coincidence isn't it? Seeing how the jacket ends up in the middle of a murder scene.'

'What if he planted it there after killing Lucy?'

Fisher screwed his face up.

'What motive?

'To frame Tom; to keep him away from his wife.'

Fisher knew from listening to the guest statements that Shane Harman had been in the main hall, enjoying being the centre of attention, dishing out autographs for most of the night. But that was most of the night, not all of it.

'Great. Another bloody suspect.'

32.

Fisher felt something like damp suede, all soft and stippled, press into his palm. He stirred and rolled over. A warm wet tongue brushed over his hand. He snatched his hand away.

'Not now Luna.' The dog started to paw at the bed clothes. 'What is the matter with you?' Fisher pushed the covers down from over his face. 'Alexa! What time is it?'

'The time is eight-o-five-am,' a stilted female voice announced.

'Shit!' He swung his legs over the side of the bed and sat up.

He'd slept through the alarm. How the hell did that happen? Then the glass or two of whisky — well, three or four — he'd sunk the night before made themselves known as he ran a rough tongue around his claggy, foul-tasting mouth.

He set out a hand and stroked the silky crown of Luna's head. 'You must be hungry, eh?'

He moved his hand and skimmed the surface of the chair next to the bed with his fingers, feeling for his dressing gown. He slipped into it, grabbed his mobile and padded to the kitchen, Luna's claws tapping out the route on the wooden floor.

With Luna waiting next to her bowl, Fisher reached into the cupboard. His heart sank as his hand delved deeper into the bag. He reached in even further. A sigh of relief escaped him as he made contact with rough, knobbly biscuits. He shook his head. Nine months on his own and he still hadn't got his shit together.

'I'll order some more. Straight away, I promise. Don't worry, I won't make you eat cornflakes again.'

The dog said nothing in reply — one advantage of a dog over a wife, he thought as he used his hand to scoop the biscuits into a clean bowl. He added a splash of water before setting it down on the floor. Bile began to rise as he bent over. He quickly straightened up and gave a rank, whisky-sodden belch.

'Better out than in, eh?' he said, before grabbing a whistle from its hook on the wall and giving three sharp blows, prompting Luna to eat.

With the dog noisily bolting her food, Fisher went to reach into the fridge, in search of something for himself, when his mobile started to ring. He pulled it from his dressing gown pocket and swiped.

'Hello?'

'Matt, it's Andy.'

'I know, I know, I overslept. I'll be—'

'There's another body.' Fisher's skin prickled. 'Jackson Cope, the gallery manager. Found dead in his home about forty minutes ago. I'm on my way over to pick you up.'

Fisher returned the phone to his pocket and rubbed a hand over his chin. It felt soft, woolly even. How long since he last shaved? He opened the fridge and reached for the milk, swigging straight from the bottle. After tipping it up to enjoy the very last full-fat drop, he chucked the empty container into the recycling bin and returned to the bedroom. He barely had time to wash, brush his teeth and throw some clothes on before the doorbell rang.

'Rough night?' Wickham said, putting the car in gear and pulling away from the kerb fast enough to make the wheels spin.

Fisher ran a hand through his unbrushed hair but stopped short of sniffing his armpits. He knew it couldn't be the ever-increasing bags under his eyes being commented on — he was wearing shades.

Deciding to ignore it, he said, 'So, fill me in.'

'When Cope didn't show for work, his assistant tried phoning him. There was no answer, so he decided to drop by the house. He didn't get an answer there either. Noticing Cope's car parked outside, he chanced a look through the letterbox and spotted Cope, on the floor, unresponsive. The ambulance crew called for a couple of uniforms to help gain entry. Cope was already cold by the time they got to him. It turns out one of the uniforms had been at the gallery Friday night and recognised Cope. Concerned it might be related, he phoned it in.'

On arriving at Cope's place, 'I take it you've got some scene suits with you?' Fisher said, climbing out of the car.

Five minutes later, after donning the obligatory all-in-one outfit, he reached for the rear passenger door, pulled a fresh dog chew from his jacket pocket and offered it to Luna, who gently took it from between his fingers. He cranked the window open and closed the door.

'That's not going to make a mess, is it?' Wickham said.

'Bill me if it does,' Fisher said, extending his white stick. 'Which way?'

Wickham pointed him in the right direction.

'Watch your head,' he said after half a dozen steps. 'The cordon tape's right in front of you. I'll lift it up but you'll need to duck. Immediately after there's a gate between two stone posts and a step.'

The gate opened with the groan of tired metal. Fisher patted a hand about. His fingers found the rough stone gate post. Moss covered its surface like a velvet glove.

'Morning gentlemen. I was just leaving,' a female voice greeted them at the door. Fisher recognised it as belonging to Dr Bernadette Cooper, one of the county's pathologists.

'Morning Bernie,' Fisher said. 'What've we got?'

'White male, approximately forty to forty-five. Probable cause of death, narcotic overdose. Ball park, I'd say he's been dead somewhere between six and ten hours. Usual caveats apply.'

'An OD?'

'White powder residue on the kitchen worktop tested positive for cocaine and traces of opioid. If the coke was high grade and laced with something like fentanyl then I'm not surprised he's dead. Obviously, we'll do a full suite of tests to give you the complete picture.'

'Any evidence he was a habitual drug user?' Fisher asked.

'No obvious signs. First time or occasional user would be my guess.'

'Okay, cheers.'

With the doctor retreating down the path, Wickham helped Fisher through to the kitchen at the rear of the house.

'The dead guy's lying on the floor between the breakfast bar and the door to the hall,' Wickham said. 'There's direct line of sight between the body and the front door. It's definitely Jackson Cope. He's in suit trousers, shirt, socks, no tie. There are evidence markers on the granite worktop pointing to small amounts of white powder. There's also a credit card and a cut-down plastic straw.

Fisher could hear Wickham moving away from him.

'Interesting...'

'What? What is it?' Fisher asked, trying to keep his irritation at bay, wondering when it was going to sink in to everyone that he couldn't see. He took a few tentative steps closer to the source of the voice. 'Where are you?'

'In the utility room next door. There's a large crate. It's been opened.' Fisher could hear the sound of something being moved around. 'There's still some packing material inside.' A few seconds later, 'It's empty. The dispatch note shows this address, but it's not Cope's name on it, it's Connor.'

Lucy Stirling's stolen pieces?

'How are you spelling that?' Fisher asked.

'Charlie, Oscar, November, November, Oscar, Romeo.'

'A play on conner as in con man, maybe?' Fisher said. 'We know Cope went to the gallery first thing Saturday. He knew about the store, with its collection of Lucy's art. It would have been easy for him to grab a few choice pieces, box them up with the rest of the stuff to be sent out. Once he'd got them, he could have stuck them somewhere safe, then sat tight, waiting for the dust to settle and the price tag on Lucy's work to climb.'

'That's one possibility,' Wickham said. 'There is another.'

'Go on.'

'What if Friday night, someone was in the process of nicking the stuff when Lucy caught them, earning her a bash over the head. Panicking, the thief stashes what they can, intending on taking them later when the coast is clear. Cope finds the stash, knows an opportunity when he sees one and sticks it in a crate to be dispatched along with the rest of the auctioned pieces. When the killer goes back and finds it all gone, they figure out what happened and last night came to collect.'

Fisher's thoughts jumped back to Frazer Marchant. Is that why he'd turned up at the gallery the next day sporting two large bags? To pick up the stolen art? But if that was the case, Cope was hardly likely to have corroborated Marchant's version of events.

In the background, voices approached, accompanied by the clatter of the foot plates that had been set down on the tiled floor, in an attempt to preserve as much evidence as possible.

'Hey Boss.' It was DS Aptil. 'Just to let you know, the team's waiting outside.'

'Lead the way,' Fisher replied. 'You been here long?' he asked, as she guided him towards the back door.

'A little while. I've been out talking to some of the neighbours.'

'And?'

'Nothing so far.'

'What about the guy who found him?'

'Cope's assistant from the gallery. Guy called Barry Keane.'

'Is he still around?'

'No. He left just after I arrived. It looked like it hit him quite hard. We got a statement then let him go.'

'Bit odd, isn't it? Junior staff don't usually go out of their way to track the boss down. And it can't be much past nine now. Cope was hardly late.'

'I asked him about that,' Aptil explained. 'Apparently the gallery is due a big delivery this morning. Seems Cope was a bit of a control freak, insisted on being the only one who could sign goods in or out.'

It was feasible.

Aptil helped Fisher over the back door step and into the garden at the rear of the property. The scent of jasmine and rose drifted lazily in the air. With Cope's death coming on the back of Lucy's murder and the possible significance of the empty crate, Fisher wasted no time issuing instructions for the house-to-house enquiries and a thorough search of the property. Soon all he could hear was snatches of conversation as everyone made their way back into the house. He was hopeful someone would have seen or heard something, even if it had been in the middle of the night. On a residential street people usually couldn't contain their inquisitiveness. Assuming the stolen items were taken from the house and related to Cope's death, this latest development could tip the investigation into Lucy's murder in the right direction. He thought about the coke. Perhaps Cope was celebrating getting his hands on art that would soon be worth a tidy sum. It certainly suggested he lied about not knowing guests were indulging in a line or two at the gallery Friday night. Not only might he have known it was happening, he might have had a good idea who was behind it. Spurred on by that thought, Fisher made a call to the team's intelligence officer, requesting details of Cope's mobile and landline activity, as well as calls made to and received by the gallery's switchboard.

He ended the call and returned the phone to his pocket. Despite the air being full of birdsong and the gentle rustle of leaves in the breeze, all Fisher noticed was the absence of noise. Indoors, the crime scene would be all hustle and bustle. Out there, he felt redundant. What could he contribute? Annoyed at himself, he roughly pushed aside his self-pity. There was plenty to be getting on with back at the station, like looking into the bidding action for Lucy's pieces. Perhaps there was someone with more than a fleeting interest in her work?

His mind made up, he tried to remember how he'd got into the garden. The problem was, he'd moved around, talking to different people. The house could be in any direction. He put out his stick and started forward. The garden was bigger than expected and it was a little while before the stick struck anything solid. He set out a hand, his fingers touching rough brick. He'd walked straight into a wall. He followed it around, hoping to find a door, only to find himself walking into a tangle of twigs and concluded he'd walked into a bush. He turned ninety degrees and started forward, hoping the house was somewhere in front of him. A garden bench, more bushes, no wall. His anxiety started to mount. He stopped again, turned back around. What was he doing, floundering around like a needy toddler without his mother to guide his way?

'Hello!' he shouted. Nothing. He huffed out a sigh, full of exasperation, then yelled at the top of his voice, 'Is anyone there?'

'Hi, do you need some help?' A voice came from nearby.

'Thank Christ. I thought I was going to be stuck out here all day.'

'This way...' A hand took his elbow and projected him in the opposite direction to the one he'd been walking in.

Inside, the man, a CSI called Jin, guided Fisher through the utility room and kitchen into the hall and then, at Fisher's request, went to find Wickham.

Soon a thunder of footfall started down the stairs.

'Looks like we might have found something,' Wickham said. 'Judging from the guy's bank statements he had expensive tastes and it wasn't all paid for by his job at the gallery. He's got monies going in, different amounts, different times. Some quite big sums.'

Suddenly Fisher forgot to be angry about being left high and dry in the garden.

'How big?' he asked.

'It varies.'

'Hundreds, thousands, tens of thousands?'

'Thousands mainly.'

'Could he have been nicking works from the gallery?' Fisher said, then immediately dismissed it. 'No. Someone would have said if stuff had gone missing before. Still, worth a check. Anything else?'

'Not so far.' Wickham said. 'I'll get back to it, if it's alright with you?'

'Sure. I'm going to head back to the office now anyway. Is your car unlocked? I need to get Luna and get out of this thing.' He tugged at his white suit.

'Should be. Do you want me to get one of the uniforms to drop you at the station?'

Fisher noticed he didn't offer to drive him himself.

'No. It's alright. I'll call Beth. Get her to come pick me up.'

'I could call you a taxi?' Wickham offered.

'I'll be happier with Beth.'

'I wasn't thinking of you.' The atmosphere developed a sudden chill. 'I mean, I expect she's busy and it's a twenty-minute drive. Even if she turns straight around, it'll put her behind by an hour.'

And all to wet nurse you, Fisher knew he was thinking.

'Don't worry. I'll sort myself out.'

'Please yourself,' Wickham said and stomped back upstairs.

33.

Fisher made his way back to the car, calling on the assistance of the uniformed officer guarding the front door. He climbed out of his scene suit before retrieving Luna from the back seat. After sending the uniform into the house for some water, he tried calling Nightingale at the office. When there was no answer, he tried her mobile, leaving a message for her to phone him back.

The sound of metal on stone came from nearby.

'I could only find a saucepan,' the officer said.

'That'll do. Cheers,' Fisher replied.

He leaned on the bonnet of the car and waited, listening to the slosh of water as Luna drank thirstily. Five minutes later, he tried Nightingale again. Still no answer.

He was toying with the idea of calling a taxi when his phone finally rang.

'Beth, at last. Where the hell have you been? Never mind. I need you to come and pick me up.'

'Sorry, I can't.'

'Why not?'

If this was because he'd put her nose out of joint then...

'I'm in London.'

'London? What the fuck are you doing in London?'

'I'm with DS Jordon.' Fisher remembered his harsh words. She went on, 'We're visiting art galleries and market stalls dealing in art, trying to find out if there's any word on the stolen items.'

'Fine. I'll sort myself out.' He terminated the call, moaning and whinging to himself as he tried to find the number for a local taxi firm.

Ten minutes later, a car pulled up across the road.

'Your taxi's arrived, sir,' the uniform at the entrance to the house called. Seconds later, 'Do you need a hand getting across the road?'

'I'm good thanks.' Grumbling under his breath, 'What do you think the dog's for?'

Once in the taxi, Luna clipped in the back seat next to him, Fisher told the driver to head for the station. Despite his best intentions, instead of using the time to plan what he was going to do back at the office, he stewed over being left to fend for himself, his ire made all the worse by the fact it was a mess of his own making. All the while, the driver jabbered on, seeming oblivious to the bad mood radiating off him. Then something the driver said found its way through the knot of dark thoughts.

'What was that?' Fisher said, suddenly alert.

'I was just saying, the gallery... shocking what happened, weren't it?' After a beat, 'We drove past it back there. You know, I had that poor girl here in the cab a couple of times. Just lovely she was. So polite. They aren't all, you know, the rich ones. Too full of themselves. Not her though. A real lady. And generous too. I know she could afford to be — rolling in it, weren't she — but you know, often the loaded ones give the smallest tips. Or no tip at all!' he said, sounding affronted. He went on, 'You know, a while back, a mate of mine asked her — that murdered girl — if she'd donate one of her pictures for this charity thing he was doing. His little boy's got this bone cancer. Horrible disease. Anyway, what d'you think she goes and says?'

The driver waited, obviously expecting an answer. Fisher shrugged.

'I don't know... Yes?'

'Ah, you're wrong... she says no.' Fisher attempted to look surprised but the driver was still talking, 'She says, "I won't give you one of my pictures... I'll give you three." Three! Would you believe it? That's what I call generous.'

It wasn't the first time Lucy's generosity had been spoken of. Seized with an idea, Fisher called to the driver, 'Hey mate, sorry to mess you about, change of plan. Can you turn around and drop me off at the gallery?'

They started to decelerate. Fisher rocked from side to side as the cabbie swung the car around.

'What you gonna do once you get there?' the cabbie asked. 'I mean, I would have thought, you know... being blind an' all.'

'I'm going to look for something I don't think will be there,' he replied, wishing he could see the other man's puzzled expression.

They arrived a few minutes later. After settling the bill — adding a sizeable tip — Fisher clambered out, following Luna onto the pavement, while assuring the driver they could manage from there. He just wished he felt as confident as he sounded. But Luna did him proud and they navigated the steps up to the gallery's entrance without incident. By the time they reached the top, a sheen of sweat had formed on Fisher's brow.

'I wondered if I might have a word with Barry Keane,' he said in reply to Molly O'Leary's enthusiastic greeting.

'Barry phoned in sick. He told us about Mr Cope. Sounds like it really shook him up.'

'Oh. I really need to talk to someone about the gallery's procedure for recording sales and gifts. Maybe somebody else can help me?'

'That would normally be Mr Cope or Barry. If they weren't in, I'd ask Bobbie. She's the office manager. Only, she's on leave this week.' After a moment's pause, she said, 'I could try Mrs Morgan? She might be able to help.'

'Eleanor Morgan's here now?'

'Yes. After Barry said he wasn't coming in, she was the only person I could think of calling. We were due a big delivery — someone had to sign for it.'

'But why her?' Fisher asked, wondering if it was anything to do with the fact she was due to inherit the gallery.

'She's the Chair of the Board of Trustees. That's like the big boss, isn't it?'

Fisher wondered if he'd known that. If he had, he'd forgotten. If he hadn't, he probably should have. Brushing aside his inadequacies, he asked to speak with her.

'She's on her way,' Molly said, as the phone clunked back onto its base.

'Thanks. I don't suppose you've remembered any more of what Miss Stirling said to you before she went up in the lift?'

'No. Sorry. No sign of any Patricks then?' She sounded disappointed for him.

'Not so far.'

The silence stretched. It didn't sound like Molly was moving much. What was she doing? Staring at his scarred face? Just then she said, 'I don't suppose I could have your autograph, could I? I kind of collect them. After the other night, I have to admit I googled you. I had no idea who you were but now I'm a real fan.'

Fisher smiled, then a moment's flush of pride was quickly swamped with self-loathing.

'I'm really not worthy,' he said. 'There are much better players out there now than I ever was. You should have got Jim Vine's autograph Friday night.'

'I did. But that wasn't what I meant. I was talking about the fact you're a hero. You saved that woman from getting the acid in her face.'

'Oh, that... I was only doing my job.'

'Well I think you're a hero,' Molly said, sliding something across the counter in Fisher's direction. 'I really would appreciate it. I've got a card here, and a pen...'

200

He held out his hand but he was left holding nothing but empty air when their conversation was interrupted.

'Detective. I understand you wanted to speak to me?' Eleanor Morgan approached with a confident stride. As she drew close, Fisher found himself enveloped in a cloud of cloying perfume.

'Mrs Morgan.' He held out his hand and found it momentarily enclosed in a cold bony grip, then swiftly released. 'Is there somewhere private we could talk?'

'I knew I'd have to get more hands-on with the place at some point,' she said once they were settled in what had been Jackson Cope's office. 'I never envisaged it being so soon.'

'You're the Chair of the Trust?'

'Yes.'

'How long for?'

'Oh, a few years now... seven or eight.'

'I thought your sister, Helen, used to run the place?'

'She did. She was the gallery manager. The Trust only deals with policy and planning matters.'

'Mr Cope was her replacement?'

'Yes. He'd been the assistant manager until then. It seemed a sensible appointment at the time.'

'*At the time*? Do I take it you've changed your mind?'

'Perhaps I'm being too harsh. He could be a little self-important, that's all. He liked being in charge too much. Let it go to his head. So how did it happen? Mr Keane didn't actually say.'

'We won't know until after the post-mortem though it looks like it might have been drug related.'

There wasn't so much as a gasp and, not for the first time, Fisher wished he could see her reaction.

'You're not surprised?'

'Actually I am. I'm not naïve, Inspector. I am aware that all sorts of people do recreational drugs. What I am surprised at is that he took so much as to kill himself. I take it it was an accident?'

Fisher ignored her question and instead asked, 'Was there ever any suggestion of him doing drugs before?'

'Absolutely not. He would have been out on his ear if there was, I can assure you.'

Fisher believed her.

'Were you aware two paintings and a sculpture of Lucy's are missing?'

'No. When did that happen?'

'Friday night, or Saturday morning. We're not entirely sure.'

'Do you think they've got anything to do with Lucy's murder? Perhaps she walked in on a robbery?'

'That's one line of enquiry we're looking into. Although there is an alternative explanation. Lucy could have given them away.'

'It was a charity fundraiser. She wouldn't have given anything away.'

'Not even as a thank-you?'

'To whom and for what?''

'How about to Mr Cope? For helping organise the event?'

'Did you ask him?'

'Yes. He suggested they might have been moved.'

'There you go then. He would have told you if Lucy gave them to him.'

'Not necessarily. He might have been worried we'd think he was lying — concerned that being found with the items might make him a suspect. We'd only have his word for it that she gave them to him, unless of course there was a process for recording gifts?'

'There must be. Let me have a look.' Fisher heard her rise from her seat, then the sound of pages turning, 'Here... there's a folder marked up Register of Gifts.' Fisher heard the sound of pages being turned. 'There are no records of any gifts this financial year.'

Fisher thought back to the scene at Cope's home.

'I understand all of the auction items were dispatched on Saturday. Is it possible to have details of what was sent where?'

'That should also be in one of these files. Let me have a look… purchases… sales… here we are, deliveries.'

'Is it true Mr Cope was very particular about signing deliveries in and out himself?'

'So I've been told,' Eleanor Morgan said with a disapproving coolness.

'Did he always use the same delivery company?'

More flicking of pages.

'It looks like it, yes. Why do you ask?'

'Things like that can sometimes be an indicator of fraudulent behaviour. I just wondered whether he had had something going with them. Maybe they set their rates particularly high and in return he received a cut.'

'Well, if there have been any shady arrangements in the past, there won't be any longer.' She slammed the file shut.

'I'm going to need to take that with me. I'd also like the sales ledger. Do you know if it's been updated to reflect the auction?'

A minute later. 'It looks like it, yes.'

'Could you take a quick look — had Mr Cope made any purchases himself recently?'

'There's nothing in the sales ledger if he did. Have the missing items been found at Mr Cope's home?'

'No. They're still missing.'

Had she expected them to have been found?

'One more check, then I'm done,' he said. 'What about purchases in the name Connor?'

After a minute of listening to the scratchy sound of pages being turned, the answer came back, no. Just as he'd expected.

With the ledgers packed into a sturdy hessian bag fetched from the gallery's gift shop, Fisher thanked Mrs Morgan for her help. He was about to return to the reception area and wait for the taxi he'd booked, when he paused at the door.

'This office… will any staff key card open it?'

'No. Mr Cope had the door to this room programmed at the highest level of security. Only a master key card will open it.'

'Master card?'

'A card programmed to open any door, including those set at the highest security, such as this one. I believe only a handful of such cards exist.'

'So how did you get in here this morning?'

'How do you think? I used a key card.'

'Yes, but whose?'

'Mine, of course. As Chair of Trustees, obviously I have the highest level of security clearance.'

34.

Fisher stared, unseeing, out of the cab window. With the revelation that Eleanor Morgan had a key card that gave her access to the rear door of the gallery, the Morgans were firmly back in the running. Had Cope somehow found out it was them and been silenced as a result? Could they have sent an empty crate to his house, to plant suspicion for the missing art on him? It was possible. But how the hell would they have engineered his death with some dodgy coke? If he'd been a habitual user, which they knew about and were somehow party to, then at a push it was possible, but none of those things rang true. Could Cope's death have simply been an accident? He would have had to have been particularly unlucky to have come across coke cut with fentanyl in the circles he moved in, but, well, shit happens. But that still didn't explain the empty crate. If Cope took the items, does that also mean he killed Lucy? If so then why was he lying dead? And if he didn't, then who the bloody hell did?

Fisher shook his head. He was going round in circles. He became aware of his heart thumping heavily in his chest. Cope's death meant the expectation on him to deliver was even greater, yet he'd never been more confused. Ordinarily he could handle pressure — hell, he'd been one of the country's top penalty takers — but this was pressure like no other. If he failed, not only could it mean Lucy's killer going unpunished but it would also see him out on his ear.

He forced his thoughts back to Lucy. Of all the possible motives, the 'robbery gone wrong' theory seemed least likely. The attack was too vicious; felt too personal. Money, lust, envy... even protecting some secret, if the consequences of exposure were damaging enough, but hot-footing it away with a handful of paintings? He just couldn't see it.

He slipped a hand down over Luna's neck and absently began to pat her with short strokes. He remembered Eleanor Morgan's comments when they'd first talked to her — how Helen had shaped Lucy into the woman she had become — and thought of Josh. Fisher knew he'd been too wrapped up in his job for far too long, relying on Mandy for the hands-on parenting stuff. But he had always tried to be a good role model. First, as a footballer, training hard to keep at the top of his game and then, when a misjudged boot had shattered his career as well as his knee cap, instead of sitting back feeling sorry for himself, he'd put the same amount of effort into learning how to become the best detective he could.

A small smile traced across his lips as he remembered Josh telling anyone who'd listen how his dad was going to catch criminals... just like Batman. The smile fell away. Yeah, just like Batman... Batman, whose mask had slipped down over his eyes so far he couldn't even see the criminals, let alone catch them. What sort of superhero was he now?

By the time Fisher reached the office, the black dog of depression was biting at his heels. He slumped in his chair. In the background, an excited chatter filled the room. At first, he thought it was the usual banter, but it quickly became clear there was more to it. Something had happened. He pulled himself up in his seat, straining to make out what was being said.

'Matt. You're back.' It was Nightingale.

'What's going on?'

'I don't know. I only just got in. The DCI wants a word.'

'Oh great.'

His shoulders slumped. All the deep breathing in the world wasn't going to help this time.

'Is Andy back?'

'I haven't seen him... His jacket isn't on the back of his chair. Do you want me to find out where he is?'

'No, don't bother. I'll—'

'You've finally turned up,' DCI Fallon interrupted, having stolen over silently. 'My office. Now.'

'Where have you been?' she asked as soon as they were ensconced in her private den. 'I was told you left the dead man's house hours ago.'

'I went to the gallery. I wanted to check on something. Has there been a development?'

'Andy has made a number of discoveries.'

Andy now, is it? Not DS Wickham. He might have known. Fisher's gut twisted as his anxiety made itself known.

'Go on.'

'He found an empty crate, like the ones the gallery use.'

'I know about that. I was there.'

'He also found bank statements. It appears Cope had been depositing large cash payments into his account for some months.'

'Again... knew that.' He wondered if Wickham had selective memory, having wiped Fisher out of his account of the search of Cope's house. As if being blind wasn't bad enough, it seemed he had somehow become invisible.

'You don't think those are important facts?' she challenged.

'I didn't say that.'

'Then why didn't you call and tell me?' Fisher opened his mouth to reply, but she didn't give him a chance, continuing, 'It's obvious Cope was in the habit of receiving payments for something other than his job at the gallery. Probably to fund his drug habit.'

'Is there any evidence he was an addict?'

'He died of an overdose.' The Falcon's disdain was palpable.

'The pathologist suggested he died as a result of opioid poisoning due to the coke possibly being laced with fentanyl. That doesn't make him an addict.'

'What's your hypothesis then? Go on, give me the benefit of your wisdom.'

'There are various possibilities. He could have been involved in drug dealing; there's also a chance he was running some sort of scam at the gallery, though I can't see that resulting in the sort of sums we're talking about. There's also the possibility the cash came from art theft. I was thinking earlier—'

'Art theft?' Warm breath hit Fisher full in the face, causing him to flinch. He imagined her leaning over the table, her face contorted with anger. 'I thought the only art reported as missing was that taken on Friday. Are you telling me there have been others?'

'Not as far as I'm aware. I think Friday's thefts were probably a spur of the moment thing. But it occurred to me that Cope could have fabricated sales. He kept a very tight rein on the paperwork. I wonder how easy it would have been to sell something for one price, then record the income in the gallery's ledger at a lower amount, creaming some off for himself.'

'How would he get hold of the cash? Wouldn't a buyer pay the gallery directly?'

'I don't know. But I'm sure there are ways. He could have been in bed with a buyer. They could have slipped him part of the payment in return for getting it for a good price. It would just mean a smaller margin for the gallery.'

Fisher thought of Frazer Marchant and his two suitcases.

'You can't just dream up your own version of events. If you haven't got a hypothesis that ties everything together then you haven't got a hypothesis full stop,' the Falcon snapped.

'Now hang on a minute!' Fisher said, loud enough to be almost shouting. 'You *asked* me to speculate. And then when I do, you shut me down. What's this really about?' Her lack of reply only confirmed what he already suspected. 'I should have known. This isn't about the case, is it? It's about me.'

'Don't flatter yourself. This is about you not being able to perform your duties adequately. You left the crime scene, leaving DS Wickham to run the show while you went back to the gallery. Again. Presumably learning nothing new. Well, I'm glad you did. I gave you a chance to prove you could still do the job, and as much as it saddens me, it seems I was wrong. Your time has run out. I will be speaking to HR about beginning competency proceedings.'

Fisher clenched his teeth. His heart thumped in his chest.

She went on, 'Earlier in the week, I mentioned that I had been looking to get a DI in from another team. Well, it seems a number of your colleagues think an outsider would be bad for morale. Therefore, to show I *do* listen, I shan't be doing that.'

Fisher's optimism peered out between parted hands.

'But you just said—'

'I will be giving Andy temporary promotion. He's more than capable of leading this investigation.'

'If you think I'm going to step aside and let someone else take over my investigation without a fight, you can think again.'

'I have no intention of taking you off the Stirling case. Andy will be running the investigation into Cope's death. Now, if it happens to be mixed up with Lucy Stirling's murder, then understandably I will consolidate the two cases under a single lead officer to bring both to a satisfactory conclusion.'

The bitch had got it all figured out. Luna's head nudged his leg, probably in response to his increased grip on her harness; it was the only way he was keeping a handle on his simmering rage.

'If DS Wickham delivers you the killer, I'll give you my badge myself,' he spat the words out. 'In the meantime, I'm going to go back out there and carry on doing what I'm being paid to do.' He stood up, shunting the chair back hard. It fell to the floor with a rattle.

'I take it that means you'll be needing DC Nightingale's assistance again?'

Fisher opened his mouth, about to tell her how he didn't need anyone's help. Only that wasn't true. After failing to find his way out of Cope's garden followed by a morning spent struggling in and out of cabs, now, more than ever, he realised just how much he needed Beth's help.

'You have a problem with that?' he said, wondering how far she'd go to straightjacket him.

'Me... no. Nightingale, well... I don't think it's appropriate for me to say. I'm sure she'll be thrilled to go back to being your...' she cleared her throat, 'assistant. Heaven forbid she should actually do some real detective work. I'll leave it to you to go and give her the good news. Oh, and a word of advice...' Fisher imagined the sly curve of a smile on her lips. 'If you want loyalty from your team, when you bawl someone out try not to do it in front of the whole office.'

35.

Fisher left the Falcon's office in a daze.

Surely, she wouldn't really go down the competency route? He'd never believed in that woman scorned stuff before. But maybe, he'd been wrong? Maybe she'd simply been biding her time, waiting for her chance?

His shoulders slumped.

What was it they say? Old sins cast long shadows. There weren't many things in Fisher's life he wished he'd never done, but slipping in between the sheets of DCI Anita Fallon's bed, after a night out celebrating the end of a big case, was one of them. His stomach still gave a sickening lurch even today when he thought of having to look his son in the eye the following day. His wife too... they might have had their problems, but she'd deserved better. Perhaps the DCI too? He remembered standing in her office the morning after, shifting uncomfortably from foot to foot, telling her that it couldn't happen again. She'd simply nodded, saying nothing in reply, marking the start of a cold rift between them.

A light touch on his arm caused him to jump.

'Are you alright, boss?' It was Aptil.

He was still outside the Falcon's office. Luna had stalled, probably due to the fact he was holding her harness as tight as a trapeze artist gripping the bar.

He gave a nod. 'I'm fine.'

He let his fingers relax and Luna led him back to his desk, where he slumped in his chair. He ran a hand over Luna's flanks and listened to her tail thump on the floor. For a moment the two of them sat, silently, the only beings in each other's world.

'Matt...' It was Wickham. Fisher turned to face him; his features blank. 'The DCI just told me the news. I swear I had no idea she was going to act me up to DI. I called to let her know about the money and the crate, next thing I know she's acting like I've solved the case.'

'And have you?' Fisher tried to keep his voice calm and even, not wanting to sound like a whining A grader who was no longer teacher's pet.

'Hardly. There's no sign of the missing art. We found no trace of any other drugs or drug paraphernalia. I have no idea whether his death is related to Lucy's murder or whether he was just unlucky and scored some bad shit. None of the neighbours we've talked to so far saw anything. I've got someone going over the CCTV from the cameras in nearby streets, but there aren't many. It's a nice residential area. It's a total fucking mystery. I don't know where to go next.'

Fisher contemplated telling him to fuck off. Then thought of the need to do right by the victims and bit back his animosity. He nodded in the direction of the chair at the side of his desk and heard it squeak as it took the other man's weight.

'Okay, well, if Cope was dealing, he would have wanted to take advantage of all the celebs he was rubbing shoulders with at the gallery on Friday night, right?'

'Sure,' Wickham said.

'So has anyone talked to Shane Harman yet, about who sold him his gear? Assuming he got it at the gallery. If he IDs Cope, then you know that's how he was getting his cash. That might also put Cope in the frame for Lucy's murder. I think it's safe to say, she'd have gone ballistic if she'd found him dealing at the fundraiser she'd organised in memory of her parents.'

'I'll get Kami onto that straight away. I did wonder if Harman was somehow involved in Lucy's murder, you know, with the coke link. I could get her to grab his clothes from Friday night while she's there. See if there's anything to link him to the crime scene.'

'I wouldn't bother with that for now. The lab'll be looking like a charity shop, the amount of clothes we've sent over. I take it you grabbed Lee and Heath's stuff for testing when you brought them in?'

'Of course.'

'I suppose Kami could broach the topic of Morrelli's jacket with Harman. See if there's any indication he planted the coke.'

'Anything else?'

Fisher thought back to the call he'd placed that morning.

'I've already put a request in for Cope's phone records. You could get someone to check them over. Look for delivery companies. Find out who delivered the crate to Cope's address and whether there were any subsequent pick-ups scheduled from the same address. Maybe he stole the art and had it shipped to his home to split up and sell on. There are probably buyers queuing up for Lucy's work now she's dead. Also, check to see if there have been any large payments into his account since Friday. Talking of his bank account — how far back do these large payments go?'

'About ten months. There's been about half a dozen payments of different amounts.'

'So that's after he was promoted to gallery manager. Take a look at the gallery's sales records and the statements from the delivery company. Compare the timings of sales and shipments to the payments into Cope's account. That lot should keep you busy for a while.'

He heard Wickham rise from his chair.

A hand landed heavily on Fisher's shoulder. 'Thanks.'

Fisher nudged his chin in a nod. He was about to slip his headphones on when the office door opened. Female voices spilled into the room with light-hearted chatter. He remembered the Falcon's parting words and his mood soured with disappointment. He really had thought Beth enjoyed working with him. It seems he'd been wrong.

'I'll be with you in a minute,' Nightingale said to whoever she'd been talking to and started towards Fisher. 'Luna's water bowl's empty. I'll just go top it up.'

'It's alright. I can do it myself,' he said, his voice flat.

He reached down and patted a hand around the floor by the desk leg where the bowl normally sat. His fingers made contact with the cold metal. He rose from his seat, grabbed his white stick and made his way to the door. He filled the bowl from the sink in the small kitchenette a little way down the corridor and started to make his way back. The water sloshed onto his fingers. The harder he tried to keep it level, the more it seemed to pour over the edge. With his attention focused on the bowl, he turned to where he thought the office door was and banged into the wall. The bowl clattered to the floor.

'Shit!'

He brushed at his trousers with a flat hand. After getting rid of most of the surface water, he bent down and, after several failed attempts, snatched the bowl up before turning around and returning to the kitchenette. As he turned on the tap, the door opened behind him.

'Let me carry that back for you.' It was Nightingale.

He turned the water off and turned to face the door.

'Don't put yourself out.'

'Have I done something to upset you?'

Nightingale was right in front of him, blocking his exit.

'No. But you will if you don't get out of my way. Aren't you needed somewhere else, where there's some proper detective work to be done?'

'What are you on about? Why are you being so nasty?' she said, showing no sign of going anywhere.

'Nasty doesn't come into it. I'm only repeating what I've been told. If our last conversation left you feeling frustrated, I'd have preferred it if you'd said something, rather than tell all and sundry.'

'Are you serious?' Her voice was thick with disbelief. 'Even if that was true, it doesn't give you the right to talk to me like you are. But, for your information, I haven't said anything to anybody.'

'The DCI seemed to suggest otherwise.'

'The DCI...? I don't understand.' After a pause, she added, 'I thought you'd be pleased with what I told her.'

'Pleased to hear how happy you are, now you're working with DS Jordon? Or maybe I should be pleased to hear that you complained about me having a go at you in public?'

'What? I didn't say any of those things. She asked me how I was getting on. I told her I was enjoying my work. I might have spoken out of turn, but I did say I hoped we wouldn't get a new DI. I said I thought it might demoralise the team. And I'm not the only one who thinks that. And as for her mentioning that you'd had a go at me — with all due respect, sir, you might want to avoid yelling at me in a busy office if you don't want people talking. It didn't bother me that you ranted at me and sent me off to work with someone else, because I know how frustrated you get, but the fact you think I went crying to the boss about it, well that does piss me off.'

The door opened then quickly closed again. Fisher dropped the bowl in the sink, grabbed the handle and pulled. The door smacked him in the head.

'Shit! Beth!' he called. 'Beth! I'm sorry...'

The sound of retreating footsteps slowed and then stopped.

'Beth?'

'Yes?' A guarded response.

'I mean it, I'm sorry. I didn't intend to insult you or anything like that. I'm just having a bad time at the moment and took it out on the wrong person.'

'Apology accepted.'

Fisher shot her a grateful smile, hoping she was facing him, then, after a small pause, 'Would you mind doing Luna's bowl for me, please?'

As Nightingale topped up the water, Fisher explained that he wanted her back, working alongside him.

'Though at the moment, I'm not sure what we're going to do,' he admitted.

'Maybe I could carry on with whatever Andy was working on?'

'I'm not sure there's much left to do. But it can't hurt to take a look.'

With Nightingale at her own desk, Fisher slipped his headphones on. The soft leather cosseted his ears and muffled out the burble of office conversations that proved a constant distraction. He thought back to Lucy's murder and let his mind roam. Could it really have been as simple as a robbery gone wrong? There was no denying the facts. Was his sense that there was more to it just a case of reading the scene all wrong?

He picked the phone up and called the CSI office number and was relieved when it was Carrie Finch who answered.

'I'm trying to get a better handle on what might have happened,' he explained. 'In my head I've got the scene showing an unusual level of violence. Am I right?'

'Absolutely. But then being bludgeoned around the head is rarely anything but.'

'But the number of strikes — one or two would have probably done the trick. I understand she sustained more than half a dozen blows to the head.'

'I'm not sure of the exact number, you'd need to ask the pathologist, but that sounds about right.'

'And the dirty water... was it actually poured over the body or could it have been from a container knocked off the table?'

'Poured over. There were actually two containers. Both were on the floor too far away from the body to have rolled. With no water on the floor in between them and the body, they had to have been empty when they were thrown.'

'You think they were emptied over the body specifically, not over her phone, which I understand was on the floor nearby?'

'...to knacker the phone?'

'Just an idea.'

'Sorry to disappoint but there was no water by the phone. It was broken though. Probably stamped on.'

Fisher thanked her, ended the call, then slipped his headphones back on.

He conjured up an image of the scene. Lucy pushing through the door to the studio. Why? Why did she go to the studio when there were still plenty of people in the main hall still willing to part with their cash? He thought about what Molly O'Leary had said and let out a sigh. Who the hell was Patrick?

He loaded the file containing the final guest list; by now everyone had been traced and a statement obtained. He set his audio-reader to play and sat back. Every so often, an eyebrow would twitch. Pop stars, TV personalities, even the famous footballer who Fisher happened to know, as well as other famous and some not so famous names, but no one who remotely sounded like Patrick.

Thinking again of the crime scene — the brutal attack, the mess — if a robbery gone wrong didn't feel right, what did? Drug-fuelled attacks often display signs of undue violence, but then so did murders motivated by jealousy or hatred. How could anyone have hated golden-girl Lucy enough to do what they did?

Golden-girl.

Fisher thought about Francesca La Salle's comments about Lucy returning to the diving squad. Was that really true? Hadn't someone said she couldn't dive anymore? The threat of Lucy's return to a sport she clearly excelled at must have rocked Ms La Salle's confidence of getting a gold at least a little. Enough for her to stop her friend from becoming real competition permanently?

He opened up La Salle's statement and ran through it once more. She'd spent most of the evening following the auction with a couple of girlfriends. He dug out their statements. They all said the same thing: apart from the occasional bathroom visit, they had all been together right up until La Salle rejoined her husband. By then Lucy was already missing. Taken at face value, the statements gave La Salle an alibi. Only Fisher didn't do face value. He knew how easy it was for people enthralled in a conversation to misjudge how long someone had slipped away for, especially when alcohol is involved. As much as he thought it unlikely she'd killed her friend, he couldn't quite rule her out. For now, she was still in the running.

36.

Luna had been lying at Fisher's feet asleep. He felt her stir. When her tail began to pat his leg, he slipped his headphones off.

'Hello?'

'It's Beth. I wondered when you were thinking of leaving?'

'What time is it?'

'Just gone six.'

He rubbed a hand over his face, feeling as stale as he feared the case was getting. While he'd been busy listening to case documents, the office had grown quiet. Time for a change of scene.

'How about we go now and stop off at the pub on the way home? My treat.'

He half expected Nightingale to cry off, but fifteen minutes later they were parked up outside what she described as a nice country pub. After ascertaining they did a decent ale, Nightingale guided him to the beer garden. Digging a tenner from his pocket, Fisher gave her his order.

'...plus whatever you want. Stick the change in a charity box if they've got one.' The note slipped from his fingers.

He was enjoying the sun on his face and the chatter of birds nearby, squabbling as they prepared to roost, when Nightingale returned. The glasses clinked as she put the tray down.

'Your pint and peanuts.'

He heard the thump of a full glass being placed on the table in front of him, then the rustle of a packet. He reached out a tentative hand. His fingers made contact with the cold, wet surface of the glass before continuing to skim the table's surface until they found the sharp edges of the foil wrapped nuts. He ripped the packet open and offered them to Nightingale. She declined and not for the first time he wondered just how thin she was, never seeming to eat.

'Cheers. I owe you one,' she said. He picked up the light chink of two glasses touching.

'Don't worry about it. I owe you a lot more than a pint, all the help you've given me.' He took a mouthful of his drink and returned the glass to the table.

'Talking of help,' Nightingale said. The sound of a second glass being put down echoed his own. 'I heard you giving Andy some suggestions earlier. I thought that was pretty generous, seeing as... well, you know.'

'You think I should have told him to bugger off and figure it out for himself?' When a reply wasn't forthcoming, he shrugged. 'Yeah, well, maybe I'll come to regret it, but I just thought... you never know, something he finds might take us that bit closer to catching Lucy's killer.' He poured out a handful of peanuts and threw them into his mouth.

'Oh. That makes sense. I thought it might be so Andy'd feel guilty about stabbing you in the back in future,' she said, just as Fisher took a swig of beer to wash the nuts down.

Beer spurted from his mouth.

'Shit,' he said, laughing, as he wiped his chin with the back of his hand. 'You've got a devious mind.'

He was patting down the front of his shirt, feeling for damp spots.

'You're alright,' Nightingale said. 'Most of it went on the table.'

Yet Fisher's hand remained pressed against his chest.

'You know, it must be quite hard to spill wine down your front.'

'Are you thinking about Carla Porter?'

'Yes. Did she say she spilled the wine or did someone spill it on her?'

'She said someone spilled it on her.'

Fisher thought about it, trying to envisage it happening. It was possible, he supposed.

They spent the next twenty minutes running over other possibilities. When the conversation started to repeat itself, Fisher drained the last of his pint.

'We done here?' he said.

'Yes.'

Her chair scraped over the patio flags.

'In a hurry to get home... Someone waiting for you?'

'Ha, yeah, right. The only thing I've got on tonight is a hot date with the telly.'

'In that case, what do you say to a bit of overtime? There's at least one more set of clothes I can think of to add to our collection.' Then he remembered his earlier musings about Francesca La Salle and added, 'For the time being, at least.'

Half an hour later, Nightingale pulled the car to a stop outside Carla Porter's house. Fisher spat out the wad of gum he'd been chewing on and wrapped it in a tissue from his pocket.

'Don't want any complaints getting back to the Falcon about having beery breath. Grab a couple of evidence bags, enough for her clothes and shoes from Friday.'

'Do you think it was blood on her top, not red wine?' Nightingale asked, sounding dubious.

'I don't know. If Porter had already tried washing the top when Molly O'Leary saw her and then said it was red wine, it's feasible. Or she could have poured red wine over herself to cover up any blood. Either way, it makes sense to get it tested.'

Nightingale rang the doorbell.

'Nice house, is it?' Fisher knew the area from his days on the beat — a densely built eighties estate only a twenty-minute stroll into town.

'It's alright. A bit small and the front garden's a mess. The woodwork looks like it's seen better days too.'

'Try again,' Fisher said, nodding towards the door.

Nightingale pressed, keeping her finger on for longer this time. Shortly they were rewarded by the sound of the latch turning. Carla Porter led them through to a stuffy front room, the smell of nicotine heavy in the air. After accepting the offer of a seat, though declining refreshments, Fisher went straight to the point of their visit.

'Miss Porter—'

'How's the investigation going? Have you made any progress?' she asked eagerly.

'We're still exploring a number of avenues.'

'But you must have some idea?'

'It's too early to say. We're trying to rule out as many people from our enquiries as possible. If you agree, I'd like to take the clothes you were wearing on Friday for testing.'

Maybe he was imagining it, but Fisher was sure he felt the room's mood change.

'What do you mean? Testing for what?'

'I understand you had something spilled down your top. We just need to be able to prove it had nothing to do with Lucy.'

'What? You think it was blood?' Her voice rose a notch. 'You think I killed her? My own sister!'

'I didn't say that. It's just routine. We're asking a number of people the same thing. Are the clothes you wore in the house?'

'Why wouldn't they be? You think I destroyed them? You do, you think I did it, don't you?'

Fisher could hear the hysteria creeping into her voice. In contrast, he kept his tone calm and measured.

'I think it would be perfectly understandable if someone spilled red wine down your top that you might have simply thrown it away if you couldn't get the stain out. Or you might have taken it to be dry cleaned.'

'What do you think I am, made of money? Of course I've still got the clothes. They're upstairs. I can't afford to replace a top just because some jerk goes and chucks his drink all over me. I paid nearly forty quid for it and only wore it the once. You can hardly see the stain now it's been washed.'

'Good. DC Nightingale, please would you accompany Miss Porter to get the items?'

'Fine!' He heard her stomp across the room.

Fisher waited. The stairs creaked, then footsteps crossed the floor above, followed by an assortment of quiet bangs and muffled voices. When they returned a few minutes later, Nightingale took the bags straight out to the car. While Fisher waited for her to return, he noticed Luna shift beside him. He set down a hand towards the crown of her head, intending on settling her down when his nose picked up a heady, musky scent that made him feel quite claustrophobic. He recognised it as the same perfume his wife was partial to. He'd hated it when she'd worn it too, only it was even worse laid over a patina of stale cigarettes.

He straightened up.

'Miss Porter?'

'Yes.' She was surprisingly nearby.

'What are you doing?'

'I'm stroking the dog. I think she likes me.'

He pulled Luna closer.

'You really think I could have hurt my sister?' Porter asked, further away now.

'In a murder investigation nobody is above suspicion.' When, after a moment or two she hadn't said anything more, he asked, 'How long have you lived here?'

'Forever.' She sounded sullen.

'You grew up here?'

'Mum bought it when I was little. In the days when she still thought we could be like a normal family.'

'Why wouldn't you have been a normal family?'

'Drink. Drugs. The different uncles I had to put up with. Take your pick.'

The hiss of a match was swiftly followed by the whiff of sulphur. He heard a sharp suck of air and then seconds later a long exhalation. Soon it was his turn to inhale the pungent aroma. He'd always hated the smell of cigarettes.

Come on Beth, what's keeping you?

'When we talked the other day, you said you'd learned about Lucy from your aunt,' he said.

'That's right.'

'You never found any paperwork after your mother died? Adoption papers or anything like that?'

'Mum wasn't exactly organised. The only things she kept were our birth certificates and a shitload of unpaid bills, which I had to find the money for.'

'Whose birth certificates?'

'Mine and Mum's.'

'Not Lucy's?'

'She was Jessica then, but no.'

Just then Nightingale returned and Fisher brought their visit to a close.

'Anything interesting to report from your soiree upstairs?' he asked as they made their way to the car.

'No stash of paintings, if that's what you mean. I did notice a couple of expensive-looking bits on her dressing table. There was a bracelet that looked quite pricey. I'm not saying it was Cartier or anything like that, but it stood out from the rest of her things that looked more chain store stuff. There was also a posh-looking pen and a coloured glass dish. Murano glass, is it? She was using that as an ashtray.'

'Make a note of everything. Somebody said they thought she was light-fingered, there might be something to it. If there is, we might just have found ourselves another motive.'

The car alarm blipped and Nightingale opened the rear door, before taking Luna's harness from Fisher's grip.

'I don't understand,' she said. 'What motive?'

'Imagine it. You're Lucy, still grieving from the loss of your parents. Your long-lost sister makes contact. Because you're a trusting soul and are feeling unusually lonely, you seize the chance to be part of a family again. Your friends and relatives tell you she's only interested in your money. You brush them off, put it down to them being snobs. Only then people start noticing things going missing. Maybe Lucy lost something too and started to wonder if her friends might have a point. Talk about biting the hand that feeds you. Everyone has said how lovely Lucy was but equally, we've also been told she was no pushover. What if she confronted Porter about it? How emotionally fraught would that conversation have been? Could have all ended in tears... or worse.'

37.

The next day Fisher spent the journey to the office in quiet contemplation, still puzzling over why Lucy had gone to the studio. The name Patrick was making itself felt, like a small stone in the bottom of a boot on a long walk. On arriving at the station, he tasked Nightingale with sending Carla Porter's clothes to the lab for testing.

'Don't forget to check the clothes against the photos first.' Somewhere in the office was a board filled with photographs from Friday's event, donated by guests in the hope it might help shed some light on Lucy's final movements. 'What was she wearing, anyway?'

A bag rustled.

'A black trouser suit, white blouse, black shoes and socks. Nothing special. It's the sort of thing I wear for work. Just off-the-peg high street stuff.'

'Socks?'

'I sometimes wear socks with trousers, though normally with boots.'

Fisher thought about Mandy, about the sort of outfits she used to wear for award ceremonies and celebrity bashes. Suggesting she might wear trousers with socks would have been tantamount to asking for a divorce. But then she would be the last person to describe herself as a pie and pint sort of girl. Perhaps if she had, they'd still be together?

He let Nightingale go and slipped his headphones on. He opened the note of the conversation with Molly O'Leary, where she recounted her brief conversation with Lucy just before the lift took her to her death. He set it to play and eased back in his chair.

Lucy had been smiling. She'd seemed excited. She'd asked Molly to wish her luck.

Why? What would make her ask for luck? It was a fund-raising event. Her pieces had sold for a substantial sum. What would have made her more excited? The prospect of making even more money, that's what.

Fisher quickly found a second file, the list of successful bids at the auction. The same person had successfully bid for both of Lucy's paintings. It was a name Fisher knew well.

He reached for his phone.

Four rings, then, 'Yo!'

'Jimmy? It's Matt Fisher.'

'Matty,' came a friendly sounding voice with a strong Essex accent. 'Long time, no see. How's it hanging?' Jim Vine and Fisher had once been team mates and together had enjoyed a run of good luck in the premier league. It was great while it lasted.

'Good thanks. You?'

'Yeah. Still killing it. I take it you want tickets?'

'Thanks, but no. I gave up going to the game when I stopped being able to see the pitch,' Fisher said, trying to keep his tone light.

'I meant for Thursday. My big birthday bash. I've hired the Topaz Club.'

'Oh, didn't realise. Happy Birthday for Thursday. But I'll pass thanks. It's not really my scene.' He almost added 'any more' but didn't want Jim to feel any sorrier for him than he probably already did.

'If you don't want tickets then...? Oh, now I'm worried. What have I done to warrant a call from the Old Bill?'

Fisher laughed.

'You sound like someone out of a naff eighties cop drama. But you're right. I am calling on official business... Lucy Stirling?'

'Of course. I couldn't believe it when I heard what had happened. So, how can I help?'

'You bought both of Lucy Stirling's paintings at the auction.'

'I did. I love her work. I actually spoke to her straight afterwards about buying another.'

'Another painting?'

'Yeah. I'm not such a fan of the sculptures. A bit ostentatious even for me.' He snorted a laugh.

Another painting — that would have made three. A spike of adrenalin shot through Fisher.

'You didn't say anything to her about scoring a hat trick, did you?'

'Yeah, I said I'd be happy to make it a hat trick, or something like that. How the hell did you know that?'

'Just something Lucy said to someone. I don't suppose you remember anyone standing nearby while you were talking?'

'There were loads of people milling around. The place was heaving.'

It dawned on Fisher that Lucy could have recounted the conversation with anyone, so who was nearby at the time was irrelevant.

'So, did Lucy actually show you more of her stuff?'

'No. There were people queuing up to talk to her. I told her I'd catch up with her later.'

'Later that night?'

'I just said, we'll talk later, or something like that.'

Fisher was nodding to himself. It all fitted.

'That everything?'

'I think so, yeah. Thanks for your help.'

'Glad to be of service. Hope you get the bastard. Oh, and if you change your mind about Thursday, let me know. It'd be great to see you.'

Fisher returned his phone to the desk. Someone gave a polite cough.

'Beth?'

'I wondered if you needed me for anything?'

'I think I just found the reason Lucy went up to the studio.' Nightingale pulled over a chair. 'I kept asking myself why she would leave a room full of people, all dying to speak to her, and go up to the studio on her own. Some sort of secret assignation is one possibility; to sell more of her work is another.'

'It's possible, I suppose,' Nightingale said.

'I haven't told you the best bit yet. I checked the auction record. An old mate of mine, Jim Vine, bought both paintings Lucy put into the auction. I just talked to him. He said he spoke to Lucy straight after the auction and told her he'd be interested in buying another. A *third* painting. He said he wanted to make it a hat trick. Hat trick. Not Patrick. I think someone overheard that conversation — or Lucy told them about it. Later, they could have told Lucy Jim had changed his mind and wanted to see some of her other pieces and that they'd sent him up to the studio to meet her. That could explain why she was so happy when Molly O'Leary saw her in the lift. She said 'wish me luck' — she thought she was going to make another sale. And probably for a tidy sum, seeing who she thought she'd be selling it to.'

'But in reality, this Jim Vine wasn't waiting,' Nightingale said. 'It was just a ruse to get her to go upstairs.'

'Precisely.'

'But that wouldn't fit with her walking in on someone accidentally, would it?'

'No, it wouldn't.'

'So it's got nothing to do with the missing art.'

'I don't think so.'

'You never thought the two were related, did you? Is that why you were happy to give Andy all those suggestions to investigate Cope and the art thefts?'

Fisher wasn't sure, but he thought he could hear the upward curve on her lips, as though the suggestion amused her.

'I wouldn't go that far but somebody needed to look into Cope. I just didn't want it to be me. My focus has always been on catching Lucy's killer. Not pissing around looking for a handful of stolen paintings.'

'So we can rule Cope out then?'

'We haven't got enough to completely exonerate him but let's just say I'm happy for our focus to shift away from him for the time being.' He fired a smile in Nightingale's direction. 'So, no Patrick. Just a cunning liar. We've just got to figure out which of them it is, given we seem to have motives galore.' Fisher sat back in his seat and ran a hand over his chin, stroking the soft stubble as he thought. After a moment he tapped both hands down on the desk in front of him. 'Beth, go see if you can get hold of a whiteboard and some pens. Let's take another look at what everyone was doing around the time Lucy was killed and map it out. See who could have realistically done it.'

As Nightingale's footsteps tripped lightly away, another tread approached.

'Matt, it's Andy. Got a minute?'

'Sure.'

'Kami called. Her kid's sick, so she won't be in today. She rang to update me on her meeting with Shane Harman yesterday. Interesting character by all accounts, although he sounds like a bit of a cliché — archetypical rock and roll bad-boy. The sort that snarls even when asking how you take your tea.'

Fisher gave a small laugh.

'Good one. And...?'

'Well, he admitted snorting the coke in the gents. He said he hadn't intended on doing anything like that, being happy to chug champagne all night, but some guy approached him and asked if he was interested in buying some coke. As it happened, he had enough cash on him for a couple of wraps. Kami got a description out of him, for what it's worth. The best he could come up with was it was some geezer in a suit who spoke like he was one of them. When Kami asked what he meant, he just said, "like all the other wankers there that night".'

'I take it she showed him a photo of Cope?'

'Yes, and it's a definite no. Looks like you were right. Cope wasn't a dealer after all.'

'Good. We're making progress at least. So, what are you working on now?'

'I'm going to take a look at those files you brought back from the gallery. Purchase and sales details, dates orders were dispatched, that sort of thing. See if I can tie them back to the deposits in Cope's bank account like you suggested.'

After Wickham left, Nightingale returned. Fisher could hear her hefting a large whiteboard across the room. It frustrated the hell out of him that he couldn't help. Not that she complained. She quickly set the board up and soon Fisher could hear the rapid clicking of keys as Nightingale opened files on his computer.

'Let's start with the Morgans,' he said. More clicking, then, 'We know what time they left, so there's only the five or ten minutes before that they're not accounted for. And then there's the possibility they parked up and slipped back in the gallery. You'll have to stick them on the board with both sets of timings.'

A couple of minutes later Nightingale said. 'Done that. Now, what about Morrelli? Have we definitely ruled him out?'

'Not at all. There's still a chance he and Georgia Bellucci were in it together.'

She read out the time they claimed to have met in the courtyard and then later when they were eventually let out by a passing waitress.

'Lucy was already known to be missing by the time Morrelli was seen in the bar, wasn't she?' he said.

'Yes.'

Fisher listened to the pen squeak over the board's surface.

'Okay, next are the two guys. Lee and Heath,' Nightingale said. 'I've been over and over the CCTV of the back door and I can't see how they got out and back in again without being seen. Looking at Heath's statement...' Her fingers skipped quickly over the keyboard. 'Oh, someone's filed a new document in his folder. Looks like the lab results from their clothes are back. Let's see.... Okay, Oliver Heath — no blood or DNA on his jacket or shirt. They did find DNA on his trousers, though it's not Lucy's. It's...' After a short pause, she said, 'I wonder if there's been a mistake?'

'What is it?'

'Hang on. I'll just see if Felix Lee's results have been uploaded... Here we are. So, no traces of Lucy's bodily fluids on his things either, but... well, it's the same as with Heath. There are traces of semen on both men's trousers. I'll give the lab a call, check there hasn't been some sort of mix-up.'

Fisher set out a hand and smiled. 'Save your embarrassment. It might not be pleasant but it's perfectly possible. Clearly neither of them gets their suits dry cleaned as often as they should.'

'No. You don't understand. They found traces of *each other's* semen on their trousers. Lee's was on Heath's and vice versa.'

38.

'Thank you for agreeing to meet at such short notice, gentlemen,' Fisher said, addressing Felix Lee and Oliver Heath. They were in Lee's lounge. Fisher was perched on the edge of a large leather sofa next to Nightingale, trying to stop himself from sliding back.

'How could we resist such a mysterious summons, Inspector?' Lee said.

'No mystery. I just thought this might be a conversation you'd prefer to have in private.'

'Curiouser and curiouser,' Lee said playfully.

'Previously, you said after the auction you both went out briefly to catch some air, leaving by the gallery's back door.' When neither man responded, he continued, 'Strange then there's no sign of you on the gallery's security cameras.' Silence. 'Well gentlemen, I'm here to dispel this little fairy tale of yours—'

'Now look here—' Lee interjected.

'No, you look here,' Fisher snapped back. 'We're trying to get to the bottom of who killed Lucy — your supposed friend — and so far, you have done nothing but lie. Well, no more. We know what you were doing, actually have evidence of it. Now, will you tell us what really happened?' Still nothing. 'Fine. Have it your own way. I'm taking you both in for a formal interview. I'll do my best to make sure the details don't get out but I can't promise anything.'

Fisher pictured the pair exchanging meaningful glances.

Eventually Oliver Heath broke the silence, 'We have to tell them, Felix.' When his friend didn't disagree, he went on, 'Felix has only been trying to protect me.'

In a faltering voice, he went on to tell a story as old as time. The two men were harbouring a secret, and not just from the police but from everyone. They were lovers. Heath had met Fran and Lucy shortly after joining the GB dive squad as a junior coach. At the time he was in the full throes of denial, fostering a misguided hope that whatever intimacy he and Lee had shared at university was down to little more than youthful exuberance. So when Fran began to show an interest in him, he reciprocated and soon the two were dating, despite the fact such dalliances between student and coach were frowned upon. But he could only deny himself for so long and eventually sought out Lee's company once again. In the years that followed the pair kept their relationship under wraps for the sake of Heath's career, having to resort to clandestine meetings whenever the opportunity presented itself: such as slipping upstairs to the second-floor store to enjoy a few snatched moments of intimacy on Friday night.

Lee took over the story, 'When I fetched Lucy's paintings, it occurred to me the store would be perfect for a bit of... well, privacy. Obviously, I had no idea anything was going to happen to Lucy, and so close by.'

'So, the bit about going out for some fresh air...?' Fisher said.

'A lie,' Heath said, his voice thick with guilt.

'So what happened afterwards?'

'What do you mean, afterwards?'

'Well, did you leave the store and return to the ground floor together?'

Heath said, 'No. We—'

In contrast to Lee's, 'Yes—'

'It can't be both,' Fisher said. 'I take it the answer is no.'

It was Heath who replied, 'We left the store together but I took the stairs. Felix went down in the lift. We wanted to limit the likelihood of anyone seeing us together. As soon as I got to the ground floor I went straight to the gents. By the time I got to the main hall, Felix was talking to someone I didn't know, so I went to the bar. Fran saw me there and came over.'

'Mr Lee?'

'That's the truth. When I went into the main hall, I saw Mack Lucas, the music video director. I went over to talk to him. Thought I'd try and touch him up for some work.'

'Which of you kept the key card?'

'That would be me,' Lee admitted.

Not that having the key meant anything, Fisher realised, seeing as both men had already gained access to the second floor. If Heath had been caught upstairs by Lucy, he could have simply followed her into the studio.

During the drive back to the station, Fisher pondered this latest revelation. Although it was always possible it was another lie, he was inclined to believe them. Yet it gave the two men a compelling motive. If Lucy had discovered them and threatened to expose their secret, what lengths would they have gone to, to keep the truth from getting out? Yet there was no trace of Lucy's blood or DNA on their clothes. Nor did it fit with the theory that Lucy had been lured upstairs on the promise that Jim Vine was waiting for her. Was that just a red herring? Had Lucy gone upstairs under her own initiative? Maybe she was going to fetch a particular painting she thought Jim Vine might be interested in and take it downstairs to him? In which case, the case against the two men looked a strong one.

By the end of the journey Fisher felt no closer to reaching the truth and when they got to the office and Nightingale asked whether they were going to carry on with the timeline, his response was lacklustre.

'I don't know. Is it getting us anywhere?'

'Yes or no?'

He heaved a sigh. 'Go on. We've started it, may as well finish it.'

With a fresh coffee at his elbow and a new timeline for Lee and Heath on the board, Fisher sank back in his chair. 'Okay. Who's next?'

'How about Francesca La Salle?' Nightingale deftly tapped at the keyboard.

'Well we know she wasn't with her husband,' Fisher said drily.

'According to her statement, after the auction she was with the rest of the party at the bar until Lucy left them. Shortly afterwards, Lee and Morrelli had a falling out about Georgia Bellucci's autograph and the group split; La Salle spent the following hour or so with her modelling friends until she saw her husband on his own at the bar and went to join him.'

Fisher nodded. 'You know, I wonder if Lee was going to tell us Morrelli was cheating on Lucy at the pool the other day, you know, before Heath turned up?'

'I wouldn't be surprised,' Nightingale said. 'Lee seems like a bit of a bitch. I don't think I'd want him as one of my friends.'

'No,' Fisher said, recalling plenty of so-called friends of his like that back in the day. He pushed the thought to the back of his mind. He needed to stay focused.

'I read La Salle's statement recently,' he said, 'and checked it against her model friends' accounts. From what I could tell, the only opportunity she had was when she went to the loo, and even then, most of the time, they went together.' He paused. 'Why is that? Why do you women go in groups? What is there to do in there?'

'Whatever you mean by *you women,* I'm not one of them,' Nightingale said. Fisher worried he'd somehow upset her, but she didn't sound upset when she went on, 'You know, when I was checking Porter's outfit against the photos earlier, I happened to notice La Salle's. She's a very striking woman and it certainly flaunted her considerable assets, but there could have been another reason for her wearing what she did...'

'Go on.'

'It was a black toga-style dress, little more than a sheet of fabric gathered in the right places. She's got great legs, by the way. Go all the way up.'

When he'd got over picturing an Amazon wearing next to nothing, the point she was making dawned on him.

'She had bare legs?'

'Probably not bare. I imagine she wore tights, but it would have been easy enough for her to take them off, use Morrelli's jacket to cover her top half, then rinse off any blood on her legs or chest in the sink by the body, before putting the tights back on. Bob's your uncle. Not a drop of blood to be seen. She could have flushed any paper towels she used down the toilet on the way back.'

'Shit.'

'I'll leave her on the board then, shall I?'

Fisher groaned. He'd all but ruled La Salle out. Out of everyone, her motive seemed the flimsiest. A bit like her dress then.

'Okay, who's next?'

'Porter.' Fisher waited. After a few minutes Nightingale said, 'She says she was with the group of friends, until they all left. Not knowing anyone else there, she stayed at the bar. At around quarter past eleven someone spilled red wine down her and—'

'I wonder whether it was done deliberately to get her out of the way?' Fisher interrupted. 'Does she say anything about the person who did it?'

'No. Only that there was a small crowd getting drinks in. She was standing behind them waiting to be served when they turned around. Someone bumped into her and spilled their drink down her front. Whoever did it was lost in the crowd. If they realised what they'd done, they didn't bother with an apology. Porter said she dabbed at it with a bar towel then went to the toilets where she attempted to wash it out.'

'She doesn't say anything about going into the staff toilets?'

'No. It just says toilets.'

'Okay, what then?'

'After she left the toilets she returned to the main hall and tried to find Lucy. When she couldn't, she asked Cope, who agreed to look for her.'

'Okay, well get that lot down.'

The pen squeaked on the whiteboard like a demented mouse. When she'd finished, Nightingale said, 'What about Shane Harman? Are we including him? Seeing as he's the only one we know had any coke on him?'

'No. Leave him off for now. I can't see him having any real motive to kill Lucy. Unless we get something more, he's out of the equation.'

'And Jackson Cope? Do we still do him?'

'You mean because I don't think it was him? What I *think* is irrelevant. Proof is what's important. Stick him on there.'

'Actually, I'm not sure I can.' Fisher could hear the click of the mouse. 'According to his statement he was here, there and everywhere. He seemed to spend the evening between the kitchen, the basement and the main hall. I'd need to go through all the statements and look for where he gets a mention and piece his movements together that way. Also, what's to say he didn't kill Lucy when he claimed to have found her body?'

Fisher screwed up his face. He'd previously ruled Cope out as the killer. Was that a mistake? Cope would have easily been able to persuade Lucy to go to the studio at the prospect of another sale.

'Is Andy around?' he asked.

'Yes. He's at his desk.'

'Go see if he's got any further with the house-to-house enquiries at Cope's place.'

When she returned, Wickham was with her.

'We've made some progress,' he said. 'None of the neighbours heard or saw anything, apart from a woman with a young baby. Turns out the baby kept her awake most of the night. She said she was walking around the bedroom, trying to rock it to sleep, when she looked out of the window and saw a man leaving Cope's. That was around two in the morning. It was too dark for a useful ID, though she did say it looked like he appeared to be carrying something. She saw him walk around the corner and a few minutes later noticed a car pull out and turn right, away from Cope's. A large, dark-coloured saloon. I've got one of the uniforms scouring the CCTV cameras in the area. At least now we've got an approximate time to focus on.'

'Any joy with the phone records?'

'Not yet. No calls were made to or from Cope's mobile that day and it doesn't look like he uses his landline much. If he did call someone, it had to be from the gallery. We're still waiting for them to send us an itemised record from their switchboard.'

Fisher blew his cheeks out and let out a long, slow sigh. They needed a break, and soon.

39.

Molly O'Leary sounded pleased to see him, or at least so he thought, picking up on the way she'd said, 'Hello *again,* Inspector Fisher.' He'd always had a thing for an Irish accent.

Wickham and Nightingale went to get the phone records and to perform a number of experiments to test the assumptions they'd used on the timeline. Meanwhile, Fisher switched his phone to silent, accepted the offer of a drink and made himself comfortable, leaning on the counter in the reception area.

'I think I may have found out who Patrick is,' he said, taking a sip of what turned out to be very good coffee.

'You have?' She sounded intrigued and he imagined a pair of green eyes flashing.

'I think she said hat trick. It was something Jim Vine, the footballer, said to her.'

'Oh! You know, it could have been.' After a short pause she said, 'You don't think he did it, do you?'

'No. Not at all,' Fisher said quickly.

'I was going to say, I never saw him apart from when he arrived and when he left. If he went upstairs, he must have used the back stairs — only someone would have noticed, a famous guy like him.'

As Fisher went to reply, a door banged open and footsteps came rushing towards them. Soon after, the lift binged. He listened to the doors slide open.

'Eighty-nine seconds,' Nightingale said.

'Seventy-eight,' Wickham replied, sounding a little out of breath.

'Miss O'Leary says the lift definitely wasn't used by anyone other than Lucy and Cope. You can hear it even in the back of the cloakroom.'

'The stairs were quicker, anyway,' Wickham said.

'Actually...' Molly said, timidly. 'I'm sure you've already thought of it, but most of the women were wearing long dresses and heels.'

'I could try coming down the stairs on tiptoe?' Nightingale suggested.

'Might as well, while we're here.' As Nightingale ran off, Fisher said, 'Any joy with the phone records?'

'Yes,' Andy said. 'We've got a long list of numbers. What about visitors?'

'I was just getting to that.' Fisher turned to face the desk. 'Miss O'Leary. Did anyone come to see Mr Cope between Saturday morning and the last time he was here?'

'Not that I know of. At least no one came to reception asking for him.'

A door banged nearby.

'Seventy-six seconds,' Nightingale said triumphantly. She didn't even sound out of breath.

'You must have raced down,' Wickham said, sounding irritated. 'You couldn't do it like a normal person then?'

'What did you just say?' Fisher asked, sounding shocked.

'I only meant most people couldn't have done it that quickly.'

'But the fact that I did, means someone else could,' Nightingale argued. 'I thought we were supposed to be looking at the art of the possible.'

'We are,' Fisher said. 'You both did a great job. I think we're done here.'

Fisher thanked Molly for her help. Wickham said something about another appointment and started for the exit.

'Inspector Fisher,' Molly said, 'before you go...'

'Yes?'

He heard the sound of paper sliding across the reception desk towards him.

'When you were here last, I asked if you'd—'

'Hang on a sec....' Fisher turned towards where he thought the doors were. 'Nightingale, can you give me a couple of minutes, please? I'll join you outside.'

Fisher found the sheet.

'Have you got a pen?' He held out his hand.

'I'd suggest you come back when the investigation is all done with,' Molly said, pressing a pen into Fisher's open palm. 'Only I don't suppose you go to art galleries much, do you?' From the tone of her voice, Fisher guessed she was smiling. In his mind's eye those green eyes were twinkling.

'Not ordinarily. Though life shouldn't always be ordinary,' he said, flashing a smile of his own. 'I hope you don't mind me asking, your eyes... they wouldn't happen to be green, would they?'

'Yes.' Then, 'Hang on, is this some sort of scam? Can you really see?'

Fisher laughed.

'No. I just conjured up a picture of you from your voice. I wouldn't have wanted to leave not knowing if I was right.'

'I thought for a minute you've been having me on.'

'No. Do you want me to write anything in particular?'

'Only your name,' He felt a little dip of disappointment. 'And phone number.' His lips twitched with a smile as he scribbled off the requested information.

'Can you read it okay?'

Molly recited his number back to him.

'At least you know how to get hold of me if you think of anything else.'

'Don't worry, I'll be in touch even if I can't.' He felt her warm touch as her fingers brushed his as she took the pen from his grip.

Nightingale was waiting for him at the top of the steps.

'What did she want?' she asked as they started the slow descent to the pavement.

Fisher wondered whether it was idle curiosity or whether she was playing with him.

'Sorry, I can't talk while doing steps. It takes too much concentration.'

As soon as they reached the pavement, he changed the subject, commenting on the results of their experiment inside. Part of him felt guilty for having wasted time flirting in the middle of a serious murder investigation. Another part, the part that responded to the surge of testosterone and adrenalin that the slight touch of Molly's fingers had initiated in him, had gone past the ability to think. He pinched his lips tight, suppressing a smile as they made their way back to the car.

40.

The following morning, Wickham must have spotted Fisher and Nightingale arrive. He joined them before Fisher had even shrugged out of his coat.

'I've given Kami the list of itemised calls from the gallery for the last couple of days,' he said. 'She's going to check it against everyone there Friday night.'

'Any joy with the CCTV?' Fisher asked.

'Still checking. I'll let you know if we find anything.'

'Detective Inspector Fisher, I want a word.' It was the DCI. 'You two go make yourself useful.'

Matt heard two pairs of footsteps recede.

'Ignoring my calls isn't a smart move, *Inspector*,' the Falcon said, enunciating his title in such a way as to make it sound like an insult. 'I don't take kindly to being made to come and find you.'

'I've been interviewing potential witnesses. I must have left my phone on silent,' he said placidly. 'What did you want me for?'

'I have to brief the Commissioner on progress before the press conference.'

'Yeah, okay. No problem.'

After a short spell, the Falcon broke the silence. 'Well...?'

'Sorry. I thought we were waiting for Andy.'

'Given up already? Probably best. Save embarrassing yourself downstream.'

Fisher took a deep breath and let it out slowly. Nice and calm.

'Not at all. I just thought you'd want to talk to us together... to save time.' He paused and cleared his throat, then said, 'You can tell the Commissioner that the investigation into Ms Stirling's murder is making good progress and we expect to have a suspect in custody shortly.'

'Really?' She sounded dubious but hopeful. 'Who?'

'I'm not a hundred per cent confident but—'

She gave an exasperated sigh.

'Oh, here we go again.'

'Not at all. I'm just trying to be thorough and there are still a few loose ends to tidy up. We don't want another fuck up, do we?'

She obviously decided to ignore the slight and asked, 'What loose ends?'

Ah, the sour sound of cynicism.

'Jackson Cope's death for one.'

'Your suspect isn't linked to him?'

'No. But Andy's still working on that side of things. He's—'

'Miss Stirling is murdered at the gallery, work of hers is reported missing. Days later Cope is found dead, an empty crate in his house, and you think the two aren't related?'

'I think Cope saw an opportunity and took it, setting off a new train of events. He probably thought no one would notice the missing items in the confusion following Lucy's death.'

'Save it. I should have known better.'

Fisher went to say something in response, but a subtle shift in air, sending the musky aroma of her perfume swirling, told him he'd be wasting his breath. She'd already gone.

Once he was sure the Falcon really had flown, Fisher pulled his phone from his pocket. He flicked a switch on the side. Several chimes rang out, signalling a number of voicemail messages: four in all. The most recent and shortest was from the Falcon. The other three were from his wife and had arrived over the course of the afternoon. He played the first message and soon sensed from the pleasant, friendly — too friendly — tone of her voice, some favour was needed. He was right. She wanted to know whether there was any possibility he could have Josh to stay on Thursday night. She must be desperate — she even used the term father and son bonding. Fisher let out a sigh. Whilst he had no specific plans for the following evening, to have a chance of any making inroads into the case he needed to keep working. In the second message a note of exasperation laced Amanda's sugar-coated words as her mask started to slip. She demanded he call her back as a matter of urgency. In her third and final message, the mask was off completely. She was probably stomping on it, crushing it underfoot, as she spoke. She informed him, in cold clipped words, that no thanks to him she was going to have to let Josh go somewhere with Frazer she wasn't entirely happy with, but seeing as Fisher hadn't seen fit to return her calls, she had no choice. And now he knew about it, maybe he'd at least have the decency to worry about Josh as much as she would be. With her words, 'Don't bother phoning back' ringing in his ears, he exited voicemail and rang her back.

Maybe she was busy or maybe she saw the caller ID and decided to play him at his own game; either way, the phone rang through to voicemail. He left a short message asking her to call him back, a worried frown on his brow.

41.

Fisher forced himself to set his concerns about Josh to one side; they would have to wait, at least until he'd spoken to Amanda. He eased back in his seat and ran over everything they knew about Friday night and everything they had learned from Lucy's friends and family, hoping to alight on something new, now his train of thought had stopped at a different station. After listening to the record of his and Nightingale's conversation with Lee and Heath at the pool the morning after Lucy's murder, he paused to consider Lee's allegation that Porter might be a little light-fingered. At the time he'd put the comment down to Lee's obvious dislike of Porter, which he'd attributed to commonplace snobbery, but was there more to it than that?

He reached for his phone. Shortly, he replaced the receiver and called Nightingale over.

'Hi. What do you want?'

'At Porter's house you mentioned there were some expensive-looking things in her bedroom. One of them was a pen, yeah?'

'Yes. With a dark blue enamel casing.'

'I just spoke to Felix Lee. That's a match for his missing Montblanc. What else was there?'

'A silver bracelet. Well, silver-coloured. It could have been white gold or platinum. And a glass bowl she was using as an ashtray.'

'Anything else?'

'When she went to the wardrobe to get her clothes out, I noticed her pick some things up from a chair next to her bed, a scarf and a pair of suede gloves. She threw them into the bottom of the wardrobe and said something about them being presents from Lucy.'

'Hmmm... Go give Francesca Heath, La Salle, or whatever her bloody name is, a call. Describe the items and see if she recognises them. Don't tell her where we've found them. If you don't get anywhere with her, try Morrelli.'

With Nightingale off making the necessary enquiries, Fisher tried his wife a second time. Still no answer. He left another message. He'd just hung up when Wickham came over.

'Kami's had some success matching the calls made by Cope the last time he was at the gallery. It looks like he rang all of the successful bidders. She spoke with the old guy, the stock supervisor. He said Cope would have called them to check they'd got their items okay. Every call leads to a successful bidder.'

'And there were no calls to anyone else?'

'No.'

'Shit. This is getting us nowhere. What about the CCTV? You must have made some progress by now.'

'We're still trying to match cars seen in the vicinity to Friday's guests. I wondered whether Cope might have called the bidders in the hope of offloading the stolen art to one of them.'

Fisher tipped his head. It wasn't a bad hypothesis.

Just then, a very excitable Nightingale arrived.

'You were right,' she said with childlike glee. 'Francesca Heath recognised the description of almost all of the items. I didn't mention the pen, seeing as we already know whose that is.'

Fisher straightened up in his seat.

'Go on.'

'Apparently Morrelli bought Lucy a bracelet for her birthday that matches the one I saw. It's Cartier and *very* expensive. And the gloves sound like a pair Lucy used to have but thought she'd

248

left in a restaurant a while back. La Salle said the scarf could be hers. She had one like it that went missing a few weeks ago.'

'The woman's a veritable magpie.'

Fisher thought about motive. Only a handful of items. Hardly the billions Eleanor Morgan stood to inherit as Lucy's sole beneficiary. Would Lucy have threatened to shop her own sister? Unlikely. More likely she'd have simply severed the familial cord once and for all and sent Carla Porter back to her previous sisterless life. That didn't sound terrible enough to warrant smashing someone over the head.

'I haven't told you the best bit yet.' Nightingale sounded like she might burst. 'I called Tom Morrelli. I thought I'd better check Lucy hadn't given Porter the bracelet. If she had, I would have thought she'd have told him out of courtesy. Anyway, he said Lucy was actually wearing the bracelet Friday night. They were in the limo on their way to the gallery when she asked him if it went with her dress. Tom thought she was only wearing it to please him, seeing as it didn't really go that well, and said so. Lucy took it off and put it in her handbag. There was definitely no mention of her giving it to Porter, who was in the car with them at the time.'

Fisher envisaged Carla Porter bending over her dead sister's body, extracting the bracelet from the open handbag. The open handbag splattered with blood and brain matter.

It all came back to the timeline.

'Beth, have a look at the board,' he said urgently. 'Could Porter have got to the studio, killed Lucy and then got back down to the staff toilets by the time Molly O'Leary saw her?'

'Yes. It's tight, but doable. Obviously, it's less tight if all she did was find Lucy dead and simply take the bracelet.'

Fisher chewed his lip and tried to clear his thoughts. After a prolonged silence he brought his hands down on the desk in front of him.

'Well, the answers aren't going to come to us while we're sitting here on our arses. We need to do something. I'll organise a search warrant for Porter's place. Beth, could you give the CSIs a ring? I'd like one of them with us. We need to get that bracelet tested asap.'

Wickham cleared his throat and said, 'Mind if I tag along?'

Fisher gave a shrug.

'Sure. Extra pair of eyes can't hurt.'

'You know,' Wickham said, 'even if you strike lucky and find Lucy's blood on the bracelet, it's still only circumstantial. Porter could say Lucy gave it to her earlier in the evening and that any blood on it must be from a previous occasion when Lucy cut herself.'

'That'll be slightly harder to argue if they find brain matter,' Fisher said.

'True, but it still wouldn't prove Porter's the murderer. Cold-blooded thief, maybe. If she did kill Lucy then you're going to need more.'

'Beth, I take it we haven't had anything back on her clothes yet?' Fisher asked.

'Some, but not all. So far they've found nothing.'

Fisher shook his head.

'If it was her, we going to have to figure out how the hell she managed to stay so damn clean.'

'How are you going to do that?' Wickham said.

'Good question. Maybe the house search will turn up a blood-spattered plastic pinny she smuggled out in that handbag of hers.'

'I don't think she's that stupid,' Nightingale said.

'I was joking,' Fisher replied glumly, wishing he wasn't.

42.

On the journey to Carla Porter's house, Fisher ran through everything they knew, trying to think of anything they might have overlooked. He thought about the jacket in the kiln — Tom Morrelli's jacket. Was its purpose simply to protect the assailant's clothes, or was it deliberately intended to implicate Morrelli? Either way, the singer was lucky that thanks to his secret assignation with Georgia Bellucci he had an alibi. If it wasn't for the fact Lucy was already missing by the time the couple left the courtyard, Morrelli would have still been their main suspect.

As soon as Carla Porter opened the door, Fisher wasted no time explaining the reason for their visit. Wickham handed her the search warrant to read, while Fisher, Nightingale and the CSI technician piled into the tiny house.

'I would have let you take the things if you'd asked,' she said. 'I've got nothing to hide. Lucy was very generous. She gave me lots of things.'

'Including a Monteblanc pen and silk scarf? Because we have reason to believe they weren't Lucy's to give.'

'I found them. People are always losing things. I keep my eyes open is all,' she said, sounding sulky.

Fisher waited with Porter, while Nightingale accompanied the CSI upstairs. It wasn't long before she was back downstairs

'Got it?' Fisher asked.

'Yes.'

'Could you show it to Miss Porter please?' Fisher waited a couple of seconds, listening to the rustle of plastic, as Nightingale displayed the bracelet in its evidence bag, then said, 'Miss Porter, tell me about this bracelet. Where did you get it from?'

'It was Lucy's.' Fisher held his breath. Was she about to admit everything? 'Tom gave it to me.'

'What?' Fisher huffed out the word. 'When?'

'It came in the post Monday morning. He put a message in with it, saying Lucy would want me to have it. I thought it was really nice of him.'

'Have you still got the note or the box it came in?'

'No. I put them out with the recycling Tuesday morning. It was only in a jiffy envelope.'

'When did you last see the bracelet? Before it arrived on Monday, I mean.'

'I'm not sure. I think... Oh!' She gave a shocked gasp. 'It was... well, it was Friday night. Lucy was wearing it but then she took it off. Tom said he didn't like or something like that. I forgot about that. Lucy did seem a bit upset. She must have given it back to him.'

Before Fisher could say anything else, there was a light tap on his arm.

'Can I have a quick word?' It was Wickham.

'Nightingale, could you stay here, please. Keep Miss Porter company.'

Wickham guided Fisher into a different room and closed the door. Fisher assumed they were in the kitchen from the smear of cooking odours in the air.

'We've found Porter's birth certificate and the death certificate for her mother in a box in the loft. Nothing relating to the adoption or Lucy's birth, or Jessica, as she was then. There's also a pile of documents relating to the house purchase. I don't know what the significance is, but it was bought outright for cash. A hundred and sixty-four thou'.'

'Don't ask me. I was only a kid at the time,' Carla Porter said, when Fisher tried to find out how a woman who was supposedly struggling to bring up two children on her own could afford such a purchase.

'And in the fourteen years that followed, before your mum died, the topic never came up?'

'I learnt a long time ago, don't ask if you might not like the answer,' Porter bit back.

Fisher pressed her for more, but the shutters came down. After taking a handful of items, they left Porter stewing and regrouped on the pavement outside like a posse of Jehovah's witnesses.

Nightingale spoke first, 'I didn't want to say anything in front of Porter, but I think I know where the money for the house came from.'

'What?' Fisher blurted. 'Where?'

'It's mentioned in the legal papers that were found in Lucy's apartment.'

'What legal papers?' Fisher asked. 'Andy...?'

'It was just some formality to do with the adoption,' Wickham replied.

'And the money?' Fisher pressed.

'I didn't see anything about money.' Adding sheepishly, 'I'll be honest, I didn't read it all — it didn't seem important. We already knew Lucy was adopted.'

'Beth, did you bother to read it?'

'I tried. Andy's right. It's some sort of contract. From what I could make out — in between the legal jargon — Mr and Mrs Stirling were to give Mrs Porter money in return for her not telling anyone who had adopted her daughter. I included it in the briefing note I did for you, but I'm sorry, I realise I should have mentioned it sooner, but, like Andy said, I thought, well...'

'How much money are we talking about?'

'I remember thinking it was a lot...' After a short pause, Nightingale continued, 'I think it was two hundred thousand... or maybe two-fifty? I scanned the document onto the system. You could check when you get home?'

Fisher shook his head.

'I don't know, if you want something doing properly...'

43.

At home, with a mug of hot tea and a packet of digestives, Fisher sat listening to the computer's stilted voice as it read from the legal document found in Lucy's apartment. It was a non-disclosure agreement between Mr and Mrs Stirling and Karen Porter, Lucy's birth mother. The document, otherwise known as an NDA, prohibited Ms Porter from telling anyone about the adoption, in exchange for which she received two hundred thousand pounds. Fisher let out a soft whistle. That was lot of money by today's standards but twenty years ago it would have been a small fortune. His face twisted into a frown. Weren't there rules around disclosing a child's original parentage? Why would they have needed the NDA?

The following morning, as soon as he got to the office, Fisher paid a visit to the force's legal team. Unfortunately, they were unable to shed any light on it. The best they could do was suggest he phone social services. Which he did. It turned out to be the right call. The council's adoption manager, a youngish-sounding man with a nasal-twang to his voice, turned out to be very obliging. After hearing Fisher describe the NDA, he asked that a copy be emailed over and promised to investigate.

He was back on the line within the hour.

'What I'm about to tell you might come as a surprise but I can't see any other explanation. Nor can our legal team.'

As he talked, Fisher's mouth fell slowly open until his jaw eventually threatened to hit the desk. His mind was working overtime. Did this change who inherited Lucy's fortune? Did Lucy actually have a fortune to leave? The implications for the investigation seemed huge.

'And you're positive?' he said, when the adoption manager finished.

'Yes. Lucy Stirling was not legally adopted. There is no record of it. In fact, there's no record of any adoptions by Mr and Mrs Stirling. When you first mentioned there being an NDA, I thought it was probably just to allay any fears the adopting parents had about the birth mother maintaining contact with the child. It's rare but it can happen, especially where the adoptive parents and the birth mother know each other. But in this case, given the sum involved and the wording of the agreement, I would say it looks like Mr and Mrs Stirling simply bought the child.'

'But why? Why not go through the normal channels?' Fisher asked.

'The most obvious reason is they'd already seen the child and she matched what they were looking for. Rather than risk beginning adoption proceedings and then finding the adoption wasn't supported, they flexed their wealth. Another reason might be one of timing. I don't suppose you know if Mr and Mrs Stirling had had a child of their own?'

'No. What difference does that make?'

'Well, if, for example, they had a daughter who had not long died, who would have been of a similar age, they could simply have let the new child — in this case Lucy — take the dead child's identity.'

Fisher started to nod.

'That would explain why they didn't adopt her sister,' he said.

'The birth mother had another child?' The young man's voice lifted a notch.

'Yes. Another daughter who would have been three or four by then. She stayed with the mother.'

'That's another reason they might not have wanted us involved. We would have needed a very solid reason to split siblings up like that. This really leaves a bad taste in my mouth. What they did was illegal. I hope everyone involved will be called to account.'

'It's too late for that. Mr and Mrs Stirling were recently involved in a fatal accident and the birth mother died years ago from a drug overdose.'

'Probably funded by the money she got for selling her baby.'

The same thought had already occurred to Fisher. He said, 'You know, I still find it extraordinary they were able to keep it under wraps all these years.'

'It would have been easy enough if they were prepared to go to the required lengths. Obviously, the NDA would have helped. The services of a lawyer would have been needed, but they can be bought. And a summary birth certificate is easy enough to create — there are people out there capable of forging all manner of official documents.'

'Indeed,' Fisher said, thinking he knew just the person.

44.

The air was cold and rain spotted the windscreen; the wipers screeched as they scraped the barely wet glass. Fisher swayed in his seat. Adrenalin coursed through his veins, overshadowing his usual motion sickness. It was a good feeling. It meant they were on to something.

'And you really think they knew all along?' Nightingale said, as she navigated twisting lanes on the way to the Morgans' residence.

'I'd stake my pension on it. They've been pulling the wool over our eyes all along. Figuratively speaking, of course. No wonder Mr Morgan wasn't happy about Porter making a sudden appearance in Lucy's life. He must have been worried to death Lucy would find out the truth. It'll be interesting to see how they react, seeing as it now means they won't be inheriting her billions.'

After a few more twisty corners, Nightingale said, 'I take it she did have billions to leave? I mean, if she wasn't really the Stirlings' daughter, should she have inherited everything in the first place? Oh... but then if the money shouldn't have gone to Lucy, wouldn't Helen Stirling's estate have gone to Eleanor Morgan anyway, as her only living relative? Or is it more complicated than that?'

Fisher's breath caught in his chest. Suddenly he wasn't feeling on such solid ground.

'Slow down a bit. I need to make a call.' He reached for his mobile and scrolled through his call history, the sound of the names and numbers filling the small space.

'Who are you ringing?'

'Lucy's solicitor.'

Olivia Rees-Bowers' voice rang out clearly through the speakers. A few quick questions later and Fisher returned the phone to his pocket.

'She sounded genuinely surprised,' Nightingale said.

'Pissed off more like. No wonder, seeing how she'd represented the family for the last twenty years and didn't have a clue.'

'At least she didn't help Lucy inherit all that money when she shouldn't have.'

According to Ms Rees-Bowers, the way the will was worded meant Lucy was rightfully entitled to the Stirlings' billions, despite not being legally related.

But Fisher was only half-listening, too busy thinking about his approach to the forthcoming conversation. They'd got motive and opportunity but, so far, hadn't a shred of evidence. That needed to change.

The car slowed and the tyres crunched as they traded the road's smooth surface for the Morgans' expensively chipped driveway. He took a deep breath. It was time to raise the stakes, friends of the Commissioner or not.

Eleanor Morgan answered the door, as aloof as ever. She showed them through to the same room they'd spoken to her husband in on Saturday morning. Fisher asked that her husband join them. He and Nightingale waited quietly while she went to fetch him.

The pair entered a few minutes later.

'You have news?' Rupert Morgan asked. The soft sound of footfall on carpet was followed by a push of air and squeak of leather as he took a seat.

'Of a kind. Yes.'

'What does that mean? I'm not in the mood for riddles.'

'All in good time,' Fisher said. 'What can you tell us about Lucy's adoption?'

He pictured both Mr and Mrs Morgan stiffening in their seats, but when Rupert Morgan replied, he didn't sound unduly ruffled. 'You'll need to be more specific.'

'Let's start with how Lucy was selected. Was she put forward by the council's adoption service?'

A long stretch of silence, then, 'I'm not sure I recall,' Morgan said with a languid tone that rankled.

'Maybe you have a better recollection, Mrs Morgan?' Fisher said.

Eleanor Morgan cleared her throat but then said nothing.

'Mrs Morgan?' he pressed.

'I was just trying to remember. The mother used to clean for Helen. When she had her second child, I recall Helen saying how she was struggling to cope with two small children and no husband. I suppose she must have said something about putting the baby up for adoption and Helen, being Helen, wanted to help.'

'Help?' Fisher snapped. 'Help would have been paying her a decent wage. Help would have been offering to baby-sit to give the woman a chance of a life. Help doesn't usually manifest itself in actually taking the child away from its mother. A mother who was already vulnerable.'

'I don't know who you've been talking to but there was nothing vulnerable about that woman. What she was was irresponsible and incapable of doing the right thing by her children.'

'If it was purely an act of philanthropy then why didn't they adopt both children?'

'I don't know,' she said, but her voice wavered, making Fisher think otherwise.

'I think you do. I imagine you know every detail. Sisters confide, don't they?'

He let the quiet fill the room.

Eventually she answered. 'Helen wanted a baby. Lucy was the right age. She was such a beautiful child with a perfect temperament.'

'And Carla?'

Eleanor Morgan's tone hardened. 'Carla was older and was already showing signs of taking after her mother. Helen thought... she thought, perhaps, it wouldn't have been a good match. The child would have struggled to adapt.'

'And she wasn't the cute wide-eyed bonnie baby your sister craved.'

'I think we've heard enough.' Rupert Morgan was on his feet now and pacing about. 'How are any of these questions getting you any nearer to solving Lucy's murder?'

Fisher ignored the other man's growing ire. 'When we spoke with you before, Mr Morgan, you made some comment about being unhappy that Carla Porter had turned up like she did, making Lucy aware of the fact she was adopted.'

'I did. And I was right to have been.'

'Why? Because after that Lucy started to show an interest in the adoption?'

'Interest? What absolute nonsense. Lucy was very much vested in the here and now. The past held no interest for her.'

'Perhaps she'd been encouraged to by her sister?'

Rupert Morgan gave a snort. 'From what I've seen that girl doesn't have the capacity to encourage a starving man to take a mouthful of food. How would someone like that encourage Lucy to do anything?'

'Well, somebody did. We found a legal document amongst Lucy's things. A non-disclosure agreement between Mr and Mrs Stirling and Karen Porter. Did you know about it?'

'I... A what?'

'A non-disclosure agreement. Surely a legal man, like yourself, is familiar with the term?'

'Of course, I know what one is. I'm just not aware of the specific one you're referring to.'

'Then let me enlighten you. This particular NDA prohibited Lucy's birth mother from telling anyone about the so-called adoption of her daughter Jessica, or Lucy as she became.'

'I know nothing about it.'

'So if I talk to the lawyer who prepared it, he or she won't point us back in your direction?'

'No and I resent the implication,' Morgan said, enunciating his words so precisely they could have been shaped with a razor blade.

'How about you, Mrs Morgan? Were you aware the adoption was fake? That your sister bought Lucy like you might buy an animal?' He though he heard an intake of breath but when it became obvious no answer was forthcoming, he continued, 'Had your sister recently lost a baby, Mrs Morgan? A daughter? Don't forget, we can find out.'

'Yes.'

'And am I right in thinking the child was called Lucy and that she died within her first year?'

'Yes.'

The room fell silent.

'Well, I think this is what you call a game-changer,' Fisher said shortly. 'We have motive and opportunity, and with both of you at the gallery that night, I doubt it'll be long before we're able to place you at the murder scene.'

'Motive? Opportunity? What utter rot,' Morgan scoffed.

'I'm sure being the eminent lawyer you are, Mr Morgan, you realise that, without a will, Lucy's entire estate now goes to her birth sister and not to your wife. In my book that's one hell of a motive for making sure Lucy died before she discovered the truth and your wife lost claim to everything.'

'Ridiculous. Such a document, if it exists, effectively removes Eleanor as sole beneficiary and does away with any reason for us to want Lucy dead.'

'That would be true enough *if* the NDA was public knowledge. Which it wasn't. If Lucy hadn't already realised its significance, it was only a matter of time before she did. It would have been in your best interests, financially speaking, for her to have died before she could let anyone else in on the secret.'

'Assuming, of course, we knew. And for the record, I will repeat, we knew nothing about any NDA in relation to Lucy. In addition to which, it seems, Inspector, you have forgotten, we had already left the gallery before Lucy was murdered.'

'Actually Mr Morgan...' Nightingale said quietly, 'that's not necessarily true. Although Lucy's body had yet to be found, it's likely she was already dead by the time you left.'

'I will not stand for such allegations,' Morgan bellowed. 'Do your worst, Mr Detective. If the only case against us is that we had a motive then you are more stupid than you look. I will enjoy seeing that smug smile wiped clean off your face when the truth comes out. Now I'd like you both to leave.'

The other man's display of confidence caused Fisher's own conviction to falter; doubt sneaked through the cracks. Had he missed something?

Pushing aside his uncertainties, Fisher drew himself tall.

'I think we've covered everything. I would like to take the clothes you wore on Friday night for testing. If you have no objection, perhaps one of you could accompany Detective Constable Nightingale to get them?'

Fisher waited for a spirited rebuff, but Morgan simply said, 'Eleanor...'

'This way...' Mrs Morgan started for the door. 'You're lucky. They've only just come back from the dry cleaners.'

As soon as they were alone, Morgan rose from his seat and crossed the room to the door.

'If you have no other questions, Detective Inspector, I shall leave you to wait for your colleague. I have a lot more important things to attend to.' The door clicked closed. .

45.

Fisher and Nightingale covered the short distance from the house to the car in silence.

'We'll give someone a laugh in the lab with these,' Nightingale said, as her boot lock blipped open. He heard the rustle of the evidence bags as she placed them inside.

'Why?'

'A pale green silk dress. Full length. I can't see how Mrs Morgan could have been anywhere near Lucy when she was attacked without coming out of it looking like a Christmas tree caught in the middle of a massacre.'

'What are her heels like?' he asked, as Nightingale relieved him of Luna's harness and began to secure the dog in the back seat.

'Virtually flat. I imagine she rarely wears heels; she's taller than me and I'm five-ten.'

'What about his stuff? He was wearing a kilt, right?' He'd heard the jokes in the office at Mr Morgan's expense.

'Yep. Blue tartan.' The passenger door slammed shut. 'You know, what I said about Francesca La Salle and her outfit...well, he's no different, is he? He could have taken the kilt off and covered his feet in a couple of plastic bags kept hidden in his sporran, then washed his legs in the sink in the studio.'

Despite the absurd, almost comical, image Nightingale's words conjured up, Matt felt like anything but smiling. He climbed in to the passenger seat and turned to stare unseeing through the window. By all accounts, Mr Morgan had left his table and went in search of Lucy shortly before they left. Had he found her? He wasn't gone long, but was it long enough?

'Beth, when we get back to the office, can you see if you can track down the lawyer who drew the NDA up? Get them in for a chat; we need some evidence the Morgans knew about the NDA and the fact Lucy wasn't legally adopted.'

'I'll get right on to it.' Nightingale put the car into gear and pulled away. After a moment, she said, 'You know, that room we were in back there, there were photos of Mr and Mrs Morgan taking part in a fox hunt. Maybe someone who can happily see a fox torn limb from limb might not have such a problem bashing someone's head in?'

'I take it you don't approve of fox hunting?'

'You do?'

'No, but I don't automatically think anyone who does is murderer material.'

'No?' A minute later, adding, 'Don't most serial killers start with animal torture?'

'Some; not all. And besides, I'm not sure blood sports fall into the same category.'

'I do,' Nightingale said with conviction. 'I think you've got to be particularly cruel and ruthless to hunt. Which is exactly what you said Lucy's killer had to be.'

Although he didn't exactly agree with Nightingale's reasoning, Fisher was far too happy at the fact she'd shared it with him to disagree. He smiled and said, 'That's a good point. You're right. I did say that. I'll keep it in mind.'

***

They hit the road, heading for Carla Porter's. Even though everything had yet to be formally ratified, Fisher wanted to be the person who told her the news, so that Nightingale could watch her reaction.

'Do you want to call, check she's in?' Nightingale said.

He gave the suggestion a moment's thought, and although it made sense, seeing how many different jobs Porter was holding down, he favoured the element of surprise.

'No. We'll chance it.'

It turned out to be a good call. His sturdy knock brought Porter hurrying to the door.

'What do you want?' she grumbled. 'You've already turned the place upside down once.'

'Miss Porter, we have some important news. Can we come in please?'

'I'm not interested. Just go away.'

'I promise you'll be very interested in what we've got to tell you.'

'Fine.' She turned and headed into the lounge, leaving them to follow. As soon as they were gathered in her tiny lounge, she rounded on them, 'Have you got who did it then?'

'No. We're still working on that.'

'So, what is it?'

With no offer of a seat or refreshments, Fisher cut to the reason behind their visit.

'Miss Porter, do you know anything about a legal document drawn up between your mother and Mr and Mrs Stirling? Something called a non-disclosure agreement?'

'A what?'

'It's a type of contract.'

'Never heard of it. Apart from a pile of unpaid bills, you've already seen everything she left. It was all here when you ransacked the place.'

Fisher went on to outline the discovery of the illegal adoption and what it meant for her, standing, as she did, to inherit her sister's vast fortune. He took his time and when he finished his explanation was met with silence.

'Miss Porter, did you understand what I just said?'

'I'm not sure. I think I... I know you're police and wouldn't joke, not about something as important as this, but I mean... is this for real? I just can't...'

'Like you say, we wouldn't joke about something this serious. But don't go on any spending sprees just yet. Apart from the fact it needs properly verifying, it's likely to be some time before you actually get to see any money. Nothing can happen until the investigation is closed and probate cleared.'

'Okay.' She still sounded dubious.

'It sounds like you had no idea...' Fisher said, 'about Lucy not being adopted.'

'No. I still can't believe it. I always thought people like Mr and Mrs Stirling were the sort to do things proper like.'

'What about Lucy? Did she ever say anything that, with hindsight, makes you think she might have known?'

'No. I'm sure Lucy would have just come out and said if she did.'

'Did she ask many questions about your childhood or your mother?'

'Not really, but what was there to know? My life's been really boring compared to hers.'

'Not even when you first made contact?'

'Maybe at the very beginning. After that she just seemed interested in doing stuff together, like proper sisters. It was really good. After all that time on my own, finally there was someone...' Fisher could hear the wobble in her voice and soon she was sniffing. In a voice thick with tears she said, 'I'm sorry. I still can't believe she's gone. I can't stop thinking about how awful it must have been. Do you think she suffered much?'

'Chances are she didn't know anything about it.'

'I hope that's true. I really do.' She blew her nose noisily. After a moment, 'It's funny how things work out, isn't it?'

'In what way?'

'It's like she's looking out for me from wherever she is.'

'I'm sure that thought must give you a lot of comfort,' Fisher said, pulling an uncomfortable smile. 'Unfortunately, from the point of view of the investigation, this latest development does make your position slightly worse in that it gives you a motive.'

The house sounded unnaturally quiet in the pause that followed. Eventually Porter responded, 'I don't understand.'

'With Lucy dead, you now stand to inherit a substantial estate.'

'But I didn't know that before you told me. And even if I did, I would never have done anything to hurt Lucy. She was my sister. I'd spent all of my childhood wondering where she was, what she was doing. And then I found her. It was everything I'd dreamed of.'

46.

By mid-afternoon they were back in the office. There was a quiet hum of activity, though it sounded a lot more subdued than it had been, energy levels dropping as the cases grew slowly cold.

After arranging for Mr and Mrs Morgan's clothes to be sent for testing, Nightingale joined Fisher at his desk. She came bearing gifts: a bowl of dog biscuits for Luna and the choice of a Mars Bar or Snickers for Fisher. He chose the Mars.

He fished in the drawer for his whistle and sloshed a cup of water over the dog biscuits. Holding the bowl out, he heard Luna come to sit next to him.

'Leave...' He placed the bowl on the ground and gave three short blasts of the whistle. In the background, the office sounds continued unaffected, as the signal prompting Luna to eat was now a familiar sound. Fisher ripped open the wrapper on his Mars. 'Well, Beth, we seem to have suspects galore. But so far, not a shred of evidence that can place any of them in the studio at the right time,' he said, taking a hungry mouthful.

'Apart from Morrelli,' she corrected.

'Who has an alibi.'

'Didn't Bellucci say she went into the hall first, so no one would see her with Morrelli? What if he went to the studio after she'd gone? There might have been time if he was quick.'

'He'd have had to be bloody quick. Also, he'd have had to go through the kitchen. Someone would have recognised him.'

'There would have been loads of waiters running around, clearing up. Would anyone look twice at a young guy rushing through?'

'But if he was with Bellucci all night, how would he have got Lucy up to the studio in the first place?'

'Oh, yeah. I don't know then.'

'And besides, didn't Bellucci say she heard the police had been called when she got back to the main hall, which means Lucy was already dead by then.'

'That's if she was telling the truth.' Nightingale emitted a soft sigh.

He knew how she felt. He needed to inject some energy into the investigation.

'Let's try thinking about it from a different angle,' he said. 'Lucy wasn't just hit over the head once; she was bludgeoned repeatedly. It was a nasty, violent attack.'

'Like a cold-hearted fox hunter might do.'

'I was thinking more like someone fuelled by hate might do.'

'We're back to Morrelli again,' Nightingale said. 'Lucy refusing to loan him the money for the tour must have rankled. We know they'd argued.'

'But she gave him the cash in the end,' Fisher reminded her.

'But he didn't know that,' Nightingale countered.

'I meant it can't have been that big a row, if she did a U-turn and gave him the cash the same night.'

'Okay, then what about one of the others? We know Francesca La Salle was worried about Lucy diving again. Could she have been angry enough to wallop her over the head? Or it could have been Heath. We know he went downstairs separately to Lee. What if Lucy saw him coming out of the store and challenged him?'

'But we've got the same problem as we had with Morrelli. If Lucy saw him coming out of the store room that means she was already upstairs. So who got her to go there in the first place? Don't forget, someone told Lucy Jim Vine was waiting for her.'

'We don't know that for sure.'

Fisher leaned back in his chair and blew out a long breath.

'Well, we're going to have to get some answers soon, otherwise the Falcon's going to rip my gonads off and feed them to the dogs. The motive points to the Morgans. How are you getting on finding that lawyer who drafted the NDA?'

'Still working on it.'

'Okay. See if you can get hold of Porter's aunt while you're at it, the one she learned about the adoption from. She might know something.' Nightingale pushed her chair back. 'Before you go, you couldn't do me a big favour and grab me a coffee, could you... and another chocolate bar?'

There was a quiet thump on the desk in front of him.

'Snickers okay?'

'You don't want it?'

'No.'

'Cheers.' He reached out, grabbed the plastic-wrapped bar and tore it open. 'You should have said. You could have had the Mars.'

'I don't eat them either.'

'You don't like chocolate?'

'Not really.'

'A woman who doesn't like chocolate... seriously?'

'What can I say?' Nightingale said, with a definite edge to her voice.

'Have I touched on a sore point?'

'They've got milk in them. I'm vegan.'

'Then why buy them?'

'I got them for you. The vending machine doesn't do vegan snacks.'

'You should tell facilities. Get them to put some vegan stuff in it.'

'And give people even more reason to take the piss out of me?'

'Why would they do that?'

'No reason. Forget I said it.'

'It's too late for that now. Why would people take the piss out of you?'

'Honestly, don't worry about it. I'm used to it. I've had it all my life.'

'Beth…'

She gave a loud sigh. 'I'm ginger… and I'm not exactly what you'd call feminine.'

Fisher had imagined her as an elfin thing with dark hair and big brown eyes. He wondered what else he'd got wrong.

'So? You are who you are and no one is entitled to disrespect you. If anyone is giving you any trouble, you need to tell me.'

'They're not. I wish I hadn't said anything.'

'Okay. It's your call, but you tell facilities *I* want some vegan food in the bloody machines.'

Nightingale was quiet for a moment, before mumbling, 'Okay.'

'I can't have you fainting on me. I'd only trip over you and break something… my leg, probably, knowing my luck.'

He knew everything was alright when Nightingale laughed.

Once he was on his own, Fisher's thoughts returned to Rupert Morgan. He slipped on his headphones and quickly navigated to the man's statement. In it, Morgan mentioned stopping to chat to a woman — a rather attractive redhead — while he was supposedly looking for his niece. When Fisher had read the statement at the start of the investigation, he'd assumed the pair had exchanged a few words in passing. Had that been a mistake?

A frown crimped his brow as he reached for his desk phone and dialled a four-digit number from memory.

'Colin Clough. How can I help you?'

'Colin, it's DI Fisher.'

'Hello sir.'

'Colin, I need to track down one of the guest statements; a woman's. One of our suspects says he was talking to her around the time we're interested in. I need to know if she corroborates his account.'

'Who's the suspect?'

'Rupert Morgan. It's possible she might not have known his name, but if it helps, he was wearing a dashing blue tartan kilt and matching bow-tie.'

A laugh came down the line.

'Leave it with me. I'll take a look at the statements, see if I can find her.'

Fisher had just returned the handset when his mobile started to ring. It was Amanda.

'I'm just about to get on the train, so make it quick.'

'What did you mean he'll just have to go with Frazer? Go where?'

'It doesn't matter.'

'I think it does. Go where?' When she didn't answer, Fisher said more firmly this time, 'Go where?'

'The Topaz Club. Me and Frazer were supposed to be going tonight, to Jim Vine's birthday party. Josh was going to be staying at a friend's but they've come down with some sort of bug. Unfortunately, I've got to head up to Manchester; one of my clients is having last minute nerves about her wedding arrangements. Frazer said he'd take care of Josh. I was thinking take-out pizza and computer games, only it turns out Frazer has arranged to meet a client at the club. He says he can't afford not to go, so he's going to give Josh my spare ticket. I'm not enamoured with the idea, which is why I called you. I thought you might want to spend the evening with your son, seeing how you let him down about the weekend. Obviously, I was wrong.'

'It's a nightclub. Josh is only fourteen. He can't go.'

'It's a private function. His age is irrelevant.'

'Okay, let me rephrase that. I'm not happy with Josh going to a nightclub with a man you barely know. And on a school night.'

'Again, if you were more involved in your son's life, you'd realise it's half-term.'

Fisher kicked himself. He knew that.

'Look. Let's not make this about me for once. Josh's only just turned fourteen. He shouldn't be going into clubs. The fact it's a private do shouldn't make any difference. I can't believe you're prepared to let him go.'

'It's not like he's going to be on his own. He'll be with Frazer.'

'Like I said, with a man you barely know.' He could feel his anger getting the better of him.

'Maybe if you had more faith in Josh you wouldn't be so worried.'

'He's a fourteen-year-old boy with hormones threatening to burst out of him like a spring geyser. I know. I was his age once.'

'He's not you. And anyway, at his age you wouldn't have looked twice at a girl if she wasn't holding a football.'

'That's only because nobody put temptation in my way. You know what these places are like, you've been to enough of them. Drink, drugs, not to mention sex...' Images of his son being lured into the gents for his first taste of coke accosted him; a chill tiptoed up his spine. 'I'm not happy with him going and that's the end of it. You need to make other arrangements.'

Snappy gave way to snarly as Amanda responded by hurling a barrage of harsh words at him. Phrases like neglecting his duties as a father and putting his job first hit him as hard as a volley of punches, before she finally cited all the sacrifices she'd made over the years. Fisher sat, shoulders slumped, waiting for her to draw breath and leave a gap long enough for him to fill. Only it never happened. Eventually she finished ranting, but before he could say a single word, her accusations were punctuated by a click and then silence. She'd hung up on him.

'Shit!' He slammed the phone down. The loud bang resonated. It was the only sound in the room. There were no clicking keyboards, no bland chatter, no harassed phone conversations.

Fisher had forgotten he was in a room full of people. Heat flooded his face. Slowly, the sounds of a busy office resumed.

He took a deep breath. Was it really that bad? It wasn't like Josh was going to be on his own at the club. And he was usually well-behaved, or at least, he used to be. But he was at an age where hormones would start to rear their ugly head.

He had to get his mind back on the case. If Amanda was happy to let Josh go, then he should accept her judgement. And so, for the next few hours, he forced himself to stop dwelling on his son and immersed himself in the forensic reports, looking for the smallest clue as to how the killer kept themselves clean while delivering the fatal blows. Would Morgan have had time to strip off his kilt, socks and shoes then wait for Lucy to amble into the studio for her rendezvous with Jim Vine? And what the hell would she have made of him, standing there half-naked? But if Morgan hadn't spoken with Lucy since the start of the evening, well before the auction, how could he have lured her to the studio on the promise that Jim Vine was waiting?

Fisher thought back to what Nightingale had said. No one knew for sure what Lucy had said to Molly in the lift. What if she hadn't said hat trick and it wasn't Jim Vine she was expecting to meet?

He slipped the headphones off and rubbed his eyes. How could they possibly feel tired? They hadn't looked at anything in such a long time. His mind drifted back to Josh. Images of his son in all manner of compromising and dangerous situations came to him. Again, his anger started to mount. A premier footballer's party in a nightclub was no place for a fourteen-year-old boy. What the hell was Amanda thinking? Lost in his own thoughts, he gave a start when a heavy hand landed on his shoulder.

'Sorry. Didn't mean to make you jump. It's Colin. I've got that information you wanted.'

Fisher took a breath, his heart still clamouring.

'You found her?'

'Yep. Carolyn Masters. Runs an art gallery in Cumbria. Must be a good-looking woman, sounds like men were queueing up to talk to her, including your man, Morgan.'

'Brilliant! Thanks Colin.'

Fisher opened Ms Masters' statement. Colin was right. The woman had barely had two minutes to herself after the auction had ended. He made a note of her number, picked up his phone and prayed she was at home. She answered on the second ring with an attractive, subtly seductive voice. Of course, she remembered the man in the blue tartan kilt, he'd been very charming.

Ending the call, Fisher dropped the handset on the base and slouched back in his seat. Unless Eleanor Morgan was in on it with her husband, and the pair had parked up, allowing Rupert Morgan to run back to the gallery, somehow getting Lucy to the studio without having talked to her, they were in the clear.

He turned towards the sound of an approaching soft tread.

'Matt. It's Beth. What time do you want to leave? It's gone half-nine.'

'God, has it really?' No wonder he felt like shit. He reached a hand down, feeling the reassuring softness of Luna's head. 'Time to call it a day.'

'You look like you found a penny but lost a pound,' Nightingale said as they made their way across the car park.

'Morgan's got an alibi for the period before he left the gallery,' he said. 'While his missus was in the ladies, nursing her bad head, and he was supposedly looking for Lucy, it turns out he was actually chatting up some woman. I spoke to her earlier. She said, she'd been talking with an elderly French couple, the husband had made a joke and she smiled just as Morgan got up from the table. Morgan caught her eye and must have thought she was smiling at him. The French couple left and he went straight over. He was still talking to her when his wife returned; he made his excuses and went back to join the rest of his party. They left straight afterwards.'

'And it was definitely Mr Morgan?' Nightingale asked. 'Careful, the steps to the car park are just ahead.'

Fisher said nothing while he concentrated on making it down in one piece, picking up the question as soon as they resumed walking.

'The blue tartan kilt doesn't leave much scope for it to be anyone else. Besides, he introduced himself as Lucy's uncle.'

'Why the hell didn't he mention this when we talked to him?' Nightingale sounded angry.

'Either he didn't want his wife to know or he was having too much fun trying to make me look stupid. Just think what a laugh he'd have explaining to his cronies how the blind detective couldn't find the nose on his own face.'

'Whatever the reason, if they are innocent, Mrs Morgan won't be very impressed when she finds out he's deliberately hindered the investigation.'

'I must be sure to let her know then,' Fisher said.

At the car, after securing Luna in the back seat, Nightingale climbed in behind the wheel.

Fisher shifted in his seat to face her. 'I know it's late but I couldn't beg a favour, could I?'

'Sure. What is it?'

'My wife's boyfriend has taken Josh to the Topaz Club, against my better judgement. I'd rather he stayed at mine tonight. Can we swing by and pick him up?'

'No problem. The Topaz Club — that's that snazzy nightclub isn't it? It's supposed to be a really cool place to hang out.'

'Which is precisely why it's totally unsuitable for a fourteen-year-old boy.'

47.

There had been a time, not that long ago, when Fisher could rely on his face or the mere mention of his name to open doors. These days he had to make do with his badge. But nonetheless it did the job and the besuited bouncers at the Topaz Club waved them through.

Inside, a dance track Fisher faintly recognised pulsed like a heartbeat and lively conversation, interjected with bursts of laughter, rose and fell as people walked by. Fisher felt insignificant yet strangely vulnerable standing there with only his white stick to lean on, having left Luna in the car enjoying a dog chew.

Nightingale flagged down a member of staff and asked for the manager.

'Hi. I'm Ginny Fox. You asked to see me?' a woman with a confident, honeyed voice said a few minutes later. After Fisher explained about Josh, she said, 'I'm sorry but it's a private event with ticketed entry. Minors are allowed provided they're accompanied by an over-eighteen who's responsible for making sure they keep within licensing rules.' Her pleasing tone contrasted with her effective refusal.

Fisher gave a cynical snort.

'And we all know how everybody follows the rules, don't we?'

'Ah, well, as with so many things, it comes down to the parents,' the manager parried. After a moment's pause, she said, 'Look, I tell you what, I'll go and find your son and ask him to come and talk to you. But if he prefers to stay here with the person his mother deemed responsible enough to look after him, I'm not going to force him to leave. How does that sound?'

'Like a good compromise. Thank you.' Fisher flashed her a grateful smile. 'Beth would you mind going with her? You know what he looks like.'

Fisher perched on a bar stool in the club's lobby, trying to pick out the familiar sound of his son's voice from the babble. Most of the chatter was female, interspersed with more resonant male voices. Occasionally he'd hear a higher pitched timbre and would sit, listening hard, until he was sure it wasn't Josh. Rising above the hubbub, came an effeminate, expensively educated drawl that sounded far too much like Felix Lee to be a coincidence. Then came the stuttering hahaha to confirm it. Fisher turned his head, following the voice's progress, wondering if any of Lucy's other friends were there. Without warning, a hand clapped him on the shoulder, almost sending him toppling from his seat.

'Matty boy!'

'Shit Jim. You nearly gave me a heart attack.'

'Sorry mate. So, you decided to come after all.'

'Not really. I—'

He didn't get a chance to finish explaining as the footballer continued, 'What are you doing sitting out here on your own? Do you need someone to take you around? Leave it with me, I'll see who I can find.'

Jim walked off as other voices approached. These ones were more than welcome.

'What's going on Dad?'

'Your mum called. Told me she was away for the night. I thought we could go back to mine and hang out. I can drop you off at home on my way into work in the morning. What'd you think?'

He steeled himself for some sort of protest but Josh surprised him.

'Cool.'

'Good. Let's go. Did you bring a coat?'

'No, but what about Frazer?'

'Where is he?'

'I don't know. I've hardly seen him.'

Fisher bristled. Should have bloody known.

'Is the manager still around?'

'Yes. I'm still here,' she said with a voice as smooth and rich as a chocolate truffle.

'I wonder if you'd do me a favour? If a guy, name of Frazer Marchant, asks if anyone's seen the fourteen-year-old kid he's supposed to be responsible for, could you tell him to give me a call?' Fisher reached into his coat pocket and pulled out a business card. It slid from his grip.

'No problem.' Fisher made to move towards the door when she said, 'Oh, Inspector, I don't know if music's your thing, but if you fancy a night out with VIP service, I'd be happy to be your guide for the night. Here...' Warm fingers pressed a card into his hand. 'Give me a call sometime. I'm sure your colleague can help with my number.'

Outside the air had grown cold. Thankfully the car was nearby.

'Did you just get hit on by the manager?' Josh said.

'She was just being polite,' Fisher said, though he'd thought the same thing.

'When we get to yours can we get something to eat? I'm starving. There was supposed to be food at that place, but it was just bits of stuff, you know, like Mum used to do when we had parties.'

Fisher tried to conjure up an image of the contents of his fridge and kitchen cupboards. He hadn't expected company.

'I could probably rustle up some beans on toast,' he said. 'Or we could get a takeaway?'

'There's a corner shop. I could go get a frozen pizza. And some Doritos. And spicy salsa. Mum never lets me have that.'

Fisher gave a grin and fished out a note from his pocket that he thought was a tenner.

'Is that enough?'

'Yeah, should be plenty.'

'We'll wait in the car,' Nightingale said. 'It's the dark blue Skoda, over there.'

Fisher and Nightingale continued across the road. Keys jangled and Fisher picked up a flicker of warm light from the flashing indicators.

The car door opened with a loud clunk. Nightingale said, 'What the hell is that?'

Fisher froze.

'What is it? What's happened?'

'There are bars of chocolate all over the back seat. The wrappers are all over the pavement.'

'Shit! Get it away from Luna now!' Fisher said urgently. 'How does she look? Has she been sick? Does it look like she's eaten any? Shit!' He'd never felt more impotent.

'Hold these,' Nightingale said, thrusting bars of chocolate into his shaking hands.

'For fuck's sake, how is she?'

'Alright, I think.' A sound like a one-armed man clapping a trousered leg emanated from the car. 'She's wagging her tail. Seems happy enough. Why don't you get in with her, give her a cuddle while I take a closer look at the chocolate? Do you think it's been tampered with?'

'No. It doesn't need to be. Chocolate's poisonous to dogs.' When he'd first got Luna, he'd been given a long list of things to avoid and chocolate was up there amongst the worst of them.

'Maybe she didn't eat any,' Nightingale said, sounding hopeful.

'She might be a guide dog but she's still a dog. She'll eat anything you put under her nose.'

'It was dropped through the open window, on the opposite side to where she's secured. She might not have been able to reach it.'

Fisher's heartbeat reduced from a gallop to a canter, but still, he wasn't entirely satisfied.

'They might have managed to throw some close enough, which she's eaten. It wouldn't take much to make her ill,' he said. Or worse... to kill her, he thought but couldn't bring himself to say.

'Hey, what's up?' It was Josh.

Fisher clambered out of the back seat.

'Someone tried to give Luna some chocolate.' Nightingale said. 'If she's eaten any it could make her ill.'

'Why would anyone do that?'

'Probably just some passing idiot,' Fisher muttered. 'Get in. We need to go. I'll call the vets, see what they say.'

Twenty minutes later they were back on the road, Josh the only occupant in the back seat. The vet, a softly spoken woman, told Fisher to keep his hopes high but his expectations realistic, whilst relieving Luna's harness from his grip. She was going to be spending the night under the vet's watchful eye, the next six to twelve hours being critical.

'Better safe than sorry,' Nightingale said in a kindly tone not dissimilar to that of countless nurses Fisher had encountered over the previous twelve months.

He gave an anxious nod and blew out a long, slow breath, before twisting in his seat to face Josh.

'Good job you're coming home with me tonight champ. I sure could do with the company.'

48.

The following morning, Fisher padded into the kitchen, weary from lack of sleep. In between worrying about Luna, there'd been the late-night call from his estranged wife, who had not been impressed by his act of fatherly love and had wasted no time telling him so. The house felt empty and lifeless; the absence of the tap-tap of Luna's claws accompanying him everywhere he went haunted his every thought. He kept telling himself it was only temporary, that she'd be fine, and then wonder whether it was too early to call the vets.

They said they'd call if Luna took a turn for the worse. No news was good news, right?

Passing on breakfast, Fisher clutched his coffee mug and listened to Josh chow down on scrambled eggs on toast.

'Why is someone trying to kill Luna?' Josh asked, between mouthfuls. 'And don't say they're not. It's obvious you don't think it was a passing idiot.'

'It might be to do with the case I'm working.'

'That must mean you're getting close.'

Fisher had thought the exact same thing.

By the time Nightingale arrived at seven-forty, both Fisher and Josh were ready and waiting. Conversation on the journey to drop Josh off was subdued. As soon as the car accelerated away from Fisher's old home, Nightingale revealed how, the previous night, she'd gone back and talked to the guy in the corner shop. Fisher's eyebrows shot up in surprise, causing the skin around his eyes to snag uncomfortably.

'It seemed obvious that it must have been a spur of the moment thing,' she said. 'I mean, who carries bars of chocolate around on the off chance? But then the guy in the shop said the only chocolate they'd sold had been around teatime and I thought I must have got it wrong. Thankfully, I noticed a CCTV monitor by the till while we were chatting — turns out they've got several cameras around the store, including one covering the sweets to deter the schoolkids from nicking stuff. I got him to show me the footage and bingo! While he was busy serving a group of lads, someone was helping themselves to enough Dairy Milk to give a dentist apoplexy.'

'So, who was it?'

'I couldn't see her face, all I know is she was blonde, quite tall and wearing a loose coat with big pockets. The guy serving said he thought he remembered a woman coming in around that time dressed like she was going clubbing.'

'Both Eleanor Morgan and Francesca La Salle are tall and blonde. Could it have been either of them?' Despite whatever theorising he'd done he'd never really pegged either woman as Lucy's murderer. Too brutal. Maybe he'd let their social class influence his thinking?

'He said the woman looked about my age, which would rule Mrs Morgan out. When I asked him for a description, he said she looked like most white women. Then, do you know what he said? Most women, apart from me. Cheeky bastard!'

Fisher once again found himself wondering what she looked like. His thoughts skipped to Amanda. When they'd first met, she used to embrace her quirks, revelled in being different and he'd found her all the more beautiful for it. The more time passed, the more she grew to look like every other wife and girlfriend. In the end there was little left of the girl he fell in love with.

'Always better to be unique is my take on it,' he said, as another idea sprang to mind. 'Are you sure it was definitely a woman? It couldn't have been a man with longish blond hair?'

'Morrelli you mean? I don't think so. The way they moved and overall shape didn't look like a man.'

'We need to get a handle on who was in the club last night. Whoever it was must have seen me standing on my own like a prize chump. It would have been easy enough to nip outside, spot Luna in the car and see an opportunity for mischief.' He pulled out his phone. 'Now what did I do with that woman's card?' he said, patting down his pockets.

On arriving at the office, Fisher set out his white stick and started towards his desk. Walking past Wickham's desk, the detective sergeant commented on Luna's absence.

'No shit. I hope she's alright,' he said after Fisher filled him in on what had happened.

Fisher mustered up a hopeful smile and said, 'Me too.' Though his stomach churned as a little voice of doubt reminded him that, sometimes, terrible things do happen.

He set off again, navigating his way through a maze of desks and chairs, swinging the stick as he'd been taught. And it was going so well, until he somehow failed to avoid a bin, which sent him toppling, landing in a heap on the floor. Thankfully nothing was damaged, apart from his pride. It was the first time he'd fallen since having Luna. With his heart still thumping he fought to control the wobble in his chin.

'You okay?' Nightingale asked, rushing over.

'Yeah. I'm fine.'

He stood up and once again set out his white stick.

'Let me help.' She gently took his hand and guided it to just above her elbow. She almost matched him for height.

He paused.

'Actually, Beth, can you take me to see the DCI? If she's in. I need to give her a heads-up on the latest developments.'

'Do you want me to come in with you?' Nightingale asked at the door to the Falcon's office.

'No. I'm okay, thanks.'

The Falcon listened to Fisher's news. In the quiet room, he could hear her breathing — fire, probably. She waited for him to finish, then said, 'Oh dear. How terrible.' And for a moment, he thought there might actually be a heart beneath the Teflon exterior. Then she said, 'Of course, I totally understand that you need to go and be with her. Tell Nightingale to come straight back after dropping you off. We can't afford to lose too many bodies.'

'It's okay. I'd rather be here, working. Keep my mind off it.'

'What about what the dog needs? Don't you think she'd prefer it if you were there, rather than on her own... abandoned?'

Fisher went to respond, to defend his choice of action, but then he saw her comments for what they were: designed to shame, to drive him from the office and off the case. Well, let her have her stupid powerplay.

He turned and started towards the door.

'Ma'am, I'll be at my desk if you need me.'

He was inching his way back to his desk, when DS Aptil stopped him.

'Downstairs called,' she said. 'Someone's turned up at reception asking for you.'

'Any name?'

'No. Sorry.'

Fisher thrust his white stick out in front and slowly made his way to the lift and down to reception. The desk sergeant must have seen him step into the corridor and directed him to the correct interview room. The small room smelled of stale coffee and body odour overlaid with a stronger feminine scent.

'Inspector,' came a voice as smooth as a good espresso.

For a moment he struggled to place it, then it came to him: the manageress; the phone call to the Topaz Club earlier.

'Ms Fox?'

'Please, call me Ginny. I brought that list of invites you asked for.'

'Thank you. You should have phoned. I would have sent someone over to pick it up.'

'I sensed it was urgent so thought I'd bring it straight in.' After a moment's pause, she continued, 'Am I right in thinking you're actually interested in who went last night rather than who was invited? If that's the case, I thought you might like the tickets we collected on the door. I brought them with me.'

A smile pulled at the tight edges around Fisher's eyes.

'What can I say? You seem to have thought of everything.'

'There's more...' Fisher's brows twitched. 'We've had problems recently, with drugs and fighting and the like, so we extended our CCTV to cover the lobby. I can email you a copy of the footage from last night if you like?'

'I would very much like.'

'Not just a pretty face, eh?' Ginny said as she slid what sounded like a cardboard box across the desk towards him. Fisher was beginning to like this woman. 'As you'd find out for yourself, if you gave me a call.'

Fisher shifted in his seat. It was definitely a come-on, and he was definitely interested. He gave her a warm smile as he reached for a carton the size of a shoebox.

'I might just take you up on that, only right now I really need to get cracking with this lot.' He tapped the cardboard.

After seeing Ms Fox back to the reception, Fisher returned to the office and gave everything to Nightingale to see what she could find. Next, he called Wickham over for a quick word, which gave him little comfort.

'I'm struggling to see how the two deaths are linked,' Wickham confessed.

'I don't think they are,' Fisher said. 'I think all Cope did was help himself to a few of Lucy's pieces the morning after her death, knowing they'd soon be worth something.'

'So how come he's dead too? An accident? A celebratory snort from a bad batch?'

'Apart from the fact that would be one hell of a coincidence, where's the rest of the dirty coke or the empty wrapper? No. I think he was in over his head with someone. Whoever supplied that coke saw the same opportunity as Cope and hot-footed it away with the contents of the crate — at least that's what my money would be on.'

'A drug dealer who knows their art?' Wickham's voice was thick with cynicism, but he must have had second thoughts as he said, 'Actually, what about Porter? She'd know how valuable her sister's work was and we know her mother was a druggie. She probably knows where to get her hands on all manner of gear.'

'Can you see Cope doing business with the likes of Porter? Besides, she hardly strikes me as some sort of drugs baron.'

Before Wickham had time to respond, Nightingale arrived, almost breathless with excitement.

'I've finished going through the stuff from the club. Lucy was actually on the invite list.'

'No surprise. They were sent out weeks ago,' Fisher said.

'Yes, but her invite was also amongst those handed in at the door. Unless she's somehow risen from dead, someone else used it.'

Fisher slouched back in his seat.

'She could have given it to one of her friends.'

'But they all had their own invites,' Nightingale said. 'Felix Lee, Oliver and Francesca Heath all went. Morrelli was invited but didn't go.'

'Didn't go or only went as far as the corner shop?' Fisher said. 'Are you absolutely sure it couldn't have been him... long blond hair and slim build?'

'I can't be a hundred per cent sure, but I don't think so,' Nightingale said. 'Besides, it makes more sense if it was someone inside the club who saw us arrive without Luna.'

'True.' Fisher turned to his computer. 'Let's see if Ginny's sent that film over yet.'

'Ginny?' Nightingale did nothing to disguise her amusement.

'Who's Ginny?' Wickham asked.

'The manager from the Topaz Club, where we were when the attack on Luna happened,' Nightingale explained as Fisher slipped on his headphones.

He quickly found the email.

'Beth, you're in charge of the controls; grab a chair. The attachment should be open and ready to play. Get it to just before we arrived and let's see what we've got.'

A couple of minutes into the film, she said, 'Frazer's just walked past.'

'What's he doing?' Fisher asked.

'Looks like he's heading towards the toilets. Probably looking for somewhere quiet to talk. He's on his phone.'

'Frazer Marchant, right?' Wickham said.

'You know him?' Fisher asked, a bit too quickly.

'He's one of the people Cope called the day he died.'

'Oh, right.'

Nightingale started to tap the screen.

'That's Porter,' she said excitedly. 'That's bloody Carla Porter. She wasn't on the list. She must have used Lucy's invite.'

'It doesn't look anything like her,' Wickham said. 'Porter's got brown hair. And look at what she's wearing.'

'Wait, I'll rewind it.' Nightingale smacked the keys. 'That's definitely Porter. She's bleached her hair and dolled herself up, but it's definitely her. Look, you can see her face clearly here.'

'Who's she with?' Fisher asked.

'No one,' Nightingale said. 'I wonder why she went?'

'Trying to step into her sister's shoes?' Wickham hazarded.

'Actually, talking of shoes... she's wearing red heels,' Nightingale said. 'She really has had a total make-over.' They fell silent as the film continued to roll. The seconds ticked painfully by

then Nightingale said excitedly, 'Oh, that's us. We've just arrived...
Now I'm just going off with the manager... Now Felix Lee and
Oliver Heath are walking past. Well, that's a surprise. Heath's wife,
Francesca La Salle is—'

'Nowhere to be seen?' Fisher interrupted.

'No,' Nightingale said. 'I was going to say, deep in conversation
with Eleanor Morgan. I don't remember seeing her name on the
invite list either.'

'Maybe she used Lucy's invite?' Wickham said. After a beat,
'So, all three women were there, which means any one of them
could have stuck the chocolate in the car and tried to kill Luna.'
Fisher's chest constricted uncomfortably. Wickham went on, 'I
take it you've sent the chocolate wrappers to test for prints?'

'Yes, but I'm not hopeful. If it was our killer, they've been
pretty good at covering their tracks so far. Though gloves would
suggest it was premeditated.'

'They could have used a tissue,' Nightingale suggested.

'Couldn't have done that at the gallery though, could they?'
Wickham said.

'No, but the murder was probably planned,' Nightingale said.
'And you could easily fit a pair of latex gloves inside a clutch bag,
pocket... or sporran.'

'But what did they do with them afterwards?' Wickham
argued. 'They'd have wanted to get rid of them as soon as possible.
For all the killer knew, we might have insisted on searching the
guests as they left. A pair of bloody gloves would have given the
game away.'

'They could have flushed them down the loo,' Fisher said.

'They wouldn't go down, would they?' Wickham replied.

'They would if they were weighted down with something. A
few coins would probably do it. Wouldn't want them bobbing
back up for the cleaners to find. I suppose we could—' Fisher sat
up in his seat and clicked his fingers. 'Cleaners... cleaning

materials. Beth, didn't you say there was a cupboard with different cleaning products in it under the sink in Lucy's studio?'

'Yes. Lucy was lying right by it. But there's no way anyone could have hidden anything in there, the CSIs would have gone through everything.'

But Fisher had stopped listening. He leaned back in his chair. Slowly things were falling into place. Lucy Stirling, a woman who had everything; a woman against whom others pale into insignificance. The savage blows, the dirty water, the smashed phone. He set a hand down by his side. The feel of fresh air under his fingers jolted him out of his reverie.

'Right. Enough sitting on our backsides. Andy, it probably makes sense for you to carry on bottoming out the business with Jackson Cope. Someone gave him the fentanyl-laced coke. Even if Cope snorted it himself, someone knew the effect it was going to have.' Fisher's brow crimped in the semblance of a frown. 'The day he died — that was the day the CSI widened their search of the gallery, wasn't it? What if seeing them there again spooked him? Perhaps he was worried they'd find something incriminating, not necessarily related to the murder. It might be worth going back over that list of calls he made. Check to see if he'd phoned any of them previously. No one can ever be entirely certain they've left nothing behind; someone only has to plant the idea that maybe they weren't as careful as they first thought to make them panic.' As he spoke, more pieces fell into place and a plan began to take shape.

As Wickham started towards his desk, Nightingale asked, 'What shall I do?'

'Call the lab. Find out why we're still waiting on results and don't take any crap off them.'

'Sure. I'll check with Colin first. He might have already chased. No point calling them twice.'

After Nightingale had gone, her words hung in the air like the ghost of an old fingerpost, pointing Fisher towards something he should have already noticed. A feeling of cold dread stole through him.

'Andy! Are you there?' he shouted. 'I've got an idea I might know who you're after.'

49.

After Wickham left, Fisher reached for his phone. Some fifteen minutes later, he ended the call and slipped his mobile into his pocket.

'Hi.' Nightingale must have been waiting for him to finish. 'I couldn't find Colin so I ended up ringing the lab myself anyway. They've promised to push our stuff to the top of the schedule.' She started to walk away.

'Beth, wait...'

'Yes?'

'What are you working on now?'

'Still trying to track down that lawyer. I did manage to get an address in Spain where he retired to ten years ago, only it looks like he's back the UK, possibly living somewhere in the Cotswolds. Oh, and I'm not having much luck with Porter's aunt either.'

'Sod's law. You know, I'm not sure how much help the lawyer's going to be anyway. Even if Rupert Morgan did have anything to do with it, the guy's hardly likely to say so now. It could be irrelevant anyway. Helen Stirling could just as easily have told her sister what they were up to. I think it makes more sense to focus on finding the aunt. We need to know whether Porter knew the adoption was fake.'

'If her mum kept a copy of the NDA wouldn't it have been in the loft with all the other paperwork?'

'You'd think, seeing as she kept all the documents relating to the house purchase. Actually, you've just given me an idea. You ever bought a house, Beth?'

'No.'

'The solicitors send you all manner of documents to sign and send back. I used to always take copies of everything in case anything went missing. I don't know why, some inherent distrust in the postal system or lawyers. Probably both. Anyway, judging from the folder full of papers at Porter's place, I'm obviously not the only one. But what if she also kept a copy of the NDA – what if that's what we've got? An early copy. Did you notice whether all the parties had signed it or were some signatures missing?'

'I'm not sure. I think everyone had signed it. I can go and check?'

'Please. I know I'm clutching at straws.'

Nightingale returned a minute later, flicking noisily through the document.

'Sorry. It's got everyone's signatures on it: Karen Porter, Mr and Mrs Stirling and the lawyer's.'

Fisher sniffed, then leaned forward and sniffed some more. He felt a jolt of excitement.

'Smell that.'

Nightingale inhaled deeply.

'It smells like stale cigarettes.'

'Which is exactly what I think it is. This document didn't come from Lucy's parents' place. I doubt if Lucy knew anything about it. What's the betting Porter planted it at Lucy's, so we'd find out about the fake adoption? Bag it up, then see if you can get hold of Colin. Ask him to get it to the lab asap. I want everything they can get off it. When you've done that, grab your coat and we'll go and pay Miss Bloody Lily Light-fingers a visit.'

Only this time they were out of luck. Carla Porter wasn't at home. According to a neighbour she'd left the house the previous morning carrying a couple of holdalls.

'Made some snarky comment about being glad to leave this shit-hole,' the woman said. 'I told her it'll be less of a shit-hole with her gone. Mouthing off like she's better than the rest of us. Have you seen the state of her place? Never cleaned those windows in all the years I've lived here.' The woman gleefully went on to give them the name of the taxi firm who had whisked Porter away.

'Where do you think she's gone?' Nightingale asked as they made their way back to the car.

'No idea,' Fisher said, searching for the number of the taxi firm on his phone. 'I can't imagine it's far.' He hit the call button. 'Not if she only took a couple of bags. Plus, she hasn't got the money yet.'

'Ever heard of credit cards?' Nightingale said.

He gave a chuckle at her cheek. At the same time, in his ear, a woman's voice said, 'A1 Taxis. Where to?'

Fisher explained what he was after. The woman, sounding like she couldn't be more underwhelmed if she tried, promised to get back to him. Still parked up outside Porter's house, they waited. Ten minutes later the woman called back and gave them what they wanted.

'Well, well, well... How about that,' Fisher said. 'Now I need to make another couple of calls. Let's see who's on the side of the angels.'

As he started to scroll through his contacts, his phone started to ring again. He answered it and silently, with the breath trapped in their chests, they listened to the voice that rang out through the speaker. A few minutes later, he hung up, flicked a finger impatiently in the direction of the ignition and said, 'What are you waiting for? And put your foot down. Don't worry about me.'

50.

Tom Morrelli entered the building and made straight for the lift. Smacking the heel of his hand on the button he was immediately rewarded with the whine of the motor. Shortly he alighted at the top floor, crossed the softly lit corridor to the door opposite and pulled a key from his pocket. After a quick, nervous look over his shoulder, he slipped the key into the lock and pushed at the polished oak door.

The first thing he noticed was the smell. The apartment had always smelled fresh, wholesome, just like Lucy. Now Tom's nostrils twitched at the funky, almost ripe, tang in the air. Stepping inside, he paused, listening. Nothing. After closing the door softly behind him, he turned and appraised the room. Cushions, usually thoughtfully positioned to adorn stylish sofas, now lay haphazardly. A small dish, overflowing with cigarette ash, sat amongst a plethora of dirty mugs on the glass coffee table, grime marring its normally pristine surface. Tom went over and picked the ashtray up, intending to empty it in the bin, but stopped and cocked his head. Music, some tinny pop ditty, was coming from somewhere nearby. He moved towards the bedroom — Lucy's bedroom — just as the door swung open.

Carla's eyes flared wide. 'Tom?'

Tom started. 'I didn't expect—'

Their words clashed like keys on a typewriter. They stopped and eyed each other suspiciously.

After a short impasse, it was Tom who spoke first. 'What are you doing here?'

'I live here.' Tom frowned, earning him a sly smile from Carla. 'This is my place now.' Her smile widened. 'You haven't heard? Turns out Lucy left me everything.'

He looked around at the dishevelled room once more.

'How long have you been here?'

Her eyes flicked to the ash-filled dish still in Tom's hand. She walked over and grabbed it off him, returning it to the table with a bang. She held out a hand. 'Key please.'

Tom reached into his pocket. He paused, closing his fist close over the cold metal.

'How do I know you're telling the truth?'

'Why would I lie? Call Lucy's aunt or the police. They'll tell you.'

He opened his hand and dropped the key into her open palm.

'Is that one of Lucy's dresses?'

Carla did a twirl, revealing a long triangle of skin visible through the open zip at the back. The dress was at least two sizes too small.

'Looks pretty good, huh?' she said, dancing to the melody snaking its way from the bedroom. 'I'm gonna get one of those personal trainers; some fit bloke. I reckon I could have a figure as good as Lucy's.' When Tom didn't reply, she tipped her chin and regarded him through narrowed eyes. 'So what are you doing here?'

'I lost something,' he said.

'What?'

He pulled a thin gold chain out from under his tee-shirt.

'A Saint Christopher. I had it before we left for the auction. I'd only been home and here before the gallery and I've turned my place upside down. It's definitely not there.'

Carla shrugged and shook her head, moving to the music, hips swaying. 'Haven't seen it.'

Tom started to scan the room.

'Have you looked in your jacket pocket? The one you were wearing on Friday.'

Tom frowned.

'What do you mean? Why would it be in my jacket pocket?'

'I saw Lucy's uncle by our table. I'm sure he bent down and picked something up. It looked like he put something in your jacket pocket.'

'Did you tell the police?'

Carla screwed her face up.

'No. It's hardly like it's got anything to do with what happened to Lucy.' She returned to swaying to the music, moving a few steps at a time, hands weaving sinuously at her side.

Tom gave a short shake of his head. He let his gaze take in the room, then started towards an antique desk. Lucy had loved that desk. She would glide her fingers over the well-polished rosewood, tracing the flow of the grain that looked as though it had been poured out. Now it was impossible to see anything other than the detritus littering its surface.

When Tom looked up, Carla was there, next to him. She grabbed his hand and twisted it back, prizing his fingers open to reveal a plastic key card. She snatched it from him and held it up inches in front of his face.

'Fucking liar! Now why don't you tell me why you're really here?'

51.

Carla Porter marched up the steps towards the gallery's entrance and walked purposefully over to the reception desk.

'Hello. How can I...Oh, hi. It's Lucy's sister, isn't it?' Molly O'Leary turned down the corners of her warm welcoming smile and adopted a suitably sad expression. 'I'm so sorry for your loss.'

'Thank you.'

Molly's smile reappeared. 'So, how can I help?'

'Friday night, when I was rinsing my blouse, I accidentally knocked my bag off the basin. I thought I'd put everything back, but I can't find a key for one of the places I clean. I'll be in real trouble if I've lost it. I wondered if you'd have a look, see if it's still on the floor?'

'It's probably better if you look. You know where you were when you dropped it.'

'I would, but I haven't got my contacts in and I forgot to bring my glasses. I can wait here in case anyone comes in. I'll tell them you'll be back in a second. Please...?'

Molly looked towards the front door; the steps beyond looked deserted.

'I suppose that'll be alright.'

As soon as Molly had gone, Tom Morrelli slipped through the front door, jogged past the desk heading for the stairs, winking at Carla as he passed. A couple of minutes later, Molly was back, shaking her head.

'I had a good look, but there's no sign of it.' Carla went to say something but Molly shot her an apologetic smile and reached for the phone. 'Sorry, I've just got to make a quick call.' Without waiting for Carla to argue, she punched in a number. A minute later, she returned the handset. 'Sorry about that. You wouldn't think it would be so difficult to get someone to come and sort out a blocked toilet, would you? Was there anything else?'

'I thought you might want to know, Tom Morrelli came in while you were back there. He went through the door to the stairs. It looked like he was in a bit of a hurry.'

A cloud darkened Molly's brow.

'Shit!' she said, racing towards the stairwell.

52.

Fisher was crouching between the folds of a long, waxy fabric — probably a raincoat — and something silky and decidedly more feminine, judging from the scent. It was only a few minutes after Molly had passed on her way back to the reception desk and already his knees were aching and his thighs burning. But he didn't have long to wait. Soon, a second set of footsteps hurried past, this time towards the toilets. He gave it a couple of minutes then quietly emerged from his camouflage of coats, unfolding to his full height. He set a hand out on the wall at his side to guide his way and moved forward. Slowly he pushed open the door to the ladies' toilets. A soft splashing noise was coming from somewhere in front of him.

'Where the fuck is it?' Carla Porter sounded angry.

'Can't find what you're looking for, Miss Porter?' he called from the doorway.

'What?' For a moment she sounded panicked. And then, calmer, 'Enjoy hanging around ladies' toilets, do you? You a perv or something?'

He could still hear water sloshing around.

'Pesky things, gloves,' he said. 'They tend to get stuck just past the u-bend. Air gets trapped in them. Stops them going all the way down. I take it you know it's possible to pull fingerprints from the inside of a glove?'

Suddenly there was a squeak of a rubber sole on a tiled floor. Something shunted into him, hard, pushing him back towards the cloakroom. He lost his footing and all of a sudden, he was falling. His head hit the tiled floor with a solid crack as Porter rushed past him.

'It's over Miss Porter!' he called.

The slap of retreating feet stopped.

He clambered to his knees and put a hand to his head, tentatively testing the rapidly growing lump.

'Miss Porter?'

His ears picked up a soft padding sound; he stiffened. Feeling vulnerable, his pulse quickened. A scratching noise nearby was swiftly followed by the waft of sulphur. Then came the squeak of her soles as she took off again. Soon the acrid stench of burning fabric accosted his nostrils. He envisaged flames licking over coats and umbrellas and a myriad of lost and found items collected over the years, dust-coated and as dry as tinder.

He staggered to his feet and shouted for help. Reaching out, his fingers touched the smooth plaster of a wall. But which wall? Disorientated from the fall and fighting a growing panic, he stumbled forward a few steps, pawing at the empty air around him. He recoiled as a heavy choking swirl of smoke filled his nostrils. Crouching down and burying his nose in the crook of his arm, he sensed a bright spot ahead; only a subtle glow, but was it fire or light from a nearby window? Which way to go? Sweat began to bead on his forehead. The already dark room was feeling even more claustrophobic. He put out a hand, felt the heat lick at it. He quickly pulled it away and shouted again. This time his calls were answered by a torrent of barks. A door banged open. Hands grabbed at him, tugging him towards them, almost pulling him off his feet. Someone else rushed past, then a loud whoosh — the familiar sound of a fire extinguisher being discharged. Stumbling out into the reception area, he took greedy gulps of clean air.

Someone pressed Luna's harness into his hand and his panic subsided.

'Are you alright sir?' Nightingale set a gentle hand on his arm.

'I am now.' He bent down and threw an arm around the dog's neck. A sudden swell of emotion took him by surprise. Since picking Luna up from the vet's earlier with a clean bill of health, he'd been so preoccupied with making arrangements for the sideshow he'd concocted to trap Porter, there hadn't been time to indulge his relief. Thankfully, just then, Nightingale's phone rang. She excused herself and left Fisher alone, giving him the space he needed to get his fragile emotions under control and stop himself from turning into a sobbing wreck.

The sound of a commotion close by brought him back to earth.

'Let go of me!' Porter snapped as someone recited her rights in a dull monotone, arresting her for the murder of Lucy Stirling.

He straightened up, sensing someone else nearby.

'Inspector Fisher, it's Tom Morrelli. Did I do alright?'

'You played your part perfectly. Thank you.'

'Oi, you! Inspector!' Porter yelled. 'Are you fucking stupid as well as blind? You should be arresting him. He killed Lucy, not me. He left something behind on Friday. He was going up to the studio to get it.'

'Give it a rest,' Fisher said. He was getting a headache. 'We know it was you.'

'Why would I kill her? I didn't know I was going to get her money.'

'We know it was you who put the non-disclosure agreement in Lucy's apartment.'

'I don't know what you're talking about.'

'You must have absolutely hated her — treated to a lifetime of indulgences and opportunities you could only dream of. The unfairness of it must have really rankled, but to have killed her because of your petty jealousy—'

'Petty!' Porter screamed. 'Petty? You have no idea what it was like to live with a mother who thinks you should be grateful to be paid to clean other people's shitty toilets. And all the while Lucy was living a life of luxury. I was the eldest. It should have been me. Lucy owed me!'

Fisher could hear the rage bubbling beneath the words. He thought about Lucy. All those blows to the head and the dirty slurry tipped over her. All that anger.

'Well she certainly paid for it. In blood. I lost my sight when another man threw acid in my face, yet I wouldn't do to him what you did to your own sister.'

'More fool you then. You don't deserve that dog of yours. I should have set fire to the fucking car.'

Fisher's fingers gently embraced Luna's harness.

'Get her out of here,' he said, in a flat voice.

53.

While Carla Porter was ushered outside and put in a marked car headed for the station, Fisher unhooked his body cam.

'Look after that. It contains some valuable evidence,' he said, handing it to one of the uniformed officers assigned to the operation.

Next, he thanked Molly for her help in the drama, then headed to the gallery's café. He sat down and took a deep breath in, relishing the rich coffee aroma lacing the air. A few minutes later came the clunk of crockery on the table's hard surface.

'You should be getting checked out in hospital, not sitting here enjoying a coffee,' Nightingale said.

Fisher lifted a hand to his head and gingerly probed the tender egg-shaped lump.

'I'll live.' He reached for his cup. As he picked it up the hot drink slopped onto his fingers but he said nothing, not wanting to draw Nightingale's attention to his shaking hands. 'I thought it went very well, all things considered.'

'You're lucky. All those coats and dusty cardboard boxes. You think your scars are bad now...'

Harsh words, but he could hear the concern beneath them and lifted the cup to his lips to avoid having to say anything in reply. He took a sip — hot but good — and could feel his adrenalin levels begin to ebb.

'I still don't see why you had to go in after her,' Nightingale continued. 'I could have done it.'

'Beth, we've been through this. If she'd seen you, she'd have done a runner. I wanted her to think she still had a chance to recover the gloves.'

'Didn't bank on her trying to set fire to the place though, did you?'

There was no answer for that.

Shortly she said, 'What would you have done if Porter hadn't been staying at Lucy's? If she'd still been at home?'

'I'd have had to tweak the plan and sent Morrelli to her place and got him to ask for her help outright. It would have been risky but I reckon it would have still worked. Don't forget, she has no idea he's got an alibi. She wouldn't have wanted to miss an opportunity to set him up again. Look how quick she was to tell us he sent her Lucy's bracelet. It would have been impossible to prove either way, seeing as there were no prints on it. Helping him to get into the studio and implicate him even more would have seemed like a gift.'

'Do you think she planned on setting him up all along?'

'I don't know. It could have been a spur of the moment thing. She knew he'd been in the studio Friday night; knew we'd find his fingerprints there. That might have given her the idea. As for the coke in his pocket, maybe she saw someone dealing coke and it cemented the decision to set him up. I know she told Cope she had no money on her, but how many women take a handbag out without their purse in it?'

'The same ones who forget their glasses when they aren't wearing contacts,' Nightingale said drily.

Fisher smiled

'Actually, she did us a favour there. Saved Molly from having to randomly throw a blocked toilet into the conversation.'

It had worked like a dream. In the same way Cope appeared to have been spooked by the CSI's reappearance and search of the gallery, Fisher figured if Porter had flushed a pair of latex gloves down the toilet when she was washing her shirt, the mention of a blockage might make her worried enough to want to do something about it.

'Do you think she flushed the autographed napkin down the toilet as well?' Nightingale asked. 'Seeing as we didn't find it in her house. It would have been the perfect size to cover the front of her shirt.'

'I shouldn't think so. It would have blocked the toilet straightaway. She probably just gave it a rinse and stuck it in her bag. If she was searched, she could say she'd used it to clean her shirt, then dispose of it with the rest of her outfit.'

'She definitely had it all figured out. So, what gave you the idea about the second set of clothes?'

'It was hearing you describe her in the Topaz Club with her glitzy dress and red high heels. It couldn't be any more different to what she wore on Friday. Why choose an off-the-peg black trouser suit from a high street chain that would be ten-a-penny in your average office, when she obviously had an alternative? It's not like she even works in an office. I imagine she had to go out and buy it specially. I tried looking at it from a different perspective — what practical reason could there be behind her choice of outfit for the gallery? First off, the black trousers were perfect. She could have wiped any splashes of blood off with a paper towel. Probably a paper towel she asked Lucy for, when she met her in the studio, red wine dripping from her shirt. That's why Lucy was bending over in front of a cupboard full of cleaning materials when she hit her. She was looking for something to help Porter clean her shirt with. After giving the trousers a wipe, any residual stains wouldn't have been visible on the black fabric. And the black socks — so obvious with hindsight — she pulled them down over her feet to keep her shoes clean.'

'The flat black shoes that were perfect for running downstairs in.'

'Exactly. Then when she got home, she disposed of the trousers, socks and signed napkin — maybe in a neighbour's bin, or the nearest clothes bank, or burnt them even — and then gave us a duplicate set for testing. It was a great plan. If she hadn't lost her temper and stamped on the phone, we'd have had nothing to place her in the studio at the right time. As it is, the shard of glass in the sole of her shoe is circumstantial at best, but every little helps.' He shook his head. 'Clever little cow.' He leaned back in his seat and took another sip of coffee.

'You can say that again. The call earlier, it was the coroner's office. I finally managed to track down Porter's aunt. The one who told her about the adoption.'

'She works for the coroner's office?'

'Ha,' Nightingale laughed. 'No. She's dead. Died earlier this year, not long before Porter got in touch with Lucy. She fell down the stairs at her home. Broke her neck. It was recorded as an accidental death. They found a pair of shoes on the floor under the body; it was assumed she tripped over them. Bit of a coincidence, the timing of it, don't you think? Bit like her mother's death.'

Fisher eased forward in his seat.

'What about her mother's death?'

'The timing of it — very fortuitous. For Porter at least. She turned eighteen and became eligible to inherit the house only a matter of weeks before her mother died. I asked the coroner's assistant if they could look up the details while I was on the phone and guess what?'

Fisher groaned. 'Don't tell me. It wasn't a drugs overdose.'

'Accidental death. A combination of alcohol and tranquillisers. The woman I spoke to said, from a quick read through, there wasn't even a mention of drug addiction at the inquest. Porter's on record as having said her mother hadn't been sleeping well and occasionally took something for it; suggested she must have inadvertently taken something after having had too much to drink. I imagine it would have been pretty easy for Porter to have

309

slipped some tranquillisers into her mum's drink, especially if she'd already had a few.'

'Nothing would surprise me. It's probably too late to do anything about her mother's death, but it might be worth making a few enquiries about her aunt, see whether anyone noticed her doting niece pay her a visit around the time of her death.' Fisher placed his mug on the table and pushed it away from him. 'Well, looks like there's still a lot to do. Time to make a move I think.'

As they approached the reception area, the tinkling sound of Molly O'Leary's laugh rang out, followed by Morrelli's boyish chuckle.

'Do you want to go over and say goodbye?' Nightingale asked.

More laughter rang out. He imagined they made a handsome couple.

'No. Let's not interrupt them,' he said and started for the door.

54.

They made the journey back to the station at a leisurely pace. Fisher arrived relaxed; even his headache was fading. Walking into the office, the rattle of keyboards and the murmur of voices slowly stopped. A cheer went up. Fisher muttered something about teamwork and started for his desk, the walk to which turned into an obstacle course of handshakes and claps on the back, backed by a flurry of 'great job' and 'good result'.

Just as he'd settled into his seat, Wickham joined him, sitting so close Fisher could smell the coffee on his breath.

'So... was I right?' Fisher asked.

'The Falcon's office is free. Why don't we go talk in there?'

Fisher's heart thumped anxiously in his chest as he followed Wickham into the DCI's sanctum. A heady perfume laced the air.

'Are we on our own?' Fisher asked, suddenly suspicious.

'Yeah. The DCI's over with the media team, recording a statement about Porter's arrest.'

After letting Wickham guide him to a chair, Fisher said, 'So...?'

'You were right,' Wickham said. 'Frazer Marchant gave Cope the laced coke. He was also the one who sold Harman the coke in the gallery on Friday, plus another couple of the guests we've called have admitted to having been approached. Of course, none of them fess up to actually having bought any. Turns out Marchant's been on Narcotics' radar for some time.' Fisher gave a soft whistle. 'That's not all,' Wickham went on. 'The Chief

Constable's Crime Squad also have him down as a person of interest. He calls himself a speciality importer. Says he can get anything from anywhere. You want a particular model Ferrari or a piece of art by a specific artist, he's your man. He tends to target sports personalities and celebrities — folk with a lot of cash to burn and a penchant for the latest toys. A raid on a lock-up he's renting has already turned up a couple of stolen high-end cars, a few dozen crates of vintage champagne and a pile of antiques. Not to mention Lucy's missing pieces and a selection of drugs, including a quantity of fentanyl-laced coke that could have been from the same batch as did for Cope. It's a proper Aladdin's cave.'

Fisher was buzzing. Who needed coke when you could get such a hit from adrenalin?

'Any indication what his link to Cope was?'

'An elaborate money laundering scam. Looks like he'd been using Cope to smuggle cash out of the country. Shipments from the gallery were sent to fake Eastern Europe buyers. A crate intercepted by Interpol was found full of cash. They're trying to get access to Marchant's overseas bank accounts.'

'No wonder Cope got spooked. So where's Marchant now?'

'Downstairs. You might want to give your wife a ring. He was actually with her at your old place when we brought him in. She was reeling by the time we left. By the way, we found nothing to suggest she had any idea what he was up to.'

'Was Josh there?'

'I didn't see him and your wife didn't mention him.'

Then Fisher remembered it was half term. Josh was probably out with his mates.

Wickham went on, 'Cope must have called Marchant for some reassurance, not realising when Marchant showed later that night and gave him a little something to help him feel better it wouldn't be long before he wouldn't be feeling anything all. Marchant probably spotted Lucy's pieces and couldn't resist. Fingers crossed he'll cough in the hope of getting a reduced sentence.'

'He hadn't bloody better — get a deal I mean. His sort are a danger to everyone they come in contact with. That man has been in the same house as my son; has taken him to a nightclub where he was touting drugs. Behind bars is exactly where he ought to be.' He paused, feeling a chill pass through him as the reality of it sank in, then said, 'So that's it then. Both cases closed. I take it you've told the Falcon all this? Your promotion should be in the bag.'

'Yeah well, I told her you're the one she's got to thank.'

'You what?'

'Like I said before, I owe you. If you hadn't pointed me in Marchant's direction, he would still be on the streets. I didn't have a clue. You were the one who twigged Cope had called him when he didn't need to, seeing as Marchant had already picked up the paintings he'd bought at the auction. Anyway, better get on. Maybe I'll see you later for a celebratory beer... boss.' He stood up and clapped Fisher on the shoulder before making his way out of the room.

Fisher listened to the door click closed. He made no attempt to move. His thoughts drifted to Amanda. Should he phone her? What could he say that wouldn't sound like he was gloating? Not that he was. Though what was he feeling, exactly? Glad such a low-life had been found out before he could do any damage to his son? Definitely. Glad Amanda didn't appear to have been involved, innocently or not? For sure. But did he feel happier now she had no man in her life? Hmm...?

He pondered the question, trying to sense any twitch of his emotional antennae. There was nothing. Maybe he'd call, ask to speak to Josh and check she was okay then. She was the mother of his son, after all.

55.

Luna tip-tapped across the tiled kitchen floor, heading in Fisher's direction. He knelt down and hugged her into him. His hand scrubbed the soft pelt of her head and she responded with a ferocious bout of licking, whining happily as her tail smacked him in the leg. Not for the first time, he gave a silent prayer she was still there with him.

Approaching footsteps scuffed their way down the hallway.

'Josh, pick your feet up when you walk.'

'Sorry. Can I take Luna out into the garden?'

'Are you dressed?'

'Yes.'

'Okay, but keep an eye on her. And if she does something you have to pick it up you know. There are some bags on the side.'

'How do you manage that, seeing as you can't see?'

Fisher thought of the ream of kitchen paper he regularly took out with him and how he'd learned to keep his hands away from his face before getting to the wash basin.

'Don't ask,' he said. 'There should be a box of toys by the back door. Try the ball. She loves playing fetch. If she shows any sign of not coming back to you, there's a whistle. Give it three blows, she should come running. You can give her a treat then, if you like. Hang on to her collar as you do it, otherwise the cheeky blighter will be off with it. But don't do it every time. Got to keep her guessing.'

Fisher heard the door open and Luna bounded outside. He made himself a fresh coffee then wandered into the garden, taking a seat at the patio table. Shortly, Josh came over and joined him.

'Luna would make a great goalie,' he said. 'She's really smart at catching the ball. I asked Mum if we can have a dog, but she says they make too much mess.'

'You know you're always welcome to come over here and play with her whenever you want.'

'Brilliant! Luna, did you hear that?'

He could hear Josh making a fuss of her. Fisher didn't try too hard to contain his smile.

'I hope your mother didn't give you too much of a hard time the other night. Coming back here after the club?'

'No. It's only you she gets mad at. I'm glad you did come though. It was such a drag.'

'You weren't enjoying yourself?'

'No. Everyone was really old,' Josh thought anyone over twenty-one was old. 'Frazer got me a Coke and made me sit on my own at a table in the corner before disappearing.' After an awkward pause, he said, 'I think him and Mum have split up.'

'They have?'

'Yeah.'

Fisher waited, wondering whether Josh was going to say something about him and his mum getting back together again. He didn't.

Fisher bent over and petted Luna.

'So, no more VIP boxes at the football then.'

'I don't mind,' Josh said, though it sounded like he did. 'I'd prefer to go with you. We could get a box.' Fisher was about to protest, when Josh added, 'Cos I know you say you don't feel safe on the terraces, what with all the pushing and stuff.'

'What about the fact I wouldn't be able to see anything?'

'When I was little and couldn't see over everyone's heads when they jumped up after a goal, you always told me just enjoying the atmosphere was enough.'

A smile escaped him. He had indeed said that exact thing.

'You got me there, champ. Okay... well maybe one day.'

'You hear that Luna? He said one day.' Fisher heard the ball bounce a little distance away and felt a whoosh of air as Luna raced after it. 'So, anyway, are you going to see that woman from the club again? The one who chatted you up?'

Fisher couldn't help but smile.

'She didn't chat me up.'

'She did too. She's pretty good looking you know.'

Fisher shook his head, laughing. He turned and headed back indoors, leaving Josh and Luna playing. He stopped just inside the back door and slipped a small card out of his jeans pocket. His turned it in his fingers as he pulled out his phone and started to scroll through his recent calls. He found what he was looking for. Finger hovering over the display, he paused. Doubt started to settle like fog, blurring his confidence, but before it could completely blot out all hope, he hit the dial icon.

'Ginny. Hi. It's DI Fisher. Sorry, I mean Matt. It's Matt Fisher. How are you doing?'

Acknowledgements

I started writing this book in the first lockdown and worked through the year to finish it in the second. Therefore, my biggest thanks must go to my husband, John, for putting up with me, day in, day out. His encouragement kept me going when I began to wonder if I'd ever emerge with my sanity intact. Besides which, he was also the lucky lad who got to read the first draft, with its clunky sentence structure, continuity errors and characters that had yet to find themselves. I couldn't have asked for anyone better to be locked down with.

Aside from John, there have been other wonderful folk who have taken the time and trouble to read drafts in various stages of readiness, without whose help the book could never have been published. In particular, my thanks go to the following:

Andrew Nattrass and his guide dog, Felix. Andrew has not only been invaluable, helping to ensure the book properly reflects life as a visually impaired person, but an inspiration, showing me how visually impaired people are able to adapt their environments to live as independently as possible. Andrew is a keen runner, cyclist and all-round action man — living proof that there's nothing you can't do if you put your mind to it.

Detective Inspector Joanna Lay, who gave up what little free time she had to read and comment on an early draft, giving me pointers and lots of little details that make the story all the more believable.

Samantha Brownley and Kath Middleton have both helped me in my journey to get this book out there are. I can't thank them enough for taking the time and trouble to give me their feedback and for continuing to provide a seemingly endless supply of encouragement and friendship to a whole host of crime fiction writers.

I am also extremely grateful to Julie Platt, not only for her fantastic editing skills, but her honest observations that helped hone the final draft into what it is today, and for helping to make Matt less of a curmudgeonly character.

Finally, I would like to thank all of my readers for their ongoing support and lovely feedback. It's what makes it all worthwhile.

Before you go...

Thank you for reading Paid in Blood, the first in the DI Matt Fisher series.

As so many readers rely on reviews to help them decide whether to try a new author, it would mean a great deal to me if you could spare five minutes and leave a review on Amazon or Goodreads.

And if you enjoyed this book, why not other books of mine, such as the DC Cat McKenzie series, which starts with A Confusion of Crows, which is only 99p from Amazon.

If you'd like to know more about me and my work, then check out my website www.susanhandley.co.uk or follow me on Twitter @shandleyauthor or Facebook @SusanHandleyAuthor

Printed in Great Britain
by Amazon